THE DIME BOX

KAREN GROSE

NOTEBOOK
PUBLISHING

First published in 2019 by Notebook Publishing,
20–22 Wenlock Road, London, N1 7GU.

www.notebookpublishing.co

ISBN: 9781913206239

A CIP catalogue record for this book is available from the British Library.

Typeset by Notebook Publishing.

To Jaime

ONE

Greta sat rigid in the hard-backed chair. The quiet was oppressive. Thoughts she didn't want to acknowledge—thoughts that crawled and lived in abandoned corners of her mind—crept into the light. What was taking the police so long to conduct their investigation? She'd recounted her story and answered each question. Only one had taken her by surprise.

What's a daughter's obligation to her parents?

Greta wasn't sure what her obligations were to anyone but herself. And she didn't know why she couldn't answer.

Except that wasn't true... She *did* know why.

If she'd answered the question honestly, the detective might have seen the raw, feral side she'd worked so hard to tame, and that, quite simply, was too much of a risk. She'd buried the past and she wanted to move forward. And so she'd left that particular question dangling, unresolved.

Minutes later, the door swung open. Detective Perez stepped into the room, walked to her desk and sat down in the chair, shuffling through a file of papers in her hand. She took off her reading glasses and laid them in front of her.

Greta's chest tightened. Even with her lawyer beside her, she struggled for air. She reached down, felt around the front pocket of her jeans, and found the coin hidden deep inside. She rubbed it, working hard to calm herself, breathing in through her nose and out through her mouth. Slow, steady breaths.

Detective Perez focused her eyes on her. "Let's go over process," she said.

Greta sighed. *Process? Again?*

"The police lay charges in an investigation," the detective told her.

She nodded. She knew. Sometimes they consulted the Crown.

"We collect the evidence."

Yep. She'd heard it all before.

"In cases like yours, I want to review the possibilities." The detective's tone made it sound like she was having an everyday, routine conversation.

Greta stiffened, jaw clenched in an effort to stay poised.

Detective Perez held her hand up and pressed a pencil to the tips of her fingers. "One: first-degree murder; two: second-degree murder; three: manslaughter."

Greta looked to her fourth. "Or no charges at all and I'm free."

The detective paused. She didn't look at Greta's lawyer as she spoke. "That's correct and—"

A cellphone buzzed, causing the words to dangle in the air. Detective Perez reached across her desk and flicked the button on the left side to silent. She smiled apologetically and glanced at her notes.

"So, between the Coroner's report and our investigation, I determine whether there's enough evidence to lay a charge." The detective stopped and looked at her. "I've made that decision."

Greta's heart thumped. Her mouth went dry. This was it. She stared back at the detective and wondered what she was thinking. *What sort of person could kill her own parent?* But the detective's eyes gave nothing away.

The phone lit up again. No sound, but Greta could feel the vibration through the desk. The detective looked down and groaned. This time she picked it up. "What?" she said. She listened. "Really?"

Greta curled into herself. To her surprise, Detective Perez stood, picked up the file of papers and left. She leaned back. Her palms left sweat marks on the chair. A hand squeezed hers gently. In the adjacent seat, her lawyer shrugged, then smiled, but not before the expression on his face had dissolved completely.

TWO

Forty-Eight Hours Earlier

Rat-a-tat-tat.

Greta muted the TV. She threw the blanket aside, stumbled from the couch and made her way to the front door.

"Oh my god," she said as she peered through the peephole. The faces of two uniformed police officers stared back at her from the dim of the hallway. She ran back to the living room and shook Latoya's shoulder. Her friend stirred as Greta shoved the shot glasses behind the cushions. A radio crackled. She retraced her steps, yanked the chain from the lock and cracked open the door.

"Ms. Greta Giffen?"

"Uh, yeah... That's me."

"I'm Officer Hatten. This is Officer Sanchez."

"How did you get up here?"

Tall and thickset with salt and pepper stubble, Officer Hatten smiled. "Perk of the job."

Greta's head pounded and she gripped the side of the door. She caught a glimpse of a man peering out from the opposite apartment over his shoulder. A cigarette dangled from his lips as he searched his pockets for a lighter. Her eyes narrowed. What the hell? Another short-term rental? A tourist? Wouldn't be her choice. No desire to move again, she'd had her studio for close to a year now and, finally, a home of her own.

"Is something wrong?" the man asked, his voice thin.

The officers ignored him.

"May we come in please?" Officer Sanchez made it sound more like a demand than a question.

Greta wondered whether she had a choice. There was no fire alarm, no announcement of a building evacuation, and if there were some sort of emergency, the tactical unit, dressed head-to-toe in black, would no doubt be standing there.

"What do you want?"

Grim, neither spoke.

When Latoya stepped in behind her, Greta waved her back and opened the door. The officers followed them inside. Two steps and they were out of the tiny hallway.

Round and red-haired, a foot shorter than her partner, Officer Sanchez' eyes swept the apartment. "Can we sit?"

Shoes littered the hall. A sweatshirt had been flung over the back of the couch. The coffee table was covered with pizza boxes and a crushed Doritos bag. Beside it, two blankets lay crumpled on the floor. Her stomach tightened at the sight of the vodka bottle, still a quarter full, standing tall and incriminating on the kitchen counter, company for the dishes stacked in the sink.

She stopped, planted her feet on the floor, and turned to face them. "What's going on?"

Officer Sanchez cleared her throat. "It's about your father."

"The asshole?" Latoya muttered under her breath.

"Have some respect."

Greta shrugged. "Because he died?"

Officer Sanchez' mouth tightened and she rubbed the base of her neck. "We'd like to ask you to come to the station to answer a few questions."

She glanced at the clock on the wall. "At nine-thirty on a Sunday night?"

"Not now. Tomorrow."

Greta crossed her arms over her chest and thought about it. She could clean her apartment. Go for a walk. Shop for groceries. Stream *The Big Bang Theory*. Or maybe even *Handmaid's Tale*. She hadn't seen Season Three. And what about *Game of Thrones*?

"Don't you want to come down so we can get your side of the story?"

She glared. Please. She'd heard that line and they never listened before. She knew those uniforms backward and forward. The dark shirt. Those shiny, black boots. The stripe along the side of the pants. The badge tacked to their chest reading *Serve and Protect* in small block letters. Did they? Who did they protect? Certainly not her.

"Do I have to?"

Officer Hatten glanced briefly at his partner. "It's voluntary, but we'd appreciate you helping us decide how to handle his death." He slipped his fingers into the top pocket of his shirt and extended his hand across the hall. "Detective Sergeant Perez is suggesting eleven."

"Not with you?"

He shook his head. "She's the boss."

What harm would it do? She had nothing to hide. "Sure."

While Officer Hatten explained what would happen, she reached out and took the card, only half-listening to what he said.

"She'll make it as quick and comfortable as she can," Officer Sanchez added.

Greta rolled her eyes. Right. Of all people, she certainly knew answering questions at the police station was the most enjoyable thing in the world.

"You need a ride?" asked Officer Hatten.

She sighed.

As he walked back towards the front door, he grinned. "Only trying to be nice."

Officer Sanchez followed her partner out. The door brushed her back as it closed.

Greta unscrewed the top of the bottle on the kitchen counter, tipped it to her lips and took a long pull. In the living room, she sunk onto the couch, flipped on the TV and, after brushing a hand across her chin, passed it over.

"That was weird," Latoya said, flopping down beside her.

She leaned over the edge of the couch and picked up a blanket from the floor.

Latoya took a sip, gold hoops dangling to her shoulders. "Why'd they show?"

"Beats me."

"Anything you want to talk about?"

"Already told you what I know."

"Want to get some advice before you go?" Latoya pointed to the TV playing an ad for a law firm. "How about them? Or call Colleen maybe?"

Cold to the bone, Greta jerked the blanket toward her and glimpsed at the screen. "It's late. Besides, what's the point? The dude up and croaked."

They spread out across the couch, legs meeting in the middle, bent at the knees, watching the rest of the show. Before it finished, Latoya was softly snoring, head back on the arm of the couch, blanket pulled up to her chin.

Though lying next to her best friend was still like being next to a heater on full blast, so much had changed from the first time in they'd slept over in grade school. She polished off what was left in the bottle, slid off the couch, crossed the room, and opened the cupboard beneath the kitchen sink, pushing it as far down as she could so she wouldn't have to take it out later. In front of the fridge, she stared into the shelves, looking for something to eat. She shivered. How long had she even been standing there?

Back on the couch, she tucked her feet beneath her, the blanket around her. Soft and warm, she thought of her mother's arms wrapped around her on those hot summer nights up at the cabin on the back patio. The edge of the fabric pressed to her nose, she couldn't capture her smell. She checked her phone, and then twisted the knob on the raggedy lamp at her elbow. The lights of the city shone through the living room window, cracked open to let in the cool night air, as she replayed the officer's visit in her head.

She barely slept. All night she tossed and turned, wondering what she should say.

***

"Detective Sergeant Perez, please."

"Homicide?"

"What?"

The constable on duty pointed to his left. "Room three forty-seven."

Greta double-checked the card in her hand and climbed to the top of the stairs. The walls of Toronto Police Headquarters were institutional white, the lights dim, and the hallway stunk of bologna. She remembered the smell because it was the only thing her father had ever cooked for her. When she found the room, she stepped straight in and stopped near the desk.

The woman was stern-faced, almost cold. "Have a seat," she said.

Greta shrugged out of her jacket and hooked it over the back of the chair. She wondered why the detective's chair was soft leather when the one she was offered was hard wood, but decided this wasn't the best time to point out the inequity. Her eyes flitted around the office. She took in its height and depth. It had an air to it. Definitely imposing. Almost authoritative. She imagined when the detective entered a room, people noticed. She was that type of person.

Detective Perez closed the file on her desk and glanced at her wrist. "It's eleven AM. Let's get started."

She frowned. No *Hello*? No *How are you*? No *Thanks for coming*? All business, her mother would've said.

Detective Perez picked up a notebook and tapped the open page with a pencil. "So tell me, Greta, where were you Saturday night?"

"At the hospital."

"At 8:30 PM?"

She studied the detective from across the desk. Perfect, pointy chin. Crisp, white shirt. Nails clipped back. Silver bob secured with a silver clip. Had she ever been late for anything her whole life? A doctor's appointment? A movie? She'd never be late for work, she guessed. God forbid she had any children.

"Probably around there."

The detective scribbled on a page. "Details are important, Greta. You might think I'm asking because I'm meticulous but I'm also asking because I care."

She pointed to the notebook. "What are you writing?"

"Specifics."

"Like what?"

"Bits and pieces I'll need to remember."

"Would it help if I talk slower?"

Detective Perez jutted her chin toward the machine on the edge of her desk. "No. I'm taping the conversation. You okay with it?"

Greta's face fell. "Is it taping us now?"

"Yes."

"Why?"

The detective looked at her. "Didn't my officers tell you this last night? I need your statement recorded."

Greta's mouth went dry. She didn't answer. She couldn't even breathe. She shut her eyes and blocked everything out around her. No, she didn't remember. She had zero recollection of that part of the conversation. She thought harder. Okay, maybe something, but it was vague. She cracked her eyes open and felt herself in the fire of the detective's stare.

"Ready?" The detective raised her pencil.

She nodded and tucked her hands under her thighs. The detective read out the date, the reason for the interview, glanced at her watch, and then added the time. "What's your relationship with your father?"

Greta straightened. "There isn't one."

"When did you last see him?"

"I told you already..." Her voice trailed off. "Saturday."

"I mean *before* he died."

"I dunno."

She could see him lying there, cold and rigid in the hospital bed, as he was probably found. But that wasn't how she remembered him. She thought back. When was their confrontation?

"Last year sometime?" *Had it really been that long ago?* she wondered.

"Can you describe what happened Saturday night?"

The pit in her stomach grew as the detective watched her and waited. How could she explain it? Less than forty-eight hours had passed, yet she couldn't account for the time she'd spent at her father's bedside.

"There's not much to tell. I took the streetcar there. Visited. Took the streetcar back. End of story."

"When you saw him, did you talk?"

"No, I don't think so."

"Did you touch anything when you were there?"

"No. The bedrail, maybe."

"Was there any physical contact at all?"

"No," she said.

"When you arrived, did you see the nurse on duty?"

She looked up to her right. Think, think. Who was it? Her mind went blank. "I don't think so."

"Did you let the nurse know when you left?"

"No," she heard herself say, but she couldn't quite picture it. Was she supposed to let the nurse know? Was that a rule? Someone might have yelled at her, she thought, but she couldn't recall what he'd said. "Maybe?"

The detective put her pencil down. "I'm missing something. You were there, at the hospital, but you can't remember? You can't remember two days ago?"

Greta dipped her head to her chest. She'd been in the room less than five minutes and already the detective thought she sounded insane or was lying. She chewed the skin on her bottom lip. "I can't be sure."

"Help me understand this..." Detective Perez blew air out through her lips. "This *not remembering* thing..."

Greta leaned forward, cradled her head in her hands and drew short, quiet breaths through her nose. "I don't know."

Detective Perez shook her head. "Well, if that's all you *do* know..." Doubt splattered every word, but she picked up her pencil and continued. "We have someone who saw you with him. So, for the record, one more time, you were there, correct?"

She nodded. "Doctor Hamid called to tell me my father was dying of cancer."

The detective lifted a hand and tucked a wisp of hair into her silver clip. Greta could tell her next words were carefully chosen. "Is this something you experience often? These lapses? For details?"

Greta looked at her, trying to determine what to say. She opened her mouth to respond, but the detective was quicker.

"All the time? Sometimes? Certain times?"

"At times."

The detective's jaw clenched and colour rose up along her neck and into the sides of her face, just like her father's used to.

"*What* times?" Her voice rose.

She sucked in her breath. *Make it stop.* Eyes to the floor, she bit her cheek. There was the taste of metal in her mouth, and she searched for the words to describe what she'd felt back in the cabin that first day.

Confusion? Anger?

Fear.

THREE

Something roused her. She jolted upright and ran her chubby hands under the blankets. She knew where to find Bunny. Face down. Out of sight. Near the foot of the bed. She and Bunny often tried to disappear, together, in that same spot. She felt his warm fabric and jerked him upwards, clutching him tight to her chest. She stretched out the frayed weave of his one and only ear and wound it around her fingers, rubbing it on the side of her cheek. Gently. Back and forth. Up and down. It was the only place Bunny still had softness.

She wiped the sleep from her eyes and stared into the darkness, squinting, straining to see. Was it nighttime? Maybe morning? She had no idea which was which.

Except for the slit of yellow that glowed around the edge of the doorframe, everything was inky black. The black part scared her, but not the yellow. Yellow was the same colour as Bunny. She pulled the sheet down to her shoulders. Shivering. Waiting. She held Bunny tight. Then she heard it. Squeaking. Good. The lock outside of the bedroom door slid open. She swung her feet from the bed and inched her way forward, the floorboards cold under her feet. Then she froze. There were sounds, faint ones, coming from the other side of the door. Scraping. Muttering. A low voice. Then footsteps. She batted her hands around to find what she was looking for. Twisting the latch, it gave way. She blinked. Eye to the crack, she inched up onto the tips of her toes. A naked light bulb glowed on the ceiling, dangling a dirty string. Shadow monsters climbed the walls as the backs of grown-ups disappeared down the hallway. Who were they? Her heart pounded as she fought the urge to shut the door. She held her hands in front of her, fingers trembling, and counted. *One. Two.* Bunny clutched to her side, she held her breath, and then opened the door.

Silence.

She crept along the length of the hallway and poked her head around the corner. The man and woman on the staircase walked like robots. Like Transformers. Heads forward, arms straight to their sides, steps matching one another. When they got to the bottom, they bypassed a room with tall windows, then they disappeared. She searched for a hiding place. There. Close enough she could see, yet far enough back to be safe. She slipped down the staircase to the bottom step. Bunny started to shake. Was he scared? Cold? She couldn't tell.

Poor Bunny.

She put her fingers to her mouth to shush him, hoping he'd be okay, then shoved him into the top of her nightgown. The long, beige one patterned with faded daisies. Like the rough patches of the wooden staircase, it had seen better days. Then, careful not to make the stair under her bum creak, she rocked forward and watched.

The woman stepped nervously, right foot to left, left foot to right, in front of an old gas stove, frying eggs in a pan. The man sat nearby, jaw tensed, watching. Waiting. His beat-up chair rattled as he pulled it up close to the edge of a small metal table making the woman jump. Her hands shook as she laid out three thick pieces of bacon in the frying pan. Though the salty scent wafted towards the staircase made her mouth water, the sizzling scared her. She scrambled back up the staircase.

The woman stopped, cocked her head, and for a moment glanced away from the eggs. Their eyes locked. Warm and brown, they invited her closer. She tucked her limp black hair that fell loosely down the sides of her face behind her ears before scooting back down the stairs and tiptoeing to the archway in the kitchen. She peered at the woman; she smiled back. Then the man. He had messy hair and wasn't wearing a shirt. Black hairs covered his chest, and his arms that rested on the table. He scratched at the bottom of his blue pajamas, then looked up and gestured to two empty chairs.

"Sit." He didn't smile.

She took a step to the one on the left. As she lowered herself to the seat, she heard the scrape of metal. Then a gasp. Then the chair jerked sideways and clattered to the floor. She stumbled, hitting her chin on the edge of the table, causing her to fall backwards. A sharp pain cut through her leg.

The man laughed. "Get up," he said, pointing to the other chair.

She struggled to the chair on her right, sat down, and put Bunny gently in her lap. The woman put plates on the table beside a dish of butter and a half-empty jar of purple jelly. Gently. Carefully. One at a time. Eggs. Bacon. Toast. Her mouth salivated, anxious to taste the sweet smoke of the bacon.

"Don't touch it," the man said.

She pulled her hand back and jammed it under her leg. How did Blue Man know what she was thinking?

"Give me Bunny."

Her eyes widened before she could stop them. She clutched him tight. How'd he know Bunny?

Blue Man stood and held out his hand. "Now."

She swallowed hard. Her eyes stung, and she tried to keep the sick from her throat.

His thick arm extended across the table and ripped Bunny from her hands. He crossed the kitchen to the bin beside the sink and stuffed him in the garbage. When he turned, his eyes bore into her. "Crying has consequences."

She didn't know what the man meant, but his words sounded ugly.

He sat back down at the table. "Let's eat."

No longer hungry, she snuck a peek at Blue Man as he piled up the plate in front of him. When he'd finished, there was no more bacon for her or for the brown-eyed woman who half-smiled. She guessed he was the boss and he was used to getting what he wanted.

She picked at the eggs on her plate and glared at Blue Man across the table. The black in his eyes made her jumpy. She bit down on her lip and stared dead straight ahead at the garbage. She'd have to wait until later to save Bunny. Knife in hand, she reached for the jar in the middle of the table and scraped around the sides. When a big blob of jelly rolled out, covering the toast on her plate, a lump welled up in her throat. She lowered the jar and wiggled half back in. Blue Man kept shoveling his fork in his mouth. He'd missed it completely.

Her head hurt. She put the knife down and covered her ears to stop the thumping. Her fingers brushed Scar. Bumpy and round, it felt like a worm. She let her fingers travel up and down. Up and down. She didn't know how Scar got there but she knew every ridge of it the same way she knew each and every lump on Bunny. But Scar was different; it was attached and it was hers. Even if he wanted to, Blue Man couldn't take it and throw it in the garbage.

The odor of grease lingered thick in the air as they ate their breakfast in silence. Blue Man speared the bacon with his fork. "Greta starts Kindergarten in September."

She looked right at him. "Me?"

"Are you stupid? Is there another Greta here?"

Was there? There were only three of them at the table. She looked down at the cracked plate in front of her and didn't dare answer.

Blue Man ran his fingers along the sides of his fork and sucked off the yellow yolk. "She's going on the bus. Got the confirmation yesterday."

The woman didn't respond. Greta looked at her. She was wearing pink pajamas. They were pretty, but ripped; little white threads opened to show bare skin on her shoulder. The man shoved the last piece of bacon on his plate in his mouth and jabbed his fork in the air. Greta had no idea what was unfolding in front of her, but the strain on the woman's face gave her a sick feeling. She looked like she was trying to be brave, but was having difficulty. *Hold it together,* she begged her, *you can do it.* The woman rallied but a tear trickled down her cheek, followed quickly by others. Greta watched the man's face redden. He slammed his fist on the table.

"Jesus, Emily. It's Kindergarten."

Greta froze. Emily? She mouthed the woman's name over and over again, carving it into her memory.

As the man mopped up the last of the runny egg yolk with a crust of bread from his plate, the woman turned to him and said, "She's four, Ian. With everything that's happened, it's too early..."

Greta clung to the woman's words. Her voice was soft and gooey. She grappled with a third name. Ian. It didn't sound real. Was it missing something?

"She's going. End of story."

Emily took a shaky breath. "Staying home another year won't hurt. I can read to her. Teach her some numbers."

"No." the man said. His voice was firm.

"What about the library instead? She loves it there..."

A switch flicked in Greta's mind. She looked at the two adults in front of her. They were her parents and they were sending her somewhere scary—and soon. Ian didn't seem to think much of the place she loved—the library, whatever that was—so she hoped her mother would take her there after breakfast. Her mood lifted. She looked at her father. Something told her to wait for his permission to speak.

"Can we talk about this?" her mother asked.

"We just did."

"Please?" she said, her voice higher.

Greta sat between them, barely breathing. Her thighs were stuck to the chair.

"I've made my decision."

"Please, Ian," she pleaded, more with her eyes than her words.

"Drop it now."

"Ian..."

"Don't make me do something you'll regret." As he spoke, a small glob of spit flew from his mouth and landed in a smear in the yolk on Greta's plate.

"Ew," she said, leaning back.

Ian banged his palms on the table, pushed back his chair and stood.

Emily flinched.

FOUR

Detective Perez snapped her fingers in the air. "Hello? Anyone home? I asked you a question."

Greta jerked her head up, back from that morning in the cabin, relieved she wasn't alone.

"What's going on? You've gone pale."

"Just tired."

"You mean hung over?"

Greta grimaced. That figured. She should've known the officers saw the bottle on the counter. Which one had the big mouth?

Detective Perez frowned. "Listen, Greta. When people don't have answers to simple questions like the ones I'm asking, it makes them look dodgy, like they're hiding something."

Heat prickled in her armpits. "It's true, though. Sometimes I forget stuff. I fell down and cracked my head open when I was little. I've still got the scar."

"Were you hospitalized for this injury?"

Greta swallowed. "I don't remember." She titled her head to the ceiling and peered into the dimness, images hovering on the periphery of her mind. "Yeah," she said, slowly. "I was."

"Do you remember the hospital?"

She gave her a slight nod. "First of all, I'm in a room lying down. It's not light. I can see shadows on the wall. Not black ones. Yellow, like canaries. Or maybe that's the wall. Anyway, I can only move my head one way and there's this row of windows. Not to the outside; into a hall. Figures, blurry ones, like ghosts in a swamp are walking back and forth." She demonstrated, her arms spread wide. "When they look in through the window, their skin is greenish brown, kind of like the colour of dead sunflowers. I don't know what they're looking at because their faces are fuzzy and they don't have eyes and—"

"Which hospital?"

She thought back to the story she'd been told. "No idea." The detective cocked her head, seeming not to understand. "I was three or four."

The detective raised an eyebrow. "Be honest with me, Greta. Are you on some type of medication?"

She started at her, wide-eyed. "You think I have a problem?"

"Crossed my mind."

"I don't even like taking pills."

The detective shrugged. "Come on. You watch TV. It's my job to assess people. Their behavior. What they do. What they say."

"And what they don't?"

Detective Perez drummed her fingers on the desk and looked at her as if she'd just proved her point. "Have your memory lapses, so-to-speak,"—her tone hard—"the ones that happen *at times*, ever been medically documented?"

Greta crammed her hands in her pockets. "I don't have a doctor. Never did."

"No checkups? No vaccinations? I find that hard to believe."

"How do you mean?"

"Withholding medical care is tantamount to neglect."

Greta looked at her. Detective Perez had no clue. Sometimes it was murder.

The detective glanced at her wrist. "Speaking of medical care, my officers are at the hospital right now talking to the staff. Anything you want to tell me before they get back?"

"So we're done?"

Detective Perez tented her fingers. "No. Don't you understand why you're here, Greta?"

She squeezed her eyes shut and thought back to what the officers had told her at the apartment, replaying the conversation in her head. Slow. Fragments. Pieces. It was coming. *There.* She popped them open.

"To help you decide how to handle my father's death."

"No."

She jabbed a finger in the air. "That's what they told me and Latoya."

"You remember those *exact words*?"

"Yes."

Detective Perez leaned in, elbows on the desk. "You, and whoever Latoya is, misunderstood."

Greta made a face. "Then why am I here?"

"The hospital called to report you were the last one with your father before he died—"

"Of cancer."

"When he did, you ran out."

"No I didn't. I left."

The detective sighed. "Do you know what a person of interest is?"

She shook her head and stretched out her legs to the edge of the desk.

"My officers didn't explain this last night? It's someone we believe has knowledge about what we're investigating. Could this be another detail you've forgotten?"

Greta retraced the conversation in her mind again. Nothing there. "One of us would've remembered."

"Meaning you or Latoya?"

She glared at the detective. If she couldn't figure that out, she had no business carrying a gun.

"I find that highly doubtful. I've worked with these officers for years and there's no way they'd shilly-shally about. They know full well how I run investigations."

"Ask them when they get back." Shilly-shally. She knew she was right.

"Maybe I will. In the meantime, let's start with some background information."

The air went thick with silence. Detective Perez reached into a drawer of her desk and pulled out a pair of silver metal-framed reading glasses. Like her hair and the clip in it, they matched. She perched them on the end of her nose, ran a fist along the crease in her notebook, and picked up the pencil.

"You're from Toronto?"

"No. Ravensworth."

"Never heard of it. Where's that?"

Greta raised her arms and waved them in a circle. "Way up in northern Ontario."

The detective glanced up and smiled. The first one. "I'm from Barrie."

She gave her a half smile back. Barrie, an hour drive north of Toronto, wasn't northern Ontario. Had the detective never seen a map? But she had nothing to gain from pointing it out.

"Born and bred." She put the pencil down. "Started working there, too. Beat cop first. Then vice. Drugs. Prostitution." She turned sideways and pointed to the wall at a picture, slightly off-centre. "That's me. Second from the left. Strange, really, but I looked a bit like you do."

Greta peered into the frame. Like hers, the detective's hair had been black, yet cut much shorter. While they were both slim, the detective wasn't five foot ten; she took up way less space. And her stiff, standard day uniform? No resemblance at all to her black jeans and scuffed-up Converse. She crossed her legs and looked away.

"After vice, I did a stint in undercover but it didn't last long. The brass yanked me out and... well, we won't go *there*," she said.

Emily's words echoed through her head. *You may not be interested in what other people say, Greta, but be kind because whatever they're telling you is important to them. Honestly, how hard can it be to sit still for sixty seconds?*

"They dropped me in homicide next. Didn't like it much at the time, but it grew on me. Truth be told, it's where I cut my teeth. Couldn't get promoted, though, so I applied to the city and, for the last ten years, I've been here, leading homicide."

She kept her face straight. Had she finished? No such luck.

"I still miss it up there. Bet you do, too. The ponds. Swimming. Ice-skating in winter. I remember when..."

And she was off again. Several minutes more ticked by. Greta listened, bobbing her head at the right parts of the story, interjecting with questions of her own. She knew exactly what the detective was doing. Trying to build trust. Nice try, but she wasn't stupid.

"Anyway," Detective Perez said, finishing up, "enough about me. Let's talk about you."

She didn't bite.

"Ravensworth. What was growing up there like?"

"Alright."

"Anything that stands out?"

She tapped her foot on the floor. "It was hot in the summer, cold in the winter. Same as here. Nothing special."

The heat in the kitchen that morning had continued through the summer. She'd spent mornings running up and down the laneway in rubber boots, peering into puddles, searching for worms, a frog if she was lucky enough to find one. Dark clouds would roll in mid-afternoon, but they brought little relief. Every so often, lightning struck and, for a half hour, sheets of rain pelted the side of the house. Though the storms never lasted long, the noise chased her deep under the sheet on her bed where she sought comfort with Bunny.

After that morning her father had eaten all the bacon, he'd stormed out of the kitchen, giving her the chance to sneak back in and fish Bunny out of the garbage. She had been relieved he was with her again, even if he was covered in grease and bacon rind. And so then, whenever the storms hit, she had held onto him tightly, not caring if he made her sheet grimy.

"It rained almost every afternoon, so I was stuck inside a lot."

"Okay, so tell me about that."

"Once, after the thunder thumping stopped—"

"The *what*?"

Heat climbed into Greta's face. "That's what I called thunder when I was a kid. Anyway, after one of the big storms, I remember my mom calling me from the kitchen to see if I wanted to make chocolate chip cookies."

"The oven? In that heat?" the detective asked. "Brave woman."

"Usually I jumped at stuff like that, but I'd been upstairs trying on her make-up and I was trying to sneak outside without her seeing me, so when she came around the kitchen corner, I pulled my sun hat over my face and tapped on my cheek, pretending to think about her question."

"Uh-oh," the detective said, "dead giveaway."

Greta ignored her comment. "My rain boots were by the front door—they were red, I think. I tried to squeeze by but I couldn't. She asked me where I'd been."

"I have kids. Grandkids. Let me guess," Detective Perez said, "you said *nowhere*."

Should she tell the detective to just stop? She opened her mouth and then closed it. Why bother to piss her off?

"My mom cupped her hand around my chin and—"

"Your pink cheeks and lips said it all?"

She nodded. "I remember telling her it was pretty. *Pretty something*, she said. Then she told me my dad would have a fit. I don't remember what I did. Maybe crossed my arms or stuck out my tongue. I do remember saying *so what?* She said it wasn't nice and when I responded that it was him who wasn't nice, she told me not to say that again because he was my father."

"How did you feel about that?"

"I dunno. I was maybe four. I probably resented it. Resented him."

"Your father."

"Yeah. She made me go and take it all off."

Greta remembered how she'd stomped her foot hard on the floor, stuck out her bottom lip, and climbed the wooden steps to the stool in front of her mother's dresser mirror. Why wouldn't her father think she was beautiful? She looked like the ladies he watched on TV. Then she heard a noise outside; it was enough to make her wipe her face as quickly as she could. The stairs creaked and her mother flew around the corner, grabbing Greta's face to inspect it.

Downstairs, a door slammed. Her father was home.

FIVE

"I take it your father was strict?" Detective Perez said.

"You have no idea."

"Mine was, too."

"Did you hate him?"

"Of course not." She paused. "Do you hate *your* father?"

Greta dug her nails into the arms of the chair. The detective would ramble on anyway, so she wasn't giving her the satisfaction of a response.

"How old are you, Greta?"

"Nearly nineteen."

"I don't think kids recognize it growing up—I sure didn't—but what I thought were my father's stupid rules back then have a lot to do with where I'm sitting now." Her face softened. "Maybe one day you'll see that, too."

Greta opened her mouth but no words came out.

Detective Perez waved a hand around her office. Near the door, a trench coat hung loose from a peg in the wall. Beneath it, a brown leather glove on the floor. To the right, a thick book and a pile of files sat on a table. Above, a corkboard stuck on the wall filled with cue cards; yellow, pink and blue, with the words Open, Pending and Conviction, the column underneath the third the longest.

"Is his there?" Greta said, searching for her fathers.

Detective Perez pointed. "Yes. Since the call came in last night."

It was on the left, the only one under yellow.

The detective clasped her hands and leaned in. "When my father was in one of his moods, my brother and I used to take off downstairs for the day to get out of his hair. I bet you and your siblings did something like that, too, right?"

Greta dragged a hand down her face. The detective knew nothing about her.

It'd been easy to stay out of his way. By the time she woke up, Ian had already left for work, so it surprised her one morning when she found him sat at their kitchen table.

She looked up from her Rice Krispies. Dark stubble dotted his chin and he was in his blue pajamas. "Aren't you supposed to be gone?"

"I live here."

"Are you sick?"

He didn't respond.

"'Cause normally you look nicer." She was thinking of the suit and tie he came home in each night.

Ian leaned across the table. "Shut up," he spat.

She froze. Her mother froze. No one moved a muscle. She'd clearly crossed a line. *Help me, Mom,* she thought. *Someone has to help me.* She tried to make herself as small as she could.

Her mother shifted her eyes in her direction. "Get your father some cereal."

She didn't need to be told twice. Off her chair in a shot, she grabbed a box from the cupboard and plunked it in front of him.

His dark eyes bore into her. "Again."

She repeated the action of setting down the cereal box ten times softly because she knew what was expected.

His caterpillar eyebrows lifted. "No bowl?"

She winced as he reached across the table and took hers. Fists in balls, she'd sat glaring at his ugly old pajamas as he ate, and then ate three more bowls in quick succession, just to prove he could. He slurped up the milk before shoving it back across the table. She'd caught it before it crashed to the floor.

After he'd left the kitchen, her mother wiped her hands on a dishtowel and rushed to hug her. Greta pushed her away; it wasn't the first time she'd been left hungry. Was it three times now? Four? She hadn't forgotten; she'd lost track.

At the front door, she found her rain boots and pulled them on. One didn't fit, and when she dug around the bottom of the toe, she pulled out an apple the size of her fist. Her mother? Then, like every morning, she ran, mud sucking at her boots, to play up the laneway.

When Greta looked back up, Detective Perez was staring at her over the top of her glasses.

"What is it?" she said. "Did you remember something?"

"No."

"Tell me."

"I guess I did. I went outside, I mean. To get out of his hair."

"That's it?"

She nodded.

"You're eighteen now, and the make-up incident was when you were four? Hang on..." She scribbled on the page. "Must have been"—She looked up—"2003?"

"How would I know?"

"Anything else from that summer?"

Greta looked at the carpet. She picked at a nail. "Maybe. Give me a second to think."

By midday, the temperature had soared and the canopy of trees stilled, thick with heat. She'd wandered back to the cabin to find her parents huddled together in the main room. The TV flickered on the plastic wrapped over the furniture, and she'd eyed the wooden cross above them on the wall. It was shaped like a T.

"Good afternoon," the man on the TV said. "Today's top story is the same as yesterday. Thursday August fourteenth is another sweltering hot day across Canada."

Sweat ran in lines down her face; the room so hot it was hard to breathe. She retraced her steps and stopped halfway back along the hallway in front of the framed photographs on the wall. She counted seven. One with the three of them, but she didn't know where it had been taken. One of her mom laughing in a green sundress, standing next to Greta holding Bunny outside the cabin. One of Greta as a baby. She lifted her hand to the side of her head. Where was Scar? She stepped forward and peered at the photo more closely. It wasn't there, but her baby head was so fat it filled the whole frame. That was funny. Another showed Mom and Ian standing with other people she didn't recognize. Ian's face was red, turned away from her mother, who was talking to another man. She looked sad. Maybe she got a sunburn that day, too? The last three photos were all of Ian. She frowned and took a step back. It wasn't fair. First, in a boat. Wait... Was he wearing red underwear? His hairy legs were stuck out and he was smiling at the camera, a fish in his hands, not seeming to care the boat was half sinking. Next, on the back patio outside the cabin; his body squished into a chair. He was laughing, and a bottle dangled from his fingers—the same one he drank from that made him fall down. After he finished it, he probably put his chin to his chest and slept there because that was what usually happened. The last was a close-up. Smiling again? She didn't understand why he smiled in pictures but not in real life. Was that what photographs were for?

In the background, the man on the television prattled on. "The summer heatwave continues to wreak havoc across North America. Fields are tinder-dry and lightning storms have been recorded in most provinces. In Ontario, residents are being asked to preserve power."

Greta stiffened. She raised her hand, like she was in class. "There was a blackout. My mom told me something like fifty million people lost power."

Detective Perez turned to her computer. "*The blackout?*" Hunched forward, her fingers flew across the keyboard. Her face brightened. "2003. I knew it. That, my dear— "

My dear?

"...was one crazy week."

As Detective Perez leaned back and launched into a full account of the events, Greta thought back, only able to recall bits and pieces.

"So let's talk about that," the detective said after she'd finished. "Did *you* lose power, too?"

"It didn't go out right away, but when my mom said it might, I remember being really scared."

"Of what?"

She paused. "The dark."

She'd hated the dark. Just the thought of the sounds that came through her bedroom walls at night made her neck damp. She prayed for the times her parents laughed and grunted, and for the silence afterwards that lulled her to sleep. But they were rare. Most nights they argued. Loud voices, in words she hadn't understood. Her mother whispered no—often. Then there would be a sharp intake of breath. Sometimes a crash and a shattering noise. Greta would wonder what had broken. The lamp? Maybe the dresser? The pictures on the bedside table?

The detective interrupted her thoughts. "You were scared of the dark when you were little?"

Her eyes narrowed. Wasn't every kid? From the detective's reaction, she guessed not.

"I guess after the blackout, you didn't have to worry, right?"

Was that what the detective believed? Her parents' fighting wasn't confined to the night. Ian's announcement about Kindergarten had hung in the air for weeks, floating in the kitchen like a hot air balloon, sinking downwards a little each day. He had refused to discuss it, and her mother had continued to fret. Greta, however, had prayed for school and for their anger to be at a greater distance. Every time she did, her heart had thumped like it would explode. Right out of her shirt, right there at the table. All over the walls and the floor. But in the weeks after the bacon incident, she'd made more sense of her surroundings and was sure of two things: one, her opinions didn't matter, and second, if she made a scene, it was of no benefit to anyone—least of all her. She knew full well: a big ugly mess meant consequences. So, when darkness came, she'd kept her prayers to herself; her own little secret, trapped between the four walls of her bedroom.

Greta rubbed her hands along her upper arms.

"You cold?" the detective said.

"No."

"Then what?"

"Then nothing."

Detective Perez eyed her, questioningly. "If you are, tell me. This building... There's something about it. Some days..."

Greta crossed her arms over her chest. Whatever. She didn't have the energy to listen to Detective Perez any longer. She was done. Trust? She wasn't feeling it. And though it'd only been once, she'd felt no guilt at all when she had looked her straight in the eyes and lied.

SIX

Detective Perez stopped mid-sentence. "You're not giving me a lot to work with here, you know..." she said, tight lipped. "Want some advice? You need to start talking."

Greta leaned forward to examine the notebook. Her summary, written in small block letters, didn't yet fill a quarter of the page—probably because she couldn't get a word in edgewise if she'd tried. She gritted her teeth to keep from swearing.

The detective put her glasses on her desk. "Cat got your tongue?"

Greta looked at her. She had half a mind to tell the detective about the kitten she'd wanted as a kid. It was a few years after her accident. She'd named it Yeshi from the moment it peaked its tiny pink nose out from the cardboard box in the front window of the pet store. Unwilling to pay for it, Ian had laughed. A few weeks later, when she spotted another abandoned on the side of the road, she'd pointed it out to him. Late for church, he'd sped by, but on the way home, when the truck slowed in its general location, her hopes rose. The wheels swerved. Then a thump. She'd gasped. That day, she convinced herself she saw it through the cracks of her fingers out of the window, back arched, head darting, paws hugging the earth. Had she? Heartbroken, she'd pestered her mother for a dog.

"No chance of that," she'd said. "I'm allergic."

Greta had arranged her pout into a smile. "Then sleep outside."

Her mother had laughed as she sat down at the kitchen table.

"Do you know my new teacher is a lady?"

Her mother had nodded and chopped up the tomato into the salad.

"Who has a moustache?"

"It's six o'clock, Greta. The table is supposed to be set. Get on it."

She remembered how she'd groaned. "Why do you always get so mad when I'm late?"

"Your selective listening pisses me off and I'm sick of telling you to do things on time."

"So start yelling at me earlier."

Her mother had shaken her head in frustration as she'd sliced into cucumber. "Shit." A bright red stream trickled from the tip of her finger.

"Ohh. You said a bad word." Greta had said, jumping down from her chair.

"Sorry. Quick, get me a band aid."

She found one in the box under the sink and stood beside her mother, watching her wrap it around her finger. Then she lowered her voice. "Shit."

Silence.

"Shi-i-i-t," she repeated.

No response.

"Shiiiiiiiiiiiiiiiiiiiit," she said, for as long as she could hold it.

"Stop it. I apologized."

"Why were swear words invented if you're not supposed to use them?"

Her mother threw her hands in the air. "Good grief, you're relentless. You exhaust me."

Greta had sulked, trying her best to get her eyes to glisten. Aware from the looks she'd been receiving lately that not everyone craved answers to questions like she did, she was disappointed her mother seemed to have joined the team.

Her mother had looked at her then and said, "There are days, my dear, that I understand why some animals eat their young."

Greta had sat still, unsure if what her mother said was true. Were there really animals that ate their own babies? When she scanned her face, her mother had grinned back. She didn't deny it.

"Come on, Greta. Giddy-up," Detective Perez said, drawing her thoughts back into the room. "It's like pulling teeth." She reached for the mouse and wiggled it on the desk. "Why Ravensworth?" She squinted at the screen. "It's way further north than I first realized."

She scowled but didn't argue. Had the detective listened, she'd have known this a half-hour ago. Was it going to take her that long to figure out the truth about her father?

"You have family up there?"

"Not my mother."

"Then your father?"

Legs wrapped around the chair, the blank page staring back at her on the desk, Greta's stomach tightened. "I—"

"Let me guess... You don't know? Or you don't remember? Because they're two different things."

"God. What's up with you? You don't have to get like that. It's simple. I got a concussion."

Detective Perez' expression darkened. "That makes you avoid answering questions?"

Words hovered unspoken in the space between them. Could the detective not see she was struggling? The things she wanted to remember she couldn't and the things she'd tried so hard to forget just kept coming.

"No. By the end of the summer, I started remembering a lot. Being sweaty. My parents yelling. The smell of the junk my mom rubbed on my scar. Oh, and the day she pulled my stitches out." She waited for Detective Perez to finish writing before ploughing on. "I even remember after one of my parents' really ugly fights, I woke up outside in the woods in the middle of the night. I was alone. I was soaking wet. I had bruises. And then these nasty red welts on my legs. But I had no idea how I got there. Wait... Hang on. That can't be right. My bedroom door squeaked. The sound still gives me the creeps. And I couldn't have opened it because they locked my bedroom door from the outside at night, and—" She looked up. The detective was staring at her, her page half-filled, fingers tight to her earring. "What?"

"Nothing."

"You asked me to tell you something so I did."

Detective Perez lowered her hand. "What's the second thing?"

"Huh?"

"You said, 'first of all'...."

"Oh, that one's different. That one's more like a voice in my head. *Rules are rules to be followed,* it says. And then I get these goose bumps and there's warm and sticky on my nose. I get trapped, you know, held down, and something's in my face. I don't know what but it tickles and sticks and tastes like a penny. Long story short." She checked to see if the page was full. It was. "I'm not sure if it's real or a—"

"Strange dream?" Hand back at her ear, Detective Perez was twisting the earring between her fingers. "They sound more like nightmares to me."

She nodded. At the time, she'd found them strange too. At about the age of eight, she'd stood in the cabin, unable to call to mind a thing before she'd gone to school. Minutes, hours, days, months could have elapsed for all she'd known. At that point, she wasn't even sure she really existed. But there was proof she'd lived in the cabin as a baby. She'd seen herself in the pictures on the walls. In photos on the mantle in the living room. In little framed Polaroids on the dresser by her mother's side of the bed. *That's my face,* she'd said, her face staring back at the camera. She'd found old paintings, too; some painstakingly drawn, others more carefree, stored away in boxes underneath the bed. Rainbows and flowers and floating butterflies, a prison horse in a meadow leaning against a rickety fence—pictures only a young child would paint. Certain she'd lived in the cabin, it was like looking out through a window in a rainstorm. She almost had it, but then the fragments would float away. And while Ian had made it clear he didn't want her there, she had known it was where she belonged.

Detective Perez leaned back in her chair, her rough, veined hands pressed together. They were mottled with sunspots, and Greta wondered whether they got that way from gardening or vacations, or even from the years she'd spent patrolling the city streets. "I'm having trouble with this. If these memories aren't real, you're wasting my time."

Greta looked at the wall. Eleven-thirty had come and gone, and the discussion was going nowhere. To make matters worse, she was hungry.

"I can't help you if you won't help me," the detective said, red-faced.

Her pulse quickened. "I'm trying."

"You certainly are."

She stopped to catch her breath. So much of her early childhood was lost, the memories faded, like pieces of a puzzle she'd never been able to solve. Hand to her head, she brushed her fingers to the tip of the scar, and ran them along the jagged edge under her hairline. What she saw stopped her from breathing at all. She pointed to the notebook, took a shaky breath and the words streamed out.

The night before school started, Greta watched her parents from her hiding place at the top of the stairs. "You need to reconsider," her mother said to Ian.

Ian smacked the TV to try to make the channel clearer, and then picked up the remote and turned up the sound.

"Please. It'll be the library all over."

He turned it up again.

"Do you want the same thing?"

Greta wasn't sure what would be the same. She loved the library and she wanted to go to school.

Ian snorted. "They were three. Little kids are stupid. They can't remember yesterday."

Her mother shook her head. "They're not the ones healing from a concussion."

Greta looked her mother up and down. Was she sick? She hadn't thrown up. If she had, she would've heard her, and Ian would've made her clean it up right away. Had she missed it? Had she left a mess somewhere he'd stepped in? Was that why she heard her mother crying? Was that what they had been fighting about last night?

Her mother lifted her knees to her chest and turned to face her father on the couch. "They'll tease her the second they see her," she said. "Her hair. Her clothes. Do you want them dancing around chanting Wretchen Gretchen again?"

Greta ran her hand along her head. Some days her hair got messy, so for school she'd try to keep it neater. She'd flatten it down on the bus in the mornings before she got there.

Ian reached for his glass. It left a wet circle on the top of the table. "Better than Feta Greta or Peta Greta or whatever the hell they called her."

Butterflies fluttered in Greta's tummy. Those rhyming words were familiar; she'd heard them somewhere before. Was her mother right? She wiped the sweat from her upper lip and wrapped her nightgown around her. Maybe school wasn't a good place to go after all.

"We dealt with it then," he went on. "Told the kids to stop. Told the parents—"

Her mother waved her hand. "But they didn't."

Ian held his glass in midair. Brown liquid sloshed over the side. "So it's my fault, is it?"

"No," she offered quickly. "I'm not saying that. Just that... Well... They didn't listen to you."

What? Someone didn't listen to him?

Cheeks red, her father swallowed the remainder of what was in the glass. "If she had my blood, she'd be tougher."

Greta straightened. She stretched her arms in front of her, rotating them to examine the undersides. They were fish-belly white. Whose blood was in there?

"How'd you do it anyway?" her mother asked.

"Do what?"

"Register for school."

"Used what we have upstairs."

"That piece of paper? Are you serious?"

She glanced at her parents. What? She had papers?

"Photocopied it at work." Ian poured himself another. "Said it's the birth certificate we got. Life isn't all peaches and roses, you know."

"That's an ignorant expression," her mother said. Greta had heard her father use it before and she hated it, too. "And," she added, "you didn't get it right."

Her stomach dropped. She liked peaches and she liked flowers. Why was the expression wrong?

"It's *cream*," her mother told him. "Peaches and *cream*."

Everything happened so quickly then. Ian's fist shot out across the couch and landed squarely on her mother's jaw. As she fell backwards, he grabbed her wrist, wrenching her towards him. She raised her free hand to protect her face. He shoved her upper body down, pinned the back of her head flat to the couch with one hand, and jammed an elbow in her back.

"Who's smart now?" he asked, venom thick in his voice.

Greta felt her nightgown dampen and her heart leap up into her throat. Ian's hands twisted her mother's head around, and he jerked it in the direction of the TV. He leaned in, inches from her ear. "Shut up, stop crying, and watch the fucking show."

Greta snuck back to her bedroom. She rolled from one side of the bed to the other, the sheet wrapped around her, clutching Bunny. She didn't hear another word. Just dead silence.

SEVEN

Greta waited for the detective to stop writing.

"Was this another dream?" she asked.

"No."

"The night before school. What was it like for you to see that?"

"Thinking about it now makes me sick."

The detective smiled and cocked her head. "Do you need a minute? How are you?"

She tried to smile back. "You know." But she knew she didn't know. Nobody knew.

"Alright. Let's continue." Detective Perez's face dulled as she turned her attention back to the notebook. "How did your parents seem the next day?"

"Like it never happened. My dad left for work and my mom and I went up the laneway."

"To get out of there?"

"Would I be sitting here if we did?"

"Point taken. Did your dad often get violent when he was angry?"

"Yeah, he did. But my mom never left him. She always acted like it didn't happen. After that fight, she walked me to the school bus."

Detective Perez looked up. "Do you think your father gave you that concussion?"

"I was a little kid. All I know is I fell down the stairs. I mean, I blame him for a lot. But that one... Well, I can't be sure."

Detective Perez paused to tuck her hair behind her ears. "Did you like school, Greta?"

"You mean Kindergarten? Absolutely."

"Come on," Greta whined. She pulled down hard on her mother's arm. "You're walking like a big lazy elephant." Her mother shot her a sharp look. "I'll miss the bus."

Emily rolled her eyes. "Relax. We're ten minutes early. It's oodles of time."

Greta stopped, held her hands out in front of her and counted. Ten minutes was the same as all her fingers, plus her thumbs. That wasn't a lot and she was right. When they got to the top of the laneway, the bus was waiting.

"See?" she said, accusingly. "I nearly got late 'cause of you."

Emily sighed. "We're here now so stop it." She leaned down to hug her but Greta did her best to wiggle away. "Good luck today. I'll miss you." Her mother turned and pointed to the side of the road. "I'll be standing right there when the bus drops you off."

Greta didn't hear her. By the time her mother turned back around, the bus was pulling away and Greta's nose was pressed to the pane, staring at the countryside passing by through the window. Thick forests of pine eventually gave way to cleared lots, handmade signs and scattered buildings, gas stations and white faded convenience stores. Then came the houses. Lots of them, all in long, skinny rows, some hidden in thick hedges, some wide out in the open, some with bikes lying outside the doors, and some with flowerpots on the porches.

When the bus slowed and pulled up in front of her new school, Tall Pines Elementary, the chaos of the first school day didn't scare her. Her heart pounded as she took it all in. Cool grass flowed to a low brick building with windows, full of paper flowers. Yellow dresses heightened the glow of the morning sun, and backpacks in neon corals and blues floated and bobbed as children ran laughing to greet one another after the long summer break.

She stepped off the bus as the school bell rang and followed a line of children inside. She stopped, put her backpack beside her on the floor, and bent down to touch it. "Hello," she said to the face staring up at her.

"Hi," it said. "Welcome to Kindergarten."

She leaned down until her nose nearly hit the floor and whispered, "Thanks. I'm happy to come but a bit scared, too."

The floor gave her a reassuring smile. "Your secret's safe with me." Then it glanced at her clothes. "You look pretty today."

She plucked at the trim on her dress and flattened the fabric against her skin. It was her favourite.

The floor continued. "Want to be my friend?"

Greta beamed at the unexpected opportunity. "Me?"

The floor nodded.

"That'd be good." She gathered up the sides of her ratty dress and sat down beside her. "What do you want to play?"

The floor shrugged. "You choose."

She tapped her finger to her lips and, as she did, looked up at the sound of snickering, straight into the faces of the children gathered around her. When a tall boy in shorts and a T-shirt with pale skin and bright red hair leaned in, she sucked in her cheeks and stumbled backwards. It was like a mop of fire was stuck to the top of his head. Even his eyebrows looked like flames. He looked like a devil.

"Nice friend," he said. "Are you a freak?"

The other kids giggled behind their hands, and a girl standing beside him in a jean skirt and white cowboy boots stepped forward. "Does your new best friend like your pioneer dress?"

Unsure what to do, Greta inched her way back on her hands and toes, grabbed her backpack, then bolted straight up and marched down the hallway, rushing in the direction the other kids had headed a few minutes before. As she stepped into to the classroom, her mouth dropped. Octagon tables overflowed with baskets of paper, and pencils and crayons. Plastic water tubs and sand boxes were filled to the brim. Boas and jackets and old people clothes hung in a dress up centre tucked into a corner. With hats. So many hats. More than she'd ever seen, even at church on a Sunday. Two large beanbag chairs surrounded by bins stuffed with books sat underneath a large window. She squealed out loud, clapped her hands, and ran across the room. As she rummaged through the books, she heard her name called. Her stomach lurched. A classroom full of eyes stared out at her from beside the teacher's feet on the carpet. She struggled out of the beanbag chair and walked quickly across the room.

"Hello, Greta," the teacher said. "I'm Mrs. Harvey."

If Mrs. Harvey was stern, Greta couldn't see it. Folded into a rocking chair, she was wearing a yellow dress that hugged her large tummy. Her curly hair was tied into a loose brown knot.

"Please," she smiled at her, "join our circle."

Greta knew it was an expectation, not an invitation, and looked around for a spot among the children, all sitting cross-legged in front of her. As two children squabbled, moving over to make a small space, she twisted in shame, folded her arms on her chest, and then sat.

Detective Perez held up her hand. "What was your teacher's name?"

She repeated it.

"Spelled as it sounds?"

"H-A-R-V-E-Y."

"And the school?"

"Tall Pines." She'd said that, too. What the hell had she been writing?

"I'll assume you spent two years in that class."

She nodded.

"How did it go?"

She paused. "A bit of an adjustment at first, I suppose, but I got the hang of it."

The first week of Kindergarten, Mrs. Harvey scolded Greta four days in a row. "Greta," she said on the first, not unkindly, "please don't throw sand from the sandbox."

She scowled and put the sand down.

"Greta," Mrs. Harvey reminded her on the second, "the water in the play table isn't for drinking."

She spat it back out.

"Greta," she begged Thursday as she showed the class how to sneeze into their sleeves and make long stringy snot worms from their elbows, "that's disgusting. And *do not* wipe your nose on the curtains. We have tissues for that. Get one and use it."

She did so, albeit begrudgingly. Why had her mother not prepared her for this?

By Friday, Mrs. Harvey had all but given up. "Greta, no hitting other children. Where are your social graces?"

Greta looked at her. "My *what?*"

Mrs. Harvey wrung her hands in despair. "You need to apologize to Hitesh." Greta stood stone-faced in front of her victim. "A heartfelt look-in-their-eyes-and-shake-their-hand-type of apology," she demanded.

"Sorry I punched you in the gut." She stuck out her hand.

It didn't stop there. The next week, each time she was reminded lying was forbidden, she couldn't shake the conviction white lies held less weight.

Yes, that outfit looks nice, when it didn't.

No, the story you're reading isn't boring, when it was.

I didn't mean to kick her, honestly, I walked into her by accident.

She survived her first trip to Principal Parthi's office after swearing ten times over she hadn't done what she had, but no matter how hard she tried to explain to Mrs.

Harvey why white lies were sometimes acceptable, she always lost the argument with one question.

"Does your father tolerate lying at home?"

"You mean Ian?"

"I mean your father, Greta." Mrs. Harvey frowned with disapproval.

Greta sighed. She had to explain everything, but most times when she did, Mrs. Harvey still didn't understand. It was tiresome. "I'm supposed to call him Ian. And no, he doesn't like lying."

Mrs. Harvey looked at her strangely and went back to her desk at the front of the class.

"Did you like..." Detective Perez eyes flitted across the page.

Again? She sighed. "Mrs. Harvey."

"Thank you."

"She was great."

"And the kids in the class?"

She flushed. That she didn't know every kid had invisible friends back then had caused her considerable grief. She muttered *idiots* through her teeth.

As a result of her frequent missteps, Greta spent most of September in the hard wooden time-out chair. When Mrs. Harvey judged her adequately reformed, she was allowed to return to the group. The first week back, she spread her arms out either side of her, lowered her nose to the table, and slurped.

"What are you doing?"

She glanced up, the eyes of her classmates upon her. "Juice."

The boy beside her rubbed the top of the table with end of a crayon. "It's from yesterday."

She examined the purple stain. That couldn't be right. "No, yesterday was apple juice and carrots." Then she licked it.

Her classmates jumped up from their seats. "Teacher," they called out, "Greta's being gross."

Mrs. Harvey surveyed the group but didn't say a word. Later that morning, she pulled Greta aside. "I need some help."

Eyes to the floor, she stared at her sneakers. A warm hand on her back guided her to the far end of the classroom, and she swiped her feet at the toys strew over the carpet. She didn't want to help. She did enough chores at home. She hadn't done anything and it wasn't fair. Beside the sink, Mrs. Harvey knelt down and cupped her ear. Her eyes widened and she leaned in and listened.

Snack helper? Her tummy rumbled.

Could she do it? She'd sure try.

Could she start tomorrow? She nodded, reached up and hugged Mrs. Harvey.

Every morning, she watched for the signal. When it came, she stopped what she was doing, went to the back of the room, found the opaque container beside the sink and, after washing her hands, pulled it to the edge of the counter. She lifted the corner of the lid and sniffed, then reached inside to taste-test its contents. Apple slices, muffins, veggies and dip, sometimes granola bars, too.

After she approved it—which always happened save for once when the broccoli was brown—she laid it out, one piece at a time, in simple, neat rows, and passed the emerald-coloured tray around the classroom. When someone was away with a cold or nits in their hair, it was her job to eat anything left over, and there was always something untouched because lice were hard to get out.

The detective's eyes darted up. "That was nice of her."

"I thought so, but not the other kids."

"Because?"

She grinned. "She let me keep the job the rest of the year."

The detective nodded. "At that age, it's hard for kids to understand different kids need different things. I'm sure you saw that at home."

"Your point being?"

"Growing up I mean, with your—"

"Brothers and sisters? I didn't have any."

Later that Fall, Mrs. Harvey gathered the class in front of her rocking chair and waggled a finger at a chart. Greta shuffled forward from her assigned seat to study the images and, when her eyes reached the bottom of the piece of paper, she sprung up from the carpet.

Mrs. Harvey glared. "Sit down."

Greta stepped over the children and returned to her place. She crossed her legs, put one hand in her lap, raising the other up high, and waited. She wiggled her fingers. She smiled. She waved. Unsure whether Mrs. Harvey could see her, she shook her whole arm so hard in the air she thought it would break. But nothing worked.

Careful not to touch the children around her, she rocked herself slowly forward and backwards, and then she grunted.

Mrs. Harvey abated. "Yes?"

She pointed to an image. "I'll do that."

Mrs. Harvey sighed, but wrote her name with a marker in perfectly formed letters beside the picture of a tree. She stood, ran her hands down the creases of her skirt, and skipped across the classroom. Brush in hand; she got down to work.

"Greta," a voice called out heatedly from across the room.

She jumped back from the easel, paint splattering everywhere.

"Stop right there," the voice said.

She fell to her knees and rubbed her sleeves across the mess. Two brown-laced shoes stopped directly in front of her.

"That's wonderful," she heard Mrs. Harvey say.

She cracked open an eye and exhaled. She wasn't being sent back to the chair.

"Tell me about this," Mrs. Harvey said after she waved a hand at the painting.

She stood, paint up to her elbows, and beamed. "It's my family."

Mrs. Harvey pointed to the smallest figure. "Is that you there in red in the middle?"

Her shoulders sagged. It wasn't obvious? Who else would it be?

Mrs. Harvey ran her finger along the page to the right. "And who's this?"

"My mother."

"What a lovely green shirt."

She cringed. "It's a dress." Ian would have a fit if her mother wore anything that short.

Mrs. Harvey gave her shoulder a squeeze. "Who's in the blue pants beside her?"

Greta peered at her teacher, hesitant. "Ian."

Mrs. Harvey's lips pressed into a thin line and she moved her finger to the left side of the easel. "What about these two?"

Greta stared at the ceiling. She wasn't totally sure. Did they look like that? "My real parents."

Mrs. Harvey stopped and rubbed her chin. She focused her eyes to the right and tapped her pencil to the painting. "So you're in care?"

Greta thought of Ian and then pointed to her mother. "Only she does."

Mrs. Harvey frowned, hands to her temples. Her eyes shifted back to the left. "Why are these two red inside?"

Greta extended her paintbrush to the image herself. "They're like me. We have the same blood."

"Ahh." Mrs. Harvey nodded slowly, then she bent down, hands on her knees, and looked her straight in the eye. "Got it."

Greta stayed silent. Of course. Why hadn't she thought of that? Obviously, a teacher would understand. Maybe Mrs. Harvey could be the one to explain it? She sucked in her breath and rose up onto the balls of her feet.

Mrs. Harvey smiled. "You're adopted."

What? She'd never heard that word before.

EIGHT

Detective Perez ran a hand across her face. "You're adopted?"

"Yeah. It's not like it's a secret or anything."

"Hadn't your parents told you?"

"My mom did. On the back patio when I was around eight."

"Why not earlier?"

Greta shrugged. "I dunno. I asked her to tell me the story of when she and my dad first met and it came up that she got me."

Detective Perez nodded. "That's very sweet."

Greta sighed. Clueless. "No. What she said. She said *got*."

"I missed it," she said, her voice low, almost apologetic. "So it was the night you found out you were adopted?"

The detective missed the point again. She wanted to slap her. "No. I knew the word. It was the first time my mom opened up about it." She stopped. "Did you get that?" She waited for the detective to answer. "Good. Because it was one of the best things she ever told me. It was late, but I'll never forget it. What she said. My Mom said she *chose* me."

That night, the wavering shadows across the back patio were gone, replaced by still black. The only light came down from a fingernail moon, luminous above them.

Greta felt warm, like toast with sticky brown cinnamon. She'd sat there and basked in the coziness of her mom's words.

"That's me," she'd repeated quietly.

Greta had peered at her mother through the moonlight and the edges of her lips pulled up into a sleepy smile. She was beautiful. In a flowered cotton wrap dress, legs tucked neatly under, folded close into the seat of the chair, she brushed the fallen strands of hair away from her eyes and tucked them back into the bun that sat loosely on the top of her head. While the story of her parents meeting had finally got better, her eyelids drooped and she drifted, in and out, in and out, with the warm, sticky haze. Her head tilted slowly backwards and hit the edge of the chair.

"So how'd it all happen?" Greta whispered, after she felt herself being lifted gently upwards and walked upstairs to her bedroom.

"It's late. Another night."

"No," she begged.

Her mother dragged her hand through her hair, loosened her bun, and allowed her hair to swing down onto her shoulders. "Okay, skooch over and give me some room."

Eyes drifting closed, she'd squeezed her skinny frame up flat to the wall and when her mother lay close beside her, the heat of her body seeping over her, she wrapped her arms around her and hung on as tight as she could.

"So, my dear," her mother had said softly, "about getting you."

Greta's eyes cracked open. From the look on her mother's face through the sliver of moonlight on the pillow, she could tell her memories were resurfacing. Vividly. She burrowed her hands in the sheets and found Bunny.

"We'd been living here less than a month when we got the news," her mother said.

She'd frowned. News? What news?

"You see, the lady from Parry Sound had explained to us that the timing of these things was never carved in stone, so when the news came—and so quickly—your father was shocked. But as appearances mean everything to him, he downplayed it all and promised to take it in stride."

Careful not to give herself away, Greta smiled a big smile. It was the first time she'd heard of Ian promising something to her mother—promising *anything*—but she didn't understand the reference to timing and appearances.

"You always ask me why you weren't born from my tummy and I don't have an answer. I can't recall what led up to it all and, frankly, it doesn't actually matter. All that matters is you're here now."

Greta wasn't so sure about that. Sometimes things mattered. Sometimes they didn't. Like the time her mother lied to Mrs. Harvey. She was sure her real mother never would've done that.

"It wasn't something your father and I talked about. It was something we accepted between us." Her mother's face turned bitter. She squeezed her eyes shut and tried to block out her feelings. "My genes were clearly a sticking point to him, but I put my foot down. Told him he'd best explore options."

Greta's mouth hung open. She'd been an option? That didn't feel right. She glared at her mother. She was smiling, proud of herself, but she had no idea why. Maybe she was a good option? She felt a little better.

"But," Emily flicked her hand in the air, "as usual..."

Greta's heart sank. From the tone of her voice, she knew what was coming. He didn't explore anything. That figured.

"I took charge and arranged your adoption myself."

Greta's eyes widened. Of course, it was her mother. The best mother in the world who stepped up and made it all happen. She was the reason Greta was here.

"When we first saw you, it was like being blown back by a tidal wave." Her mother looked at her with the warmth in her eyes that made Greta feel a bit safer. She grinned. She loved her mother so much sometimes.

"Your father cried. Messy tears, all over. I turned my back so he didn't see me staring."

What?

Red-faced, Greta sat up in her chair. "Can you believe it? No crying was the second rule on the list. The one after silence."

Detective Perez looked at her strangely. "The list?"

"The one on the fridge. Never mind. At the time, I didn't really believe he cried anyway—it was another lie— but I remember thinking that, if he had, I'd hate even him more. It was so unfair, all of it. I thought about all sorts of consequences for him, like being forced to drink poison or being hit by the truck like my cat, maybe even pulling his toenails out one by one. I was so mad. I wanted him dead. I thought about..."

Detective Perez stared at her, stone-faced.

"Now what?" she said.

"Then your thoughts became true, didn't they?"

The question dangled mid-air between them. She wanted him dead but she hadn't thought about killing him. Not that day. She scoffed. "It's completely different. I was a kid. Didn't you have an imagination like that?" The expression on the detective's face wasn't one she'd seen before, so when she gestured for her to continue, she shrugged. Guess not. "Anyway, then my mom told me what happened when I got to the cabin."

"When the lady handed you over," her mother had said, "you were wrapped in a tiny green blanket, soft as butter. You had this head full of incredible thick, black hair. And these amazing crystal-like blue eyes. Who knew babies were born with blue eyes? I remember looking at your long, slender fingers and knowing you'd be tall."

Her mother had been right. She was taller than all the other kids at school.

"That made your dad happy. He'd been clear what he'd been stuck with the past three years was too short. A little too plump. Definitely too chatty. Could you turn down the volume? A little bit more. No, right off. Keep it there now."

That part of her story had made no sense. But whatever.

"Your father called you Gretchen after a great aunt on his mother's side."

She'd wondered what her real father would've named her. She waited for her mother to go on, but she stopped. Had she fallen asleep? The muscles on the side of her cheeks moved. She was thinking. Maybe about the name Gretchen. When the bed shifted, she closed her eyes and waited.

"When you got older, we shortened your name up. Gretchen became Greta. Like a nickname."

She was aware of that; like honey and sweetheart and dear. Her mother called her those names all the time.

Then her sheets straightened and the wood creaked and her mother's feet faded across the floorboards.

Detective Perez smiled. "Sounds like you and your mom had a good heart to heart that night."

Greta nodded.

"And what about your father? Did he ever talk to you about your adoption?"

She smirked. "You're joking, right?"

"Why would you say that?"

"I tried once and I paid for it."

"So you never brought it up again?"

She stood and jabbed a finger in her face. "He's nothing to me."

The detective didn't bat an eye. "Sit down, please. Let's talk about it."

She made a rude noise. "The bastard didn't care I existed."

NINE

Greta stood at the edge of the main room, a white envelope in her hand. She passed it to her parents.

"Can I go?" She stood and waited; hopeful.

"Sure," Ian said after he read it.

She took the invitation back. "Can we leave now?"

He leaned back on the chair, his ankles crossed and hands behind his head. "The party's Thursday."

"You'll take me?" she asked.

"No." He reached for his beer can and drained it.

Her face fell. "Then how do I get there?"

He swiped his hand across his mouth, belched and stood. "You're in Grade Two, dipshit. Figure it out."

When Ian left the room, Greta turned to her mother.

"Don't look at me," she said, palms up. "I don't have a car."

She groaned. "You don't even have papers."

Her mother batted a hand in the air. "Details, Greta, details."

She tugged at the bottom of her shirt. Those weren't details; they were rules. She'd seen Ian pass papers through the front window when he was stopped for driving too fast. Wait... Was her mother suggesting she'd drive without them? Ian would never allow it.

"Then I'll walk," she said.

"To Clear Lake?" Her mother's eyes widened. "It's twenty kilometers."

Greta sat down beside her. "So? That's only forty there and back."

Her mother groaned. She took the invitation from her hand and left the room. When she returned, she reached across the couch and batted her on the shoulder. "Latoya's mom said you can take the bus home with her."

"Tomorrow?"

Her mother shook her head. "Thursday."

Greta paused. "She's coming to the party, too?"

Emily sighed. "It's at her house."

Greta hugged her mother and ran upstairs to her room. She couldn't wait to share the news with Bunny; only one question he had made her head spin. He asked it softly first, then over and over, until he became so loud she shoved him under her pillow. Why had *she* never had a birthday party?

Four days later, when the bus dropped them off at the bottom of the driveway of a blue and gray shuttered house, Greta's jaw dropped. The front yard was fenced, the flowerbeds full, and streams of balloons floated at each side of the porch. A stone pathway led to the front door. As soon as they stepped inside, a wave of warm air laden with cinnamon flicked at her nose. Her mouth watered.

Down the hall, Latoya threw her backpack on a chair, her lunchbox on top, and sat down at the island in the kitchen. She pointed to her left. "Mom, this is Greta."

A woman with tight hair and deep brown eyes looked over her shoulder and gave her a smile. Greta waved and climbed onto a tall chair beside Latoya as her mother shut the fridge and placed a white casserole dish on the counter. Her tummy rumbled. Hotdogs? Kraft dinner? Soup? Shepherd's pie? At least she wouldn't be eating cereal again for supper.

"Right, girls, I need you out of my kitchen," Latoya's mother said as she leaned into a cupboard and rummaged through a sea of bottles. "I'm fixing roti and oxtail."

Latoya took Greta by the hand, and she trailed her through the house, flip-flops slapping on the tiled floor. It reminded her of the TV show Ian didn't know she watched after school. The walls were white. The furniture was white. Everything looked new. It sparkled. Like the rest of the house, Latoya's room was filled with toys. Heat rose in her cheeks when she thought of hers. Not much more than a closet; and the paint was cracked, leaving winding patterns to chase through sleepless nights in her mind. And the single mattress tucked into the wall was lumpy, with coils that dug into her back, leaving marks; and though the summers were hot and the threadbare sheet was all she needed, winter was worse and she was constantly cold.

When Latoya's mother called them downstairs, the first thing Greta saw was a kitchen full of people. Some were standing, others sitting, but all were talking and laughing. She squeezed between the adults, looking up at them as if their appearance might answer her question.

"The kids are out there," she heard someone say.

With a hand shading her eyes, she stood in the back doorway. On the grass, girls on a blanket sat laughing in front of a table. When she saw what was on top, her stomach dropped.

"I gotta pee," she told Latoya through her squint.

Back upstairs in her bedroom, she searched through her desk and found what she was looking for. She picked up a marker and wrote her name on a piece of paper. She maneuvered her way back through the adults in the kitchen and, when finally outside, took the biggest present she could find and pressed the card onto it.

Unfamiliar with party games, all Greta could do was her best. At dinner, she piled her plate so high that, by the end of the meal, her stomach ached. When it came time to open the presents, she positioned herself on the blanket next to Latoya. The sun cooked her head as her best friend opened her gift. Latoya's mother and her grandmother exchanged a glance as Latoya hugged her. The bright red scooter was a hit.

By mid-evening, with the guests gone, Greta settled with Latoya in the living room. Her father, in corduroys and slippers, read a book while her mother flipped through a magazine. Her brothers, both older, knelt side by side at the coffee table and put the pieces of a skyline together in a puzzle.

"Bath time," her father announced fifteen minute later as he dropped his book in his lap.

Latoya groaned and, while she did what she was told, Greta watched out the front window. She couldn't see a single set of headlights on the street.

Latoya's mother glanced at her wrist. "I'm sure he's on his way," she said, reassurance warm in her voice.

When Latoya returned, hair wet, in pajamas, she climbed onto her father's chair, snuggling her nose in his shoulder. He smiled and wrapped his arms around her. Greta pulled her eyes away.

"Should we call?" Latoya's mother asked, stifling a yawn.

Greta stared at the carpet. Even if she wanted to, she didn't know the number.

"I'll get the class list." Latoya's mother disappeared to the front hall and, when she returned, there were lines etched across her forehead. "There's been some sort of mix-up."

Greta's cheeks burned. She pictured Ian on the couch, his face pressed into the plastic. She could almost smell the stink of the drool spilling out of his mouth.

She gave the best-surprised look she could muster.

The pencil stopped scratching the page and Detective Perez motioned to the chair. "I appreciate how that might have made you feel back then."

"He forgot me."

"There's thousands, maybe millions, of parents who get caught up late at work every day. Meetings. Special projects. A call from the boss. Traffic alone is a disaster."

She sat, arms at her sides, nerves ragged. "He was home."

"Maybe he fell asleep."

"More like sleeping it off."

Another taunting silence ensued. That hadn't been the worst of it. After she'd put on the pajamas Latoya's mother laid out and wormed her way into the makeshift bed on the floor, the blanket wrapped around her, thick, soft and warm, all she could think of was Bunny. Like every night, the lock outside her bedroom door would be bolted tight. She prayed he wouldn't wake up in the middle of the night in the dark, alone, missing her, and wondering where she was.

Detective Perez looked over the top of her glasses. "Let's move on. What about mental health issues in your family? Any history?"

Greta looked up. "What? I don't know."

"If there are any—and I'm not saying there are—it'd be nothing to be ashamed of. The whole stigma thing drives me crazy."

"Nice word choice," she remarked. "For your information, detective, my generation knows a lot more about mental health than *yours* does. Genetics. Hormones. Stress. The environment. Which, by the way, you wrecked. Back in the day, as my mom would've said, you hid your shit under the rug."

Detective Perez nodded in agreement. "It was a different era, I'll give you that." She folded her hands in front of her. "I'd like you to focus on your father. Did he have—"

She smacked her palm to her forehead. "He was born like that."

"And your mother?" said Detective Perez.

"What about her?"

"Anything up with her mental health?"

"I don't think so." Then she stopped. "Except maybe once. A whole year was out of whack."

TEN

"Your eyes look like scary marshmallows," Greta told her one morning over breakfast. "They're white and puffy and shiny inside."

Her mother glanced up from her coffee cup and rested her chin in her hands.

"Are you sick?" she asked.

"No, honey. Just tired."

She put her spoon down. "A little or a lot?"

"A bit."

"Are you gonna be slow? Or are you cranky?" She didn't want to miss her bus.

"Neither," said her mother.

"Then what?"

"It feels like storm clouds all around me."

Though Greta looked out the kitchen window, the morning sky clear and bright and blue, by the time the bus dropped her off after school, she knew something was up. Her mother wasn't standing waiting for her at the stop. She ran down the laneway to the cabin.

"Hello?" she called out.

No answer.

She pressed the front door shut. The kitchen was empty and dark, and down the hall in the living room, the TV was black, the chairs on the back patio empty.

"Mom?" she called out again.

A gnawing pain filled her stomach. She rushed upstairs and opened her bedroom door, covering her nose with her hands. It stunk of boiled cabbage. "I'm home," she whispered.

Her mother didn't stir.

"You forgot me," she said louder.

Still no response.

She dropped her hands to her sides and leaned down close to the edge of her mother's head. "Hey."

Emily squinted through the darkness. "That you, Colleen?"

She pulled a face. Who else would it be? "Who's Colleen?"

"An old friend. Just forget it... I was half-asleep. Go watch TV."

She didn't move an inch. "Is it the storm clouds?"

Her mother nodded. "You see them?"

She didn't know what to say. She'd looked for them all day. On the way to school and outside at recess and on the way home on the bus, but she couldn't find them.

"Kind of," she told her so she didn't feel bad.

Her mother patted her head, covered her ears with her pillow, and rolled over.

Greta found Bunny in her room and went downstairs. Desperate to know more about storm clouds, she flipped through the channels on TV. Were they invisible? Dangerous? Would the power go out again? Were they magic?

After school each day, whenever she found her mother in bed or on the couch, Greta searched for the clouds; she'd look on top of the covers, on the dresser beside her make-up, and underneath the mattress where the dust bunnies lived, but she never found them.

***

"Depression's complicated," Detective Perez said.

In no hurry, Greta took a slow, deep breath. "She was always sleeping. Stopped brushing her teeth. She had these cracked, flaky, dry lips. She didn't eat much either."

The detective nodded. "Unless someone's been there themselves, we're still learning what to do with it."

Though she tried to piece together what she knew, not a lot of it came back. "I knew she was unhappy, but back then I didn't understand why."

"Were there services up there to help?"

"I told you: we didn't do doctors."

"Right." The detective cleared her throat. "That must have been tough."

She pulled her hands over her face and sighed. "Not really. It didn't bother me half as much as the lying."

It was a late afternoon in December.

"Greta is going through a difficult time," she heard her mother tell Mrs. Harvey as she eavesdropped on their phone call. Happy her mother had finally come out of her bedroom, what she overheard stunned her. Maybe she'd heard wrong. She shut her eyes, straining to capture the conversation from the steps of the wooden staircase.

"She clung to my knees when the school bus pulled up, begging to stay home."

She hadn't. And it was Lie Number Two. She was flattened. Her beloved Mrs. Harvey would think she was a baby. Her prized Snack Helper job would be at risk.

Greta pushed herself off the bottom step and stormed into the kitchen, waiting for the conversation to finish. She counted to one, two, three; silently fuming. After her mother hung up the phone, she exploded. "What's wrong with you?" The strength of her voice echoed through the kitchen and bounced off the dingy white walls. "You know why I cried at the bus stop. You pinched me hard under my arms."

Her mother turned, startled, but didn't respond, not even to defend herself.

Greta took a step back. Who *are* you? Where is my *real* mother? *She* wouldn't have forgotten what happened. What did you *do* with her? Her *real* mother would know the truth.

She yanked up her sleeve and pointed to each one of the bruises. Purple and yellow and brown. The impostor took them all in.

Greta waited. A. Full. Awkward. Minute.

Her mother pursed her lips and chewed slowly on the bottom left corner. Greta knew the look. Contrite action was needed—and fast. She told her she didn't like it either when the kids called her Wretchen Gretchen but that, deep inside, she didn't care. The hurt was her mother's, not hers. She didn't pick her own name.

Lie Number Three came months later when Principal Parthi discovered Greta wasn't in school. He called the house to investigate, and her mother said she'd kept her home for the day to help with the spring-cleaning, claiming four hands made for easier work than two. But it didn't add up. Ian was home, so there were actually six hands, not four, and cleaning day was Saturday. That's what the rules taped to the refrigerator said. She couldn't read them yet, but she'd heard them so often she was absolutely certain it was on the list. She listened to the rest of the conversation, waiting to see what would happen.

"Principal Parthi, I'm fully within my rights to keep my daughter home now and again to help out with the chores."

Pause.

"I understand that."

Pause.

"Well, I'll have to check with my husband."

Longer pause. She cleared her throat.

"Then she'll be on the bus Monday morning." Her mother placed the phone in the receiver.

"Why are you still lying?" Greta asked.

Her face turned deep red. "I'm not."

"And now you're lying again."

"Greta, I can keep you home if I want to." She knelt down beside her and held her arms out. "Besides," she smiled, "when we're both home together, we're not lonely, are we?"

She stepped away and put her hands on her hips. "I'm not lonely. I have Mrs. Harvey."

Emily winced.

"*And* I have the kids at school."

Her mother pushed herself up from the floor. "When we're together, we're safe."

She looked at her mother. Had she gone insane? School was perfectly safe. Mr. Parthi said it was, and she'd heard him say it more than once. "If you need to be safe, you should find your own school for grown-ups," she told her.

Her mother's face clouded over. Greta could see from the way she was staring off in the distance, she was thinking. Good for her. Maybe she'd go find one—but if she did, there was something she needed to know. "Whichever one you choose," she told her, "you probably can't lie there."

A sharp crack rang out through the office. Greta stared wide-eyed at the detective.

"Sorry. Dropped my notebook." She stretched her arm down under her desk. "I can see why you were upset. Why do you think she was doing that?"

"Because of my father. She felt better when I was around." She pressed a hand to her chest. "All she and I had were each other."

The detective ran a finger across the page. "You just told me you had friends at school."

"It wasn't until right after that."

Detective Perez frowned. "So you weren't telling the truth?"

She raised her hands in the air. "I was. The timing's just disjointed."

Monday morning found Greta standing at the water table when a voice to her right said, "Nice you're back." The voice belonged to Latoya. She wore a purple dress with thick woolen tights, and had carefully braided pigtails perched high on her head. She was small, unlike Greta's tall. Her rich cocoa brown complexion contrasted with Greta's porcelain skin. Latoya spun her tugboat around an imaginary route in the oversized plastic tub. "Why is the sky blue?"

Greta pushed her limp black hair back from her face. She'd never thought about it. It just was and always had been, except when it rained. "I dunno," she said. She was happy one of her classmates was talking to her. "How small are the people on the radio?" she asked Latoya.

Latoya pinched her fingers together. 'Teeny weeny tiny, like this."

Greta flashed a grin. "Do you know the man who comes into your room at night to make sure you're asleep?"

Latoya turned to face her. "What?"

"And if you aren't, he gets mad?"

Latoya shook her head side-to-side. "Nope."

"Well, how long does someone have to stay under the blanket, like they're dead, until the man goes away again?"

Latoya paused. She stirred her boat around in the water. "I don't think that's true for Earth. But if it was true for far away, like somewhere in a monster movie, I'd guess about six minutes."

Greta considered Latoya's answer and thought it sounded right. A long time, but not too long. This girl was smart. To be sure, she asked her one more question. "Do you know if, when bees eat flowers, their farts smell like flowers?"

Latoya laughed. The space between her two front teeth showed. "Of course, silly. What else would they smell like?"

Greta picked up her tugboat with her left hand and steered it across the surface of the water. Then she stretched out her right, inching her fingers along the cool plastic side of the tub, until she found Latoya's.

ELEVEN

"Is this the same Latoya who was at your apartment last night?" Detective Perez said.

She smiled. "The one and only."

The detective flipped through the pages of her notebook. When she stopped, she said, "Her last name is—"

"Jackson."

Detective Perez wrote it down and underlined it twice.

"Want to talk to her?" She reached around the back of the chair, dug through her purse and pulled out her phone. "She knows about my parents. School, too. Grade One sucked. We had this teacher, Mrs. Stanton. If Ian ever came to school, I swear they would've been best friends. They both loved silence." What she didn't tell her was that, while Ms. Stanton repeatedly smacked the little silver bell on the side of her desk to bring order to her classroom, Ian demanded that everyone at home have a clearly marked and accessible *off* button. Greta's, he'd told her, was located on the side of her head. "And they both thought kids learned by repeating stuff a thousand times."

"Sounds familiar," Detective Perez sighed.

"When Latoya and me told my mom Mrs. Stanton was too strict, she promised we'd adjust, and when I told her Dad was an asshole, she promised he'd change, too."

"Did he?"

"It was all lies." She held out her phone. "Call her if you don't believe me."

"Latoya? How long exactly have you known her?"

"We're like sisters."

"I didn't ask who you were. I asked how long you've know her."

"I told you. My whole life. She'd do anything for me."

"That's what I'm afraid of. I'm sure you understand why that's a problem."

She shrugged and put her phone in her purse as a narrow-faced woman stuck her head through the doorframe of the office.

"Astra?"

Detective Perez craned her neck in her direction. "Are they back?"

"No, but I searched up the vic's background like you asked."

When the woman stepped into the room, Detective Perez took the document from her hand and skimmed through it. After a short silence, she turned back to face her.

"I'm confused. In your words," she looked at her notebook, her tone sour, "your father was an asshole. But it says here," she fluttered the piece of paper in her hand, "he was employed as a Deacon at a church." She put it down and planted her palms on the desk. Her voice rose. "I don't know a single deacon who acts like a jerk."

Greta's chest trembled. "Right. And you know all of them?

"Of course not."

"It's an expression." Her mother turned around and peered into the back seat. "It means you need to save for the unexpected."

"What I'm expecting is a bag full of candy."

Her mother's back stiffened and she turned away. "No need to be saucy, Greta. If you ever decide to start saving, I've got a dime box for you."

She opened her mouth to ask a question, but Ian caught her eye through the rear view mirror. He was mouthing her mother's words. Her mother looked at him in disbelief. When he started to laugh, her mother's head dropped, and it took a moment for Greta to notice her shoulders were shaking, too. Furious with them both, she closed her mouth and leaned her head on the back of the seat as Ian drove along the tree-lined streets. She knew the route to the downtown core by heart and could tell exactly where he'd turn off to get to the parking lot beside his office.

Ian Giffen, Municipality of Bracebridge.

As the truck pulled in, she stared at the sign. She didn't know why he had one but, from the very first time she'd seen it, she'd guessed he was someone important. She waited until the engine was shut off and then jumped out of the car and hugged her mother.

Ian smoothed the wrinkles from his Sunday suit and came around to their side and hoisted her up on his shoulders. He poked her hard in the side.

"Where are we going?"

He laughed as if he didn't know.

Greta ignored the pain in her ribs and played along. "Candy store, candy store, candy store." Light and free clinging tightly to his head, she kept her hands to the sides, careful not to touch the top because he didn't like to have one hair out of place. He turned around and jogged down the street.

"Wait for me," her mother called out.

Ian ignored her. In high heels and a dress, she ran behind them, trying her best to keep up. When Ian stopped to talk to friends on the street, she waved her arms to let him know she'd nearly closed the gap. Just as she got close, he looked her way; solid, calm and confident. Then he sped off again. The sign for the old-fashioned candy store appeared in the distance. Greta's mouth watered, evaporating any desire to wait. She pleaded with Ian to go inside.

"Go get 'em, tiger." He ruffled her hair with his hand, a rare gesture of affection.

Greta pushed the door open. She shut her eyes as a strong, sugary smell hit her. Opening them, she inspected the familiar glass jars lined up in rows on the counter and recited the names of the candies out loud. Caramels, Pixie sticks, Tootsie rolls, Licorice pipes, Wild strawberries, Cherry sours, Gummi freedom rings, Laffy taffy, Swedish fish. She knew which ones cost a dime and which ones cost less. Her favourites cost a penny. She took a brown paper bag from the pile on the counter and began to fill it up.

As the weight of the bag grew heavier, her mother pushed open the door of the store behind her. "Don't forget my cherry sours," she said with a smile.

She hadn't. Though her mother had taken forever to catch up, they were her favourite and she'd already stuffed five in the bag. As she grabbed two Pixie sticks and a Caramel for Latoya, an unfamiliar voice called out.

"Emily?"

Greta took her eyes off the glass jar and watched a strange woman approach her mother.

"It *is* you. Well, I'll be damned," she said, smiling.

Her mother's eyes widened with surprise. "Colleen... It's so good to see you again."

She recognized the name, but when Colleen hugged Emily tightly, Greta noticed her mother didn't hug her back quite as much. She was looking around the store, eyes darting left to right, scanning the aisles in front of her. Why was her mother so scared of her old friend? Her stomach knotted, and she put her candy bag on the counter in front of her and studied her.

Colleen wore make-up on her eyes. Her long brown hair was cut prettily, and she didn't dress like them; she wore nice jeans and a soft, stylish black leather coat. She was fancy. She got the sense she was not someone good and that Ian would be mad.

Colleen leaned towards her mother and touched her arm. "You alright?" she heard her murmur. "Is he here?"

When Ian walked through the front door of the store, she turned around and finished counting out her candy. Bag full, she walked to the front of the store and waited, but they didn't come to the front. They were huddled together at the back of the store with Colleen, talking in sharp whispers. She couldn't hear what they were saying, but she could tell from their faces they weren't happy.

Without warning, Ian broke away from the conversation and charged up the aisle to the cash register. "Let's go," he insisted. "Now."

Greta moved quickly. She handed her bag to the cashier, who smiled sweetly and took her five dimes. Her mother strolled calmly to the front of the store, took her hand, and pulled her out of the way as Colleen brushed by abruptly.

On the street outside the store, Ian's mood soured instantly. He shot her mother a look Greta knew spelled trouble. She braced herself. "Did you know?" he snarled at Emily.

"How on earth would I? I was as surprised to see her as you were."

Ian got right up in her mother's face. "Oh, I know how you could have. You've already proved that, haven't you? Don't get me started."

Her mother paled. "She's entitled to be in the candy store as much as anyone else. It was a coincidence."

"Coincidence my ass." He spat a big, white blob on the street. With his face bright red, he clenched and unclenched his fists. He stepped forward, snatched away Greta's candy bag, and jammed it in the garbage can.

Greta watched in disbelief. "But I got everything perfect. You can't take that."

"Oh, yes I can." His look reduced her cry to a sniveling whimper. "And I just did."

"But why?"

Ian fumed.

"Tell me why." Her voice was shrill and desperate.

He lowered his face to hers and growled. "Life's not fair, kid. And I don't want to hear one question from you."

"Then close your dumb ears!" she screamed back.

Ian's eyes bulged. He shot up and backed away from her, then turned on his heel and strode up the street, leaving them in his wake.

At home where no one could hear, the yelling started. Greta watched her parents fight from the top of the stairs. Her father's eyes were glassy and his words unclear. She tried to make them out.

If you ever tell anyone, I'll fucking slit your throat.

Her eyes widened.

Same goes for...

She leaned forward, but his sentence trailed off. Colleen?

And hers too.

Who's too?

All fucking three of you. Don't think I won't.

Her tummy ached. Was she in trouble now, too?

The fighting went on for ages. Her mother tried to get him to listen, but it was like he couldn't hear or didn't want to. Greta's ears hurt from all the noise, and so she gave up, went to her room, curled into a ball, and pulled her sheet up over her head. Even the soft weave of Bunny's ear couldn't calm her; not this time. Colleen had wrecked Sunday, and it was an eternity until the next one.

Greta hated her father, and whoever Colleen was, she hated her, too.

TWELVE

Detective Perez peered over the top of her glasses. Long lines ran across to the bottom of the page of her notebook, words capitalized, underlined and crossed out.

"If what you're telling me is true—"

"It is."

"Your mother must have been scared, too."

Greta laughed bitterly. "She wasn't scared of him. She put up with him."

The detective whistled through her teeth and made a dipping motion with her head. "In which case, that's a strong woman."

Something about the detective's comment finally put her at ease, though she couldn't quite tell what it was. She twisted around the back of the chair, pulled her phone from her purse again, and punched in the passcode, flicking through the pictures on the roll with her thumb. The Xiangzis. Her teammates. Shots of Bracebridge. Goofball Latoya. An endless stream to choose from, but only one taken before she had turned fourteen. She tapped on her mother's face and passed it over to Detective Perez. "It's a little older," she explained. Detective Perez examined the screen and, when she glanced up, Greta added, "The picture I mean."

The detective passed back her phone. "Tell me more about her."

She dropped the phone back into her purse, groped through the folds in the side, and found her chapstick. She ran it around her lips. "Chatty and loveable."

It was the second hottest summer Greta could remember—well-above normal temperatures. She gave up wiping the sweat dripping from her forehead and let it run freely in rivers down the sides of her face. The ice cubes in the hand-squeezed lemonade her mother had made had melted in minutes, and the little pithy lemon pieces sunk, pooling together on the bottom of the glass like a knot of worms.

"Why's it so hot?" She unpeeled her thighs from the faded green and white plastic patio chair. They'd had those same chairs forever.

"We can't control the weather," her mother said. "Besides, if we didn't have it, what else would we all talk about?"

Her mother always told her people in Canada loved to talk about the weather. Each time she met somebody new, the conversation always started in the same way... Rain. Sun. Snow. Humidity. *Hey, can you believe the...?* It was always a case of insert-the-weather-of-the-day. It was like the typical Canadian's greeting.

That afternoon, two main roads had collapsed in the heat. The municipality cordoned off the highway because of the size of the sinkholes, but as the cottagers had started to come north for their vacations, they needed the road crew to work double-time. Ian was scheduled to work late that evening, and then his boss told him he'd be working the night shift all week. While it wasn't his preference, any evening she had with her mother at the cabin by herself was a rare opportunity to stay up late and talk or watch what they wanted on TV.

She waved her hand at the back of her neck and flapped her shirt. "Tell me about when you and Ian met."

Emily rolled her eyes and gave her the not-this-again look. Her mother had told her the story when she was younger, but she didn't remember it clearly. Now that she was eight, she wanted to hear it again. Maybe then she could figure out her family's secrets? Why Ian hated her so much and why she didn't have any memories as a little kid.

"It was July 1996. Your dad and I fell in love in The Hammer."

She leaned back on the patio chair. *That's so weird,* she thought. How anybody could fall in love in a place named after a tool was beyond her, but she wasn't asking questions this early on in the story or she knew her mother would stop talking altogether.

"It was love at first sight," her mother said.

"Like the googly-eyed Lady and the Tramp love? When they sat down at supper in the fancy restaurant and ate spaghetti together?"

Her mother laughed. "I was sixteen."

Yuck, Greta thought, her mother was old. *Sixteen is pyramid ancient.*

"We spent every day of that summer together, your dad and I. A couple of days with Aunt Hannah—"

She eyed her mother. "Aunt Hannah? Who's Aunt Hannah?"

"My sister."

"What?" She hadn't seen a single photo of her mother's sister anywhere around the cabin. Not on the walls or in the living room. Not even in her mother's bedroom. Had her mother drunk the worms in the bottom of the lemonade? She tried to keep her voice even. "You've never said anything about her before."

"We're not discussing it." Her mother looked wearily at her lap. "And don't bother with the third degree. It was a long time ago."

She examined her mother's face in the early evening light and knew it wasn't worth pushing. Though she'd always wanted a sister to hang out with, she decided she'd have to file Aunt Hannah away for later.

"After six months," her mom said, "your dad and I were so in love we started a new life together."

"What was wrong with your old one?"

"It's an expression."

She'd never heard any adult say anything like that before, but decided to believe her. "Keep going," she directed, adding "please."

"We bought a couple of newspapers. The Brantford Expositor. Maybe the Toronto Star? I can't remember which one, but we checked out the classifieds for somewhere to live. That was back in 1996, before things were online."

She nodded, knowingly. "Yeah, you guys lived in the dinosaur age. You had to drive to see your friends. We can speak to ours anytime now, like on Facebook." Not that Greta did because they didn't have internet at the cabin but, even still, she knew how it worked. She'd been on Facebook at the school library. "And you listened to music on black shiny discs as big as car wheels. Or on tapes the size of a book."

"Eight tracks," her mother said. "They were called eight tracks."

"Whatever. Now we have iPods that get, like, hundreds of songs. Not that I have one like everyone else in my class." Pleased the way she'd worked in that subtle hint, she hoped a little guilt would pay off on her next birthday. "I'm so happy I'm not a pioneer lady like you. It would've sucked."

Her mother frowned. "I'll have you know 1996 was an interesting year, Greta. Ontario had a wicked tornado outbreak. And Marc Garneau flew off on his second space mission."

She grimaced. "Good to know."

Her mother's history lessons annoyed her. She was always doing it and she knew her lame tricks. She'd be right in the middle of a good story and then she'd wreck it by weighing it down with useless details; inconsequential facts no one wanted to know and nobody cared about. It was like her mother thought she was too young to realize she was trying to open her eyes to the world beyond their northern Ontario neighbourhood.

She sat up in her chair, clenched her jaw tight, and glared at her from across the patio, so mad at the way she started the story—the story she asked to hear. She didn't want to hear anything else. She didn't care how she and Ian met—she didn't like him anyway—and she wasn't interested their history anymore. She picked up her glass, went back inside, and slammed it in the sink. When her mother joined her on the couch in the main room, she grabbed the TV remote off her lap and turned up the volume.

The next morning, Greta tiptoed out of her bedroom, crept down the wooden staircase, and stole out the front door of the cabin. Then she ran. Down the steps. Around the side of the house, sprinting past the stone patio, heels kicking up dust on the dirt path. No time for dilly-dallying. She raced through the backyard. When she reached the end of the grass, she crossed her legs in front of the rotting structure, raising her eyes to the sky.

"Please, don't make it squeak."

She knew it was no use—and couldn't wait any longer.

"One, two, three."

The door groaned. Feeling her way, she shifted forwards a little, then an inch to her left, far away from the crack on the seat. Held together with a screw, one wrong move meant drowning face first in the brown muck underneath. "Ewww," she moaned, covering her mouth. It didn't work. She held her breath too.

Greta didn't understand why some people called an outhouse a privy. It wasn't private. Whole colonies of flies buzzing around her head made it their home. After her eyes adjusted, she waved her hands to command them.

"Okay, shut up and listen," she told them, then she paused, making sure she had their attention. "Jones family, you have the floor. Santos family, you take the bench. And McKenzies, this morning you've got the roof."

But the flies didn't listen; they buzzed all around, their families mixed together.

Then *Whomp*. Greta jumped, nearly falling off the seat.

"What ya doing in there," she heard Ian yell from outside. He shook the walls of the latrine.

Greta groaned. What did he want?

Whomp. Whomp.

She felt the rough seat shift beneath her butt. Her face grew hot and she gripped the sides of the bench. "Not funny," she said.

"It's coming down, Greta, it's all coming down," he said, laughing manically. He rattled the boards outside. Greta felt like she was sitting in the midst of an earthquake. Then it stopped. Ian opened the door and peered inside, a tree branch clutched tight in his hand. He stared at her, her pants down around her ankles. He smirked.

"When it falls," he said, "I'm not jumping in to save you."

"Get out," Greta warned him. Her bottom lip quivered. She threw the roll of toilet paper at him.

Ian poked her legs with the branch—hard. She lifted them up and, when she did, heard the toilet seat creak. Her back broke out in a sweat. She reached down to the floor of the latrine and felt around the damp boards. She found the rock she had hidden, just for emergencies like this, and hurled it directly at Ian. It hit him on the forehead.

"What the—" he said, dazed. He brought his hand up to his face. When he dropped it, there was a red smear on his fingertips.

Greta's heart leapt into her throat. She felt his dark eyes upon her. He took two steps forward.

"I'm gonna shove you down that bloody hole."

Greta stood quickly, pulled the outhouse door closed, and snapped the inside hook down through the eye. She clutched the inside handle. "You're such an asshole," she muttered.

She felt the door rattle in her hands. The hook slipped but she held on as tight as she could. She screamed at him, "I'll cut your throat while you sleep if you ever do that again."

Ian grunted, pushing his full weight on the door. A loud popping sound rang out and Greta felt the door give way. One by one, Ian's fingers curled round the inside of the boards. She cowered back as his arm snaked through the gap and flailed around erratically, swatting at the hook. Suddenly, she heard her mother's stern voice nearby.

"Ian, that's enough."

His arm dropped. There was quiet for a moment, and then a slap before something fell to the ground. Greta shot straight up from the seat and peered through the knot in the wood. Her mother's cheek burned an angry pink. Ian stood, his fist raised above her.

"Leave the kid be," she said.

His fist swung. Another thud. Greta heard her mother moan. Then he disappeared from her sight. She counted to ten five times over, unlocked the door, and pushed it open. Her mother rolled to her side slowly, wiping blood from her nose before getting to her feet.

"Honey, you're okay." She passed over the roll of toilet paper. "Finish up."

Greta sat back down on the seat and rubbed her eyes with the palm of her hand. Red-faced, she stared at the ground. "I hate him."

"We'll go for a walk."

"I hate those, too."

"Come on. I'll tell you the rest of the story."

Detective Perez traced a finger along her jawline. "I'm beginning to see why you didn't like him."

She blurted a little laugh. "You think?"

"It's a good thing you and your mom are so close."

"We did everything together. She knew everything about me back then." Greta struggled to speak through the lump in her throat. "The stuff I liked to eat, what I thought about, my dreams, my favourite colour. We shared all our secrets."

It was kind of true, just not the whole truth. Because, as it turned out, her mother had kept secrets she never dreamed of.

THIRTEEN

Greta sauntered around the corner to the front of the cabin and to find her mother waiting for her on the porch. After she kissed her on the forehead, they fell in step beside each other, the gravel crunching under their feet. Neither spoke of Ian's stupid outhouse games, his clenched fists or Emily's bruised face.

"We lived in four places in three years," her mother said after they made their way up the laneway. "The first was in Lindsay in a widow's basement. It was freezing with snowdrifts five feet high."

Greta stopped. She was pretty sure that was taller than she was. Was it taller than her mother?

"And there wasn't a lot of light because there was foil wrapped over the windows."

"Was the old lady a vampire or something?" Greta remembered a book she'd found in the library that explained how vampires stayed in the dark because they thought if they went outside they'd burn in the sun. She stuck her teeth over her bottom lip.

Her mother laughed. "No, not those either. It keeps the house cool in the summer and it's cheaper than curtains. I think she just forgot to take it off for the winter."

"I get it," she said. But she didn't. She was in the midst of doing a double-check, walking quickly through their cabin in her mind.

It was made of long, knotty, logs stacked together in a way her mother described as having character. Two small four-pane windows framed either side of the wooden front door. The windows were identical in shape, and looked almost like the Japanese origami she'd made at school in Craft Club. Inside the front door, just on the left, was a closet. Beside it, a towering wood stand to hang sweaters and jackets. The kitchen was inside the front door to the right. A long beige counter stretched under the light that filtered in from the window, next to the fridge and stove. That was where the rules were posted, stuck to the side of the fridge. By the end of Grade Two, Greta was able to read them. They were written in her father's hand:

Silence is golden.

No crying.

Speak only when spoken to.

Tell the truth.

Clothes were made to be modest and cover the body completely.

No games allowed in the house.

No TV after 7pm.

Saturday is for cleaning.

Sunday is for church.

Down the hall from the kitchen was the main room. A window stretched from the floor to the ceiling, welcoming in daylight that bounced off the plastic wrapping the furniture. On the left side of the main room, a crooked wooden staircase had been built straight up close to the wall; the stairs moved when she walked up and down them, no matter how carefully she trod. The second floor, with its oddly peaked roof, extended the width of the cabin. She'd learned the hard way that Ian

stopped at the front door, she turned to Greta. "Well, never mind then," she said, shoo-shooing it away. "What matters is that the old lady asked us to move. So we found a new place in Peterborough."

The sun faded, leaving the northern sky a deep crimson red, yet the heat of the day remained. Ian was at work so, after dinner, Greta suggested they head to the back patio to hear the rest of the story.

"Where's Peterborough?" she asked.

"About 45 kilometers east of Lindsay," her mother said, settling in a chair beside her.

Greta had no idea how far that was. She'd heard her father say the laneway was a kilometer long, so the distance between Lindsay and Peterborough would be like running up and back forty-five times without stopping. No rest. If it weren't so hot tomorrow, maybe she'd try. "Was the new place nice?"

"The ground floor? It had a living room with a stone fireplace, a bedroom, and a tiny kitchen at the back. It was tucked in the middle of a Victorian row house on the edge of the Trent River. We lived in Number Six, with neighbours on both sides."

"Was there tinfoil on the windows?"

"No, we had big open windows like here in the cabin." She pointed over her shoulder to the back outside wall.

"Then curtains?"

"Yes. They were blue like a robin's egg, and they had flounces."

"Sounds lame." Greta thought about it. "Why did you and Ian have curtains there and not here?"

Her mother closed her eyes while Greta sat and waited. "Back then, your father didn't want anyone looking in," her mother said.

"Was he doing something he shouldn't have been? Like breaking the law?" She'd seen handcuffs in her parents' bedroom, the same ones Officer Pappas had strapped to his black belt when he came to visit at school. Her mind was spinning—right out of control. "Was Ian a criminal? Is that why you have handcuffs in your dresser?"

Her mother snorted. "Of course not. And you shouldn't be snooping in our room."

She ignored her. "Then why don't we have curtains here?"

"Look around, sweet child. What do you see? We've got privacy ten miles in each direction."

Greta stared out into the forest. Her mother had a point. Besides the red flowers her mother planted around the small, smooth white collection of stones every year, all she could see were trees and bushes. The forest was so dense she couldn't even see through it. "What did you do in Peterborough?"

"Dad looked for a job, but almost everything was taken by the students from Trent University trying to make money for school."

"Did you go to university, Mom? At Trent?"

"No, sweetheart," she said. "It wasn't in the cards for me."

Greta looked over to see if her mother was serious. She was.

"Within a couple of weeks, your father found something part-time at The Lift Lock. It was physical work, outdoors in the late evening heat. But it left our days free to do what we wanted."

She wasn't sure what her mother liked to do. She always did what Ian told her to, but maybe that was her choice, too; after all, they were married and she was pretty sure that's what married people did—together stuff.

"Some days we packed a lunch and went to the Sandy Lake Beach in Buckhorn for a picnic. Other days we walked through the trails at the Riverside Zoo. We saw camels, two-toed sloths, yaks and emus. On hot days we stayed home and walked out our back door and just jumped in the river."

Greta's eyes narrowed, blade-thin. Something was off. "That's not true," she said. "You're scared of water."

Her mother looked away, her face clouding against the long shadows across the length of the patio, and gazed far off deep down into the ends of the back yard. Greta imagined inky pools full of wild animals, lions, cheetahs, and wild boars, long in the tooth and short on patience.

"So what's the deal?" she said.

"You know the lock's dual lifts on the Trent Severn-Waterway? Back then, they were the highest hydraulic boatlifts in the world," her mother said. "A true Canadian treasure."

Greta groaned. Here we go again. She would not be sucked into the history game. Not this time.

"How'd you jump in the river, Mom?" she repeated, determined to uncover the truth. "You can't swim."

Her mother looked right through her and bypassed the question. "Your father did his best that summer. He worked hard but, with all the stress, he missed a couple shifts. Maybe more than two. Probably a few. When his boss called, he told me to say he was sick. I did but his boss didn't believe me, and so Ian lost his job. With money tight, the landlord evicted us."

"What does that mean?" Greta thought she already knew, but she wanted to be sure.

"Leave, darling. We had to leave our house by the river. So Dad and I packed up what little we had as fast as we could before the police showed up at the door."

Detective Perez tapped her pencil on the desk. "Stop for a sec. Did your mother say anything else about these evictions?"

"No."

Tap, tap.

"Did the police ever show up?"

"I don't know. She never said and I was maybe nine years old when she told me."

Tap, tap.

"Did she say why not?"

Why the detective asked the questions she did was beyond her; she didn't appreciate her game of cat and mouse. She thought back to all the events that had led up to that point.

"Understood. But those details would've been good for me to know."

"You? I wasn't thinking about you. I was digging for myself. Looking for hints she'd drop. And that night she was pissing me off like you are."

The detective tossed her pencil down, causing it to roll across the desk. "Did you get what you wanted?"

"No." She reached out and shoved it back.

Back on the patio, Greta's long bony arms were covered in goose bumps and the mosquitos had worsened in the mid-evening air. They were using her ankles as an all-you-can-eat buffet, turning them red and swollen. She yawned, unsure whether she could go on. If she couldn't, she knew there might not be another chance to hear the rest of the story. Love. Two houses. Eviction. Police. She knew there were things that didn't add up. But what were they? She decided to change her approach. Tone it down a little. Be gentler on her mother. After all, she used to be her best friend—until she got real friends, like Latoya.

"Mom..." She allowed her face to reflect mild surprise. "That's crazy. You had to move again? I feel bad for you."

Her mother looked at her, the corners of her eyes crinkling. Her mouth turned slowly into a smile. Greta smiled back at her. "It wasn't the worst thing that happened," her mother said.

She stopped dead in her tracks. Was this the moment? Was her mother about to tell her whatever she'd been hiding? Adrenaline cursed through her body and gave her the second wind she needed to stay awake. "What do you mean?" She made sure to match her mother's sweet, low tone. "About it not being the worst thing, I mean."

"Oh," her mother said, waving a hand in the air. "It's just one of those adult expressions."

She kicked the legs of her chair.

Her mother appeared not to notice. "Remind me. Where were we?"

Heat rose in her cheeks. "You and Ian were evicted. You said Ian wasn't a criminal but I think he was, and I bet you know he was, too. You're just not saying."

Her mother shot her the warning look. She caught it but she was frustrated; she had asked her mother to tell her the story because she wanted to hear the whole thing. The truth—the *whole* truth. Nothing that wasn't true. It pissed her off. It was like she didn't want to tell her the story. She stuck out her lip, pouting.

"The third place was Bracebridge. We'd never been that far north before. By the time we got there, the fall colours had spread through Muskoka, covering it like a blanket. Yellows, reds and oranges, all floating from the trees, spinning on the breeze, leaving a river of colour that ran through the streets of the town." She leaned forward, half-smiling, lost in thought. "It was beautiful. How can anyone go wrong living in a town like that? It's home to Santa's Village—a Christmas theme park." She looked at Greta. "Coincidentally, do you know Santa's Village sits at a 45-degree latitude, exactly halfway between the equator and the North Pole? How cool is that?"

"Cool, really cool," she shot back. How would she know? Her parents hadn't bothered to take her.

Her mother looked away, as if she'd read her mind. "Dad got a job with the municipality before we arrived. The same one he has now."

"Keeping the roads safe." She'd seen all the cars on the road on the way to school, not to mention in the parking lot at church on Sunday.

"And full-time meant benefits."

"Like prizes?" she asked. Was that why the furniture in their main room was wrapped in plastic?

Emily laughed. "Health insurance and holidays."

Greta smirked. Another lie. They'd never been on a holiday.

"It was like we'd won the lottery."

"How much money does Ian make?"

Her mother looked as puzzled as she felt. "No idea. I've never asked him. He takes care of the finances."

Greta's chest tightened. Wasn't that the truth—more for himself, no doubt. She'd seen the faces of the families who watched them scour the hand-me-downs at BFT. BFT was what the kids called it. Bracebridge Fashion Boutique. But it wasn't. It was Bracebridge Thrift. It made her angry how her father bought shiny new shoes and white shirts with button-down collars when all they ever got were second-hand sweaters and long pants. She made a mental note that the next time she was on the computer in the school library, she would find out how much money a full-time worker in Bracebridge was paid.

"Our third place was quaint," her mother told her.

"That's weird," she said, scrunching up her nose.

"Exactly. Whimsical. A summer cottage. No water, and the old well around the back was dry as a bone. Dad's new friends came to help us out."

She kept her face straight. *Dad's new friends...* Like someone like him could ever have any. In the eight years she'd been in the cabin, she couldn't remember a single time they'd had visitors.

Greta was exhausted. Her mother had said four houses, and so far she'd only covered three. She pinched herself to stay awake because the fourth was hers: the cabin in Ravensworth. Would Nancy Drew fall asleep with a mystery smack dab in front of her? Not a chance—and she wouldn't either. She stifled a yawn.

"Were you happy back then?" she asked.

Her mother raised a hand to the chain around her neck, twisting the little pink bead back and forth. "Moving eighty kilometers to the boonies?"

From her tone of voice, Greta knew the answer. "Why move where you don't want to live? It's not like you were married. I would have kicked his butt to the curb."

Her mother laughed. "It's complicated. When you're older, you'll learn relationships have ebbs and flows."

No, Greta thought, *I won't*. And she didn't know what ebbs and flows were, but they sounded disgusting.

"Anyway, it was immaterial. When Dad first showed me the cabin, he'd already made the down payment."

"So just pay another."

"It was small but well-kept for a hunting camp. He had to drive to work in Bracebridge but he was convinced we were moving on up."

Greta mulled. "So Ian wanted this place and he got it. He wanted privacy and got that, too. Plus he could drive to work." She waited for her to confirm. Her mother didn't say a word. "Hello? Did *you* get anything out of this?"

Her mother's jawline twitched, and she turned and looked across the table. She smiled. "Darling, I got everything I wanted. I got you."

FOURTEEN

"**M**uffin?" Detective Perez nudged a white cloth bag across her desk. "I made them last night."

The question was so unexpected it threw Greta off guard. What was taking so long? And she didn't want a muffin. She wanted to turn her down but knew it was a bad idea, and so she reached out and took one anyway. The tiny, wet purple blobs sprinkled across the top brought to mind days spent picking wild blueberries in the shrubs at the far end of the property with her mother. She poked at the fruit.

Detective Perez frowned, reached into the bag, pulled out a knife and a container of butter, and pushed them across the desk. "Let's get back to your father," she said.

Greta picked up the blade like she might slice her in half. "Didn't you hear me? I'm done with him."

The detective sighed, watching her.

"I didn't do anything. If I did, why would I agree to come here?"

"Unlike him, you still have the ability to make that choice."

She thought back to the frantic moments after the candy store and the outhouse, and everything else that happened. "He's not the victim here. Why aren't you asking about me?"

The detective paused, the muffin poised an inch from her mouth. "You?"

Greta stabbed at the muffin. "Yes, *me*. I'm not telling you anything more about that asshole or what happened at the hospital until you know how *I* survived."

Detective Perez sighed. "Fine. If you must."

On the first day of Grade Three, Greta ran around the playground, desperate to find Latoya. The fact she hadn't been picked up along the bus route hadn't set off alarm bells; Latoya wasn't the type of person who liked to be rushed, and her mother often had to drive her to school. After the bell rang, Greta followed the line inside and stopped, her eyes wide, her guard up. The teacher at the front of the room was a man. He had broad shoulders, dark brown hair, a blade-thin nose. Did he like to drink in the evenings like her father? When her classmates were seated, he held out a file and read names from a list.

"'Scuse me, Mr..." She hesitated as he hadn't yet introduced himself. "Mr. Teacher, you've made a mistake... You forgot Latoya."

The class giggled. She held her breath as he examined the piece of paper, watching him triple-check it. After what felt like five minutes, he looked up over the silver moon-shaped glasses balanced on the end of his nose. "What's your name, little one?"

The giggling exploded like fireworks. Cheeks deep red, she sunk down into her desk. Who was this man and where had he come from? While the expression reminded her of the ones her mother liked, she imagined her father would think he was a dipshit, too.

"Greta," she whispered.

"Mine is Mr. Ennis." He pointed to the blackboard where he'd written his name in capital letters using chalk. More snickering from the class. "There's no Latoya on the list."

She didn't understand it. Latoya was gone. She'd vanished; vaporized into the ether.

For the rest of the morning, Greta sulked bitterly and hoped Mr. Ennis had made the biggest mistake of his career. But then, at recess, she found out Latoya and her family had moved away during the summer—to someplace called Orillia. Her best friend hadn't said a word. Not a whisper. Not a call when she knew they had her number. Her heart shattered into a thousand pieces, each one flung like pebbles across the playground.

With no time to grieve (she'd seen what happened to kids who played alone), Greta set out to acquire a new best friend. Secrets... Everyone had them—and she kept secrets well. They were an art form; one her family provided perfect training to master. She'd learned it technically didn't matter whether you had a one or not; the power was in the illusion you did. Undisclosed information people didn't know they wanted until they had it.

That afternoon, the playground pipeline flooded with juicy gossip. Principal Parthi hits Mrs. Stanton to make her obey him. The shy kids looked on from afar in wonder. Principal Parthi has handcuffs in his office for when she won't.

The news spread like wildfire. The cool kids flocked to her side. Had anyone seen them? Someone said they had. Then somebody else confirmed they had, too.

Without a word, Greta stood, letting them dig deep in the dirt as she held court to consider their speculation. A lift of an eyebrow, a perfectly placed smile, and a mischievous grin were all it took until every kid on the bus wanted to sit beside her or asked her to eat lunch with them the next day.

The following morning, Greta could feel the eyes of the teachers on her a little more closely than usual and, after Mr. Ennis talked to the class about the disturbing lies floating around the playground, he took them out into the back field to run. He pointed to the track. "Five times round." The class stood with their mouths open. Mr. Ennis, who doubled as the school's track couch, crossed his arms over his chest. "Get moving."

When the class thought they'd die if they ran any farther, Mr. Ennis told them they were sufficiently warmed up to participate in a series of races. The class groaned in unison, but Greta was secretly thrilled: she'd run up and down the laneway at home as far back as she could remember. When Mr. Ennis lined them up in groups of six, she bent down on the track and listened for the signal.

"Go!" he shouted.

Greta burst ahead. Her arms flailed in the air and she ran every race as if her feet were on fire, barely touching the ground. When the heats were finished, she was the only one in the class lined up for each final race and, by the end of the afternoon, she was the fastest runner in every competition.

Back in the classroom, a boy shot brownish-green vomit from his mouth in a projectile fashion, splattering everyone in the back row, and while most of the kids slumped in their desks, exhausted, Greta still had fuel left in her. Even with her socks full of holes and her running shoes course against her soles, she could run all day long. It was what she dreamed of at night. She could run forever.

Greta was eight, and wise enough to know something at home was collapsing around her. She worked hard to be the peacemaker, yet there was only so much she could do. Ian burned with a flame of fury. His whole body shook with rage. Her mother stayed silent, and her meekness fuelled his fire. She was used to the long silences by then; her parents ignored each other for weeks. When Ian came home from work each night, Greta stayed upstairs in her room. Only suppertime was unavoidable.

"These are butt ugly," she told her mother one night as she set the plates out on the table.

Emily looked over her shoulder. "They have character."

She held one up to the light; pitted and chipped. How had she not seen that before? Had they always been that way?

"Why are they so beat up?" She examined the other two. "They're three different colours."

Her mother shrugged and dropped a handful of chopped carrots into a pot. "They're all the thrift store had."

Greta rolled her eyes. Of course. They had someone else's cast offs. "It's disgusting."

She sat down at the table and ran her finger around the rim of a plate. *Where did you come from?* She imagined herself as a tiny unseen speck on the side, watching snippets of the lives of the people who owned them before they did. In their kitchens. In their backyards. In their main rooms. She bet their last life had been better. She imagined there had been mountains of food. Laughter. Maybe birthday parties. Maybe they'd even been part of a set. But now, all singles had been tossed out or given away. Where was the rest of their real family? Where was *hers*? What did her real parents look like? Did she look like her mom? Her dad? Did she have brothers and sisters? What happened? Why hadn't they kept her either?

"Can I see my birth certificate?" she asked.

Her mother sighed. "Your timing's not great, Greta. Your father will be home soon."

"Later then?"

"Another day."

"Every adoption has papers. I want to see them."

"You'll be ready for all that when you're older."

"How old?"

"Twelve."

"No, now. What's the big deal?"

"There isn't one, so drop it and take your fingers off the plates. One day we'll get new ones."

Greta pouted. It wasn't right. Four years was a long way away, and Ian had a job so surely they could get new plates now. He had his own parking space. New shoes. An endless supply of bottles. She pointed to the cheque made out to the church tacked up on the fridge.

"We *have* money." Her face burned when she thought of her clothes. They weren't as stylish as what the other kids wore and because her haircut was plain, she kept it wrapped up in a ponytail. Her sneakers had holes that soaked her socks in the rain and she still had the pink backpack she'd been given on the first day of school. So where was the money? What was it for? *She* needed some.

"Mom," she said sweetly, "can I get an iPod?"

"Are you kidding me? We can't even afford plates."

All Greta heard her mother say was they had money but the money they had wasn't for her. For things she needed. For things she wanted. She was well aware of the difference. "Fine. I'll buy one myself." She knew she couldn't, but she said it anyway, just to be difficult.

"That's a great idea."

"What?" She hadn't expected that as her answer.

"This is why I've been telling you to save your money."

It was what her mother had told her every Sunday on the way to the candy store, and she hated when her mother was right. She always rambled on about something. What was it called? "About that dime box thing..."

When her mother turned from the soup, the look on her face made her cringe. Oh no. She lay her head on the table. Here we go with the history and it's gonna start with those four stupid words. The dial clicked on the stove and her mom sat down at her side. "Back in the day," her mother said.

Greta groaned.

"There were public payphones all over."

She looked up and half-smiled, pretending to be interested.

"When they were invented in 1946, the phone company charged five cents for a call, but in the early 1950s, the phone company doubled it. People were outraged. Ten cents was a lot of money—twice what they were used to paying."

She scoffed. So what? "The payphones in Bracebridge cost fifty cents. Ten cents is a good deal. If they didn't want to pay, they shouldn't have made any calls."

Her mother frowned. "They had no choice. There were no cell phones, and some people didn't have a phone in their house. They relied on those public payphones. To book a doctor's appointment. To keep in touch with family."

Would she ever get to the point? "Can we get on to the dime box thing?" she asked after she made a mental note to look up the pay phone business in the school library. It was interesting, but her mother didn't need to know.

Her mother folded her hands on the table. "Because people never knew when they needed to make a call, they kept a box to save their dimes in. That's why they're called dime boxes."

A box for dimes? What did they look like? Were they big? Were they small? How many dimes could they hold? What if there were too many and the box overflowed onto the floor? Consequences would be dealt with in her house. Ian would be sure of it.

Her mother left the kitchen and, when she returned, she was holding a red wooden box in her hands. Greta jumped up and grabbed it. "Is this a real one?" she asked, examining it.

Her mother nodded.

She opened it. There was nothing inside. She lifted it to her nose and sniffed. Musty. She shut the lid and held it high. There were designs carved into the outside and she ran her fingers slowly along the smooth ridges. Then she turned it over. "Look. Someone's initials."

Her mother's face darkened. She crossed the kitchen and stood in front of the stove.

Greta pointed to the bottom. "Who's D.S.?" she said.

"Beats me, sweetie."

She put the dime box on the table. "Where'd you get it?"

Her mother picked up the ladle, stirred the soup, and filled two bowls on the counter. "At an antique market in Bracebridge years ago." After she brought the soup to the table, she dug a hand into the side of her dress and pulled something out of her pocket. She handed it over.

"What this?" Greta asked.

"Your birth certificate."

She unfolded the sheet.

Greta Giffen.

Birth date: July 16, 2000.

Birthplace: Parry Sound.

She looked up. "It's a photocopy. Where's the real one?"

"No more questions, Greta," her mother said. "Your father's late, so eat your soup and stop bugging me."

Greta put the copy of her birth certificate in her dime box. Pleased she got one of the two things she wanted, she'd ask for the original and her adoption papers another day. If her dad wasn't around then, maybe she'd ask her mom about her old friend Colleen and what she'd overheard the night her mother and her father were fighting.

Later that evening, she hid her dime box beneath her bed. Under her sheet with Bunny, she thought about all the money she'd spent over the years at the candy store. Had she saved some of it, she could have bought an iPod. Had she saved it all, she might've had enough to go to Orillia and see Latoya. The pillow damp, she swiped her palms across her cheeks. Her heart hurt. It was as if she'd been swallowed up. She still missed her.

FIFTEEN

Detective Perez picked up her phone and punched in some numbers. "Where're Sanchez and Hatten?"

She rolled her eyes.

"Astra... Who the hell do you think it is?"

Consternation and another eye roll.

"Remind them I have next to zero background here."

She paused as she listened to the speaker on the other end of the phone.

"They found *what*?" She wrote something down. "I need to see it. Are they on their way now?"

A longer pause filled the room.

"Then have them send it to me ASAP." She punched the screen again and put the phone down. "Okay, Greta. I've noted what you've said. The lies you told to avoid becoming an outcast and the wooden box you got from your mom. Are you done?"

Greta's cheeks burned. "No. That's not how I got through my father's shit."

"We're here to discuss what happened in that hospital room prior to your father dying."

"Back to him already?" That figured. "I ran—and, no thanks to him, I got pretty good at it."

Detective Perez tented her fingers in front of her. "You realize I'm only putting up with this to get to the end—"

"Back then, he gave me the same smug look he did Saturday night. But I dealt with it."

***

"I'd like to speak to you at recess," Mr. Ennis said shortly after Spring Break.

Greta peered out from under her bangs, not moving an inch in class all morning. What type of trouble she was in? Had Mr. Ennis heard the rumour she had started earlier that year? She hoped not.

The bell rang and her classmates filed out, leaving them alone. He cleared his throat from behind the desk. "You're a runner," he said.

Her shoulders relaxed but she kept her distance from the back of the room. "Kind of."

"Interested in junior track? The other girls are older, but I think you'd do fine."

She held her face still and worked hard not to reveal what she already knew. She'd run races with the older girls and beaten all of them. She was confident she could beat them again.

"Practices are in the back field at lunch. Three times a week." He passed her a note. "Your parents need to sign this tonight. See you out there."

At supper that evening, Greta waited for Ian to pour syrup on his pancakes and make his way through his favourite meal. He put his fork down and slurped his coffee. She slid the note across to him.

"No garbage on the table," he said, shoving it back at her.

"It's not garbage. I need you to read it. And sign it."

"What is it?"

"Permission to run on the school cross-country and track teams."

"No."

Her mouth dropped. He hadn't even read it. She glanced across the table at her mother who looked down at her plate. She'd signed it the moment she got home from school. "But why not?" Greta asked.

"Because I said so."

Ian slammed his empty coffee mug on the table. He stood and left the kitchen.

Greta went upstairs to her bedroom and fell in a heap on her bed. Her mind was spinning. Suddenly, it stopped. She blew her nose and rolled over. Her feet touched the floorboards and she slipped downstairs. There was nobody in the kitchen. She stood in front of the fridge and stared at the cheque tacked up to the door. *St. James Church. One hundred dollars.* She double-checked the bottom right-hand corner. She looked left, then right, and pulled it out from beneath the magnet.

Back in her bedroom, she took Mr. Ennis' crumpled note from her pocket. Smoothing out the creases, she laid it flat on top of the cheque. She held her breath, lined up the two pieces of paper perfectly, and examined them.

"Crap." She couldn't see through.

She lowered her nose to the paper, her finger tracing each loop and line she could make out. They were faint, but she followed them slowly, practicing, almost like a doctor performing surgery. Once. Twice. Ten times over.

"Shit." She still couldn't see it.

There had to be an answer. Her back ached. She sat up and stretched. There was no way she was giving up.

She wiped the sweat from her forehead and went to open the window. Then it hit her: she grabbed the note and the cheque off the floor, holding the two flat up together against the pane. She could see her father's signature in front of her, clear as day. She picked up the pen.

When Greta showed up at practice the next day, the older girls gave her a hard time; about being a baby; about her ratty sneakers; even the way she looked when she ran. The teasing dissolved the first time they went around the track together and she left them in her wake. In the weeks they practiced as a team, Greta's speed and discipline made them forget her ugly clothes and awkward gait, and on the morning of the first regional meet of the year, she won every race. She beamed with pride as her teammates high-fived and slapped her on the back. She was one of them.

The short race, saved for the afternoon, was the last. Greta overheard a group of parents calling it *the event* of the regional meet. She didn't understand it.

"What's the deal with the hundred-meter dash?" she asked after she sat down on the ground in the holding area beside her teammates.

The team captain glanced sideways, stretching, head down to her knee. "It's the race for the real athletes."

Greta looked around the tent. "Isn't that everyone?"

The captain smirked. "No. Some are wannabes."

"Giffen," the race director shouted, interrupting their conversation. Clipboard in one hand and a chocolate donut in the other, he was the only one who didn't look the part. He pointed over his shoulder. "Heat One," he told her. "Lane Three."

She walked out to the track. As she looked down the home straight, the competition came forward and joined her. Some crouched. Some stood rigid. She bent down and pressed her hands to the ground. Then she put her feet in the blocks, raising her hips, and kept her head tucked down the way Mr. Ennis had taught her. She listened for the official.

"On your mark."

A hush spread over the crowd. Her body tensed and she took a deep breath and held it.

"Set."

The gun fired.

She exploded out of the blocks. She locked her head forward and pushed her body up. Her arms swung to the rear, and at thirty metres, she felt smooth on the balls of her feet. At fifty meters, elbows slightly away from the sides, she took a fast look left. Then right. No sign of the other runners. At seventy meters, she had company. Six girls surged forward and all she saw was their backs. Decelerating into the finish, she leaned her chest forward and crossed the top of the line. Seventh place? She'd been completely blown away. Bitterly disappointed, she didn't make the finals.

After the meet, the team, tired yet victorious, boarded the bus. When they arrived back at Tall Pines, Mr. Ennis asked Greta to stay in her seat. He sat down beside her. "Tough one, huh?" he said.

She turned away from him, shoulders slumped.

"It's the thrill of victory and the agony of de-feet."

What? She didn't respond.

"Here." He handed her a box.

She prayed it was a sandwich. While no one on the team appeared to notice, she was the only one who didn't have a lunch. Whether Ian hadn't bought sandwich meat or he'd eaten it all again himself wasn't top of mind. Either way, though, she was starving.

"Go on," Mr. Ennis said. "Open it. You may like what's inside."

She took the box and lifted the lid. Her face reddened and her mouth froze in an O. Inside was a brand new pair of running shoes.

Back at the cabin, she slid her hand down beneath her bed, pulled out the box, and slipped the new shoes onto her feet. From the top of her bed, she stared down at the two large lumps sticking out from under the sheet. Her heart soared, and she fell fast asleep.

It was just past one o'clock of the biggest race of the season. Between the runners, the teachers and the parents in the park, Greta had never seen so many people gathered together in one place in her life. She hoped her parents might have considered coming, but when she remembered how she got there in the first place, her throat tightened and she felt sick.

"Ready, Greta?" Mr. Ennis asked after he found her stretching her legs out on the field.

"I think so." She was. Her new running shoes made her invincible.

Coach Innis gave her a skeptical look. "Five kilometers is a long way and it's your first big one. Go out there, run fast, and have fun."

She looked at him dumbfounded. Her speed gave the team hope the season would end better than last year's mediocre finish. She wasn't there to run fast and have fun; she wanted to win the whole race.

Coach Innis scanned the crowd. "Your parents here?"

She leaned forward and touched her nose to her knees. "They're busy at work."

"Oh." He looked confused. "I was hoping to meet them today."

"Maybe next time." She tried her best to put an end to the conversation.

Mr. Ennis didn't seem to notice her discomfort. "I'll cheer you on then." He sat down beside her. "Look what I brought." There were ten shiny dimes in his hand.

Greta laughed out loud. She'd forgotten their conversation on the bus ride home from regionals; her new running shoes had erased everything that day from her mind. She told Mr. Ennis if he wanted her to run faster at the next meet, he was going to have to cough up and pay her.

"How much?" he'd asked.

"Ten dimes," she'd told him.

"Really?" He'd looked totally surprised.

"Yep," she'd said. Ten or she was done.

It was supposed to have been a joke. The warning horn blared, and girls from every school approached the starting line. Mouth dry, coins tucked in her pocket, she stood and jogged over to join her teammates. *You've got this.* Her heart pounded. You've got this.

The final horn sounded and she stepped out quickly. For the first kilometer, she kept pace near the front of the pack. In the second, her body relaxed, her breathing slowed, and she hit her stride. By the third, she was well out in the front with five runners she didn't know. She sized them up. If she wanted to win, she knew she was going to need to pick up the pace.

In the fourth kilometer, she pushed forward. She passed three girls, yet was still trailing the fastest. The fifth and final kilometer was the most difficult part of the race; the route took her past a large pond, wound through a dirt path in the forest, and ended with a climb up and down a steep grassy hill. The two girls were neck and neck. As they ascended the hill, Greta focused forward, sped up, and passed her competitor. Beads of sweat ran down the sides of her face. Her legs screamed, but she held the pain in, showing no emotion. As she crested the hill and rounded the corner, she caught sight of the finish line. Mustering one last burst of speed, she blew down the hill and tore through the paper banner.

The crowd roared and Mr. Ennis stood at the finish line to congratulate Greta. She caught her breath, pumped her fist in the air, and gave him a high-five. The Northern Ontario Junior Elementary Cross Country Track Championship had never been won by a Grade Three student before. She'd made history—and added ten shiny new coins to her dime box.

***

Greta waited for Detective Perez to respond, but she twisted in her chair and kept writing. After a few seconds, she looked up. "Let's take that break."

That was it? No *congratulations*? No comment? Not so much as a smile? The woman was untouchable. She reached around the back of the chair for her coat.

"Did you bring someone with you?" the detective said. "Latoya perhaps? Your mom?"

Everything spun. For a second, she thought her heart would stop. "What? My mom? My father killed her."

SIXTEEN

Detective Perez's face bulged. "Your mother's dead? Why didn't you say something before?"

"I'm saying so now."

"But I had no idea."

"Isn't that your *job*, detective?"

Silence descended in the space between them. The detective's face reddened. "I'm not a mind-reader. If you think—"

"Here's what I *think*," she fired back. "All you care about is him. You don't care about my mom, and you sure as fuck don't care about me."

The detective raked her hands through her hair and moaned. "This kind of muddles things."

Blood roared to her ears. Barely able to make eye contact, she couldn't believe what she heard. Her chest tightened, her whole body shook. Muddles? For who? Her mother's murder changed her whole fucking life.

"When did this happen?" the detective asked.

Greta thought of the dark years she could never seem to outrun. She longed for the days with her mom on the back patio at the cabin. The moments they walked down the laneway in the summer; Mom in her green sundress, head thrown back, relaxed and smiling, the soles of her feet rusty brown, the afternoon sun bouncing off her auburn highlights; and Greta, beside her, holding her slim wrist, listening, trying her best to understand. She wished she'd captured them in her bare hands like a firefly in a jam jar. If she shut her eyes tight, she could still feel a little warmth from those days, the warmth of their connection living on.

"First your mother. Now your father?" the detective repeated. "How?"

She sunk into the chair and pulled her hands to her face. It was all so much more complicated than that. She had no idea how to explain it. A hand touched her shoulder, and she wrenched away, sucking in air. When she opened her eyes, Detective Perez was crouched on the floor beside her. A hand squeezed hers, the skin peppery and cool.

"Take your time, Greta," the detective said. "Talk to me."

That summer, Greta had had trouble sleeping. For years, following one or, at most, two cracks in her bedroom ceiling a couple of times over was enough to send her to sleep at night. But when she was nine, following every single crack's route couldn't exhaust the thoughts that ran wild through her head. When she did manage to drift off to sleep, she would dream she could see herself running naked outside the cabin. She had no idea what the dream meant, but no matter how hard she tried, she couldn't make it stop. Each night it jolted her awake, and her sleepless cycle started over again.

She heard everything going on in the cabin through the night. The comforting noises and the scary ones. She remembered sitting at the top of the wooden stairs when she was small, hidden in the shadows, watching her parents fight. She could tell when they were coming by the static in the air. She knew their rhythm by heart. First, Emily's voice rose; next, a door would slam; then Ian's deep, booming voice would echo, followed by a crash. Objects would fly through the air or he would flail his fists. But Greta always felt the same. She longed to leap off the stairs to help her mother, but instead she would crouch with Bunny, holding her hands over her ears, watching as her father's strength grew. It was like he was Hulk—a superhero she'd grown to loathe. Superheroes didn't beat up their wives... Or did they?

By morning, the static in the air and the thunder and lightning of the fight would have blown over. Her mother and father would always carry on as if nothing had happened, and Greta often wondered if what she'd seen had actually been a dream. But now her sleeplessness filled in their story. All the fights her mother had previously minimized came into focus, and she was no longer confused about what was and wasn't real. Ian was a monster.

How the devil got into her father was an enigma. It tormented her. She couldn't understand how he'd been asked to be a deacon at the church when he was a devil at home. Didn't God know? Didn't He see everything, like Santa? But then, she'd long since lost her belief in the magical man who would visit at Christmas; he never came, after all. And as for God... well, her faith in Him was wavering, too. 'Cause, really, He should have known. And if He didn't, her father was the best evidence she had that God wasn't doing His job well.

How did it all start, she would wonder. Was he born a sharp-clawed monster, wrapped in blankets by his parents? Her mother never would have dated someone like that. She hated long nails and always made sure Greta's were cut close to the edge. More likely, he was born a sweet, cherub-faced baby and later on transformed to a savage in his teens. Her mother had always warned her to stay away from teenage boys because they did a lot of weird things alone in their room. She guessed this was one of them.

Despite the sleepless nights, the summer passed, and Greta returned to school, defeated by the violence she heard each night. Her parents never discussed it. When she tried to talk to her mother alone, she couldn't look her in the eye. The only thing that kept her alive was running. As the pain in her heart multiplied, feeling her feet against the ground and the wind through her hair soothed her. And, while the new school year meant a new teacher, Mr. Ennis remained her track coach, which filled her with warmth and a sense of home. She was part of a team; it was where she belonged. Lunchtime practices became her lifeline, and as no one cared what she did at home as long as she was quiet, she snuck out each night to run after supper, too.

By spring, familiar with every footpath and trail within a five-kilometer radius of the cabin, Greta swept every race, including the hundred-meters, and won the Junior Track Championships a second year in a row.

The day after the championships, Principal Parthi burst through the door of her classroom. He didn't bother to knock, just barged inside, red-faced, waving a newspaper around over his head. When he stopped at the front of the room and held out the *Bracebridge Examiner*,

Greta's mouth dropped. Where was the team photo? Her picture—Greta's, alone, without her teammates—was on the front page. Bile filled her mouth. What if someone saw it?

Mr. Parthi's voice shook. "Tall Pines Junior Track Team Does It Again." Light filled his eyes.

Greta shrunk in her seat. The photo wasn't pretty; her arms were relaxed and her form streamlined would make Mr. Ennis happy, but her mouth hung open and her nose dripped with snot. She waited for her classmates to snicker, but they applauded and congratulated her instead. Proud of being part of a winning team, proud of herself, she'd inched her way back up and, by the end of the afternoon, her anxiety eased.

Early the next morning, Greta wound her way through the trails in the woods. Lost in thought, she stopped in front of a rusty padlocked gate at the perimeter of the property, turned around, and picked up speed, making her way back through the dry shrubs and thick trees as fast as she could. Mosquitos gnawed at her face as she bounded up the steps and opened the front door of the cabin. Ian, home from the night shift, blocked the doorway.

"What the hell is this?" he spat.

Greta glanced at his hand and her heart froze. Her face stared out from the page. He pulled her inside, threw her to the ground, and sat on top of her.

"Answer me."

He grabbed a fistful of her hair, jerked her head backwards, and slammed it down hard on the floor. The framed pictures in the hallway rattled, and one smashed into pieces on the ground. Greta saw stars.

"Are you stupid *and* deaf?" he screamed.

She couldn't breathe. She squirmed and twisted for air.

"Why do I have to find out what you're doing behind my back?"

She didn't answer. When he shifted his weight, she thought her back might break.

"I never gave you permission to run," he yelled. "So *ask* me."

She didn't need to: she'd won. He had no choice. He'd never risk his precious reputation.

"Do it." His hand tightened. "You'd better do it now."

Her eyes welled. She couldn't take the chance. It was too important. She struggled to speak through what was left in the space in her throat. "Can I run school track?"

He slammed her head on the floor again.

Somehow she managed to speak. "Please."

"That's my good girl."

The sound of his voice gave her chills. He pushed his weight off her and lowered his face to hers. His breath on her cheek smelled like a warm gym bag. "I don't give a shit what you do," he said.

They both knew that wasn't true. She rolled over and flipped him the finger. Ian stood, pulled his foot back, and gave her a swift, hard kick in the ribs. Eyes shut, bone-tired, she drew in a breath and curled inward. The fight drained out of her.

***

The sun rose and dawn faded. Greta woke, pulled on her socks and shoes, and tiptoed out of the house. With Mr. Ennis' encouragement, she recommitted to training each morning that summer—but not with his goal of winning the Junior Track Championships a third time and not with the school's hope of appearing on the front page of the newspaper again. She still cringed when she remembered the photograph. *Their* dreams weren't her motivation; she'd become acutely aware the constant pain in her heart, the type that cut it straight through, was temporarily soothed under the strain of a strenuous run.

Everything at home was fermenting; an earthy decay that left an aggressive, acidic aftertaste in her mouth. Her thoughts and opinions went unrecognized. She lived like a ghost. At night, Ian demanded total obedience. She lay in bed, unable to sleep, and heard everything.

"I'm not asking you... Put the book down."

Pictures flashed before her eyes; scenes she tried hard to forget. Ian's eyes bulging as he strode across the kitchen. Her mother, jaw tense, lowering the book to the table.

"Give it to me," she heard him snarl. His face would be rigid and red.

There was no use arguing because it always led to something worse. She heard him grab it from her hands and throw it in the garbage. Just like Bunny. She knew her mother would be left sitting in the chair immobilized, her face ashen, frozen in fear. She'd felt that fear, too, and she knew it wasn't enough for him.

Greta's heart pounded in her ears as Ian slammed her mother hard up against the wall and punched her close-fisted in the face. Her mother cried out and fell, and Greta knew she'd be holding her hands upward to protect her head from what was yet to come. Fists clenched, her father used her body as a punching bag, inflicting more pain than he felt. Head in the pillow, nauseous from the dull thump of pounded flesh, she willed it to stop. She wanted to go down and help her, but she couldn't move. Her own bruises, rimmed a yellowish-green, hadn't faded, and she didn't want to add to her collection. The clock ticked by in silent minutes. When she thought it was over, her father lifted her mother up and shook her with such force she was sure she heard a snap. Then silence. Then something fell on the floor. She imagined her mother, limp as a rag doll.

Greta scrambled out of bed and flew down the stairs to the kitchen. Her father stood, his hair a mess, his hands spread on the counter, staring out the window. To his right, her mother had dragged herself across the room, her trail marked by a bloody smear streaked across the floor.

"Mom," she said. "Wake up. Please."

She bent down and cradled her head in her lap, unsure of what to do. Ian stooped, fists clenched, and looked her in the eye. She dropped her mother's head and cowered backwards to make herself tiny.

"Greta," he whispered, his breath hot on her neck. A shiver ran down her spine. He rubbed his hand gently along the top her arm, and hot urine flowed down her legs, drenching her beige nightgown. "Greta," he said after he closed the gap between their faces another inch. He gave her a penetrating, unrepentant stare, then he pulled away from her and left the cabin.

His look had stopped her short. After what felt like an hour, with her legs weak, she crept across the kitchen floor. The back of her mother's head was covered with thick, congealed blood. She took a tea towel from the sink and pressed it gently to her nose and lips to try to stem the blood. Eyes glazed, her mother groaned softly, her skin translucent. Every movement painful and slow, she sat with her all night, safe beside her in the silence. How she thought they were safe there, she didn't know.

The next morning, daylight spilled across the kitchen. Her mother's face was unrecognizable—deep purple—and she could barely walk; her body stiff and swollen. No amount of make-up could cover the damage. Not this time.

Greta counted fourteen days her mother was housebound, waiting for the sprains to heal and the bruises to fade.

From that fall forward, Greta felt helpless; she couldn't bear to see her mother beaten down. When Ian wasn't with them, she saw her in a totally different light. She was free to be herself. When he worked late, they watched TV or sang silly songs and played tag through the house. When they baked chocolate chip cookies, her mother never worried about the crumbs in the sheets. She smiled, picked them up, and popped them back in her mouth. Then, when the plate was empty and her mother said she was still hungry, she reached down the bed for her toes. Greta didn't believe her when she insisted they tasted just as good. Her mother's sure didn't when she tried them.

Great's fear and hopelessness eventually morphed to anger, and she took that anger with her when she ran. She hated her father. She hated herself for not helping her mother. She hated her mother for being so weak. She hated the adults who weren't helping her. The adults underestimated children, thinking they didn't know what was going on, and who lied to them. Why didn't adults just tell the truth? They told kids to. Why couldn't it be that simple?

When Principal Parthi appeared at the door of her classroom six months later, the look on his face told her everything she needed to know. Something was terribly wrong. He was with another man she half-recognized. Was he a visitor? The guidance counselor? She wasn't sure. He stood beside him in a crisp navy blue suit.

Principal Parthi looked straight at her. "Can I see you for a sec?" he said.

She looked left and right. "Me?"

"Yes," he said gently. "And bring your backpack and coat."

Heat rushed to her cheeks, and she could feel the eyes of her classmates all over her. She had no idea why she was in trouble or how much, but from the pit in her stomach, she assumed it was a lot.

Her friends whispered as she slunk silently between the rows. The time it took to get to the front of the room was longer than any five-kilometer race she'd ever won.

She grabbed her things from the peg at the front of the room and stepped out into the hall.

"Hi Greta. This is...." Mr. Parthi mumbled.

She didn't hear the name. Mr. Parthi closed his eyes, swayed back and forth, and pinched the bridge of his nose. He hadn't said a word, but what passed between them confirmed she was going to be in need of some 'guidance'.

"Your mother had an accident this morning," he said slowly.

She blew warm air out through her nose. Though Mr. Parthi's voice sounded unusually high, it seemed she wasn't in trouble after all. She wanted to dance on the spot. "Is she okay?" she asked.

Mr. Parthi coughed and jerked his thumb to the suit on his left. "Mr. Katz here will explain." Then he took a step back and turned the conversation over.

She had an ugly feeling about what Mr. Parthi had said; he'd avoided saying anything much at all. What was he hiding? She'd been in situations like this before. Her stomach dropped and she shivered. Why didn't adults just tell the truth?

Before Mr. Katz opened his mouth, from the way he knelt down in front of her and looked her straight in the eye, she knew something terrible had happened at home. She covered her ears with her hands and crouched down on the floor in a ball, bracing herself for the impact. When it hit, it hit hard.

Over and over. And over again.

SEVENTEEN

"I'm sorry," Detective Perez said.

Greta sat silent, eyes cast to the floor.

"For you. Your mother. For the short time you had with her."

When she looked up, Detective Perez rocked back on her heels, her hands gripped together so tight her knuckles were white.

"I should've known," she said. "I had no idea what you've been through."

"Yeah," Greta agreed, "you should've. And how about you give it a try? Instead of trying to pin my father's death on me, think for a moment what it's like to know my father killed my mother."

The detective sat back behind her desk. "Go on, please." Her hand shook as she picked up the pencil.

Mr. Parthi and Mr. Katz explained her parents were home together that morning and there'd been an accident in the kitchen. Her mother was baking and fell backwards, hitting her head on the edge of a small metal table. Rather than helping her right then and there, her father, distraught, lost his senses. This was common, Mr. Parthi assured her; anyone in the same sort of crisis might find himself or herself in a similar state. Mr. Katz told Greta her father had then jumped into his truck and drove as fast as he could to get help from a neighbor, but they had no idea which neighbor it was when she asked—nor did she because, ten years into her life, she still hadn't met one. When this neighbor returned with her father to the cabin, it was apparently too late. Her mother had passed away.

That was the story. That's what they said. Her mother had *passed away*.

Passed.

The word echoed in her mind. Passed what? Passed where? What were they were trying to tell her? She wasn't stupid. She knew the truth. Passed meant *dead*. So why didn't they say that? Her mother was dead. She'd died. She pictured her bleeding out from a gash on the back of her head in the middle of the kitchen floor. When Greta thought things couldn't get any worse, they did. Mr. Parthi opened his arms to comfort her.

"I'm sorry, Greta," he whispered sadly.

Sorry? Was all that he had to say?

Her despair boiled over. She ran down the hallway, smashed the stairwell door open, and tore outside to the back of the school. When Mr. Parthi and Mr. Katz caught up to her, she was on the edge of the track, head in her hands, inconsolable. They sat down beside her. No one moved. No one said a word. Greta cried until she couldn't cry any more. When she lifted her head, heavy with grief, she focused her eyes straightforward. "There's more to the story," she said, resolutely.

The two men looked at each other. "What do you mean?" Mr. Parthi's face was creased with concern.

The secrets she'd held for years bubbled to the surface. She didn't try to stop them; she needed them to be in the open, for everyone to hear. That way, if anyone wanted them later, the missing pieces of her mother's life had been told. She didn't want to take the chance anyone could make something up. Like they all thought they knew what happened. They didn't. They couldn't. They hadn't been there. They didn't have a clue.

She let it all spill out.

"My mom and dad don't get along." She knew calling her parents by their first names made adults uncomfortable so she didn't. "My father was sent home from work and he wasn't happy about it. His boss forced him to finish his leftover vacation days. He told him it was a use them or lose them situation. This week he's been restless and cranky. A real asshole. He and my mom had a huge fight last night. I heard it all."

Greta stopped and took a deep breath. Mr. Parthi and Mr. Katz waited for her to continue.

"When I woke up this morning, I could still feel the tension from the fight. I told my mom I'd stay home with her but she told me I should go to school. She's had years of dealing with my father's moods; she can usually ride them out pretty well."

Mr. Parthi and Mr. Kristensen exchanged glances.

"So I made my lunch. Mom felt bad because my dad hadn't been to the ATM and there was nothing to eat in the fridge. I made a butter sandwich and stuck it in my backpack and when I left for school, she was still alive."

She started sobbing. Mr. Katz put his arm over her shoulders and walked her inside the school. While she sat in his office, waiting—for what, she didn't know—she pulled out the sandwich and threw it hard against the wall. She wanted to go home, curl up underneath the covers of her bed, and disappear off the face of the earth.

Mr. Parthi drove her home early afternoon. Down the laneway, rocks pinged the underside of his car. As he pulled into the barren patch of grass outside and squeezed his car between Ian's truck and an OPP cruiser, from the front seat, she could see the cabin was dead still. Reluctant to go in, she summoned up her courage, got out of the car, and opened the front door. Mr. Parthi followed along behind her. Past the kitchen. Down the hallway. To the main room where her father and the officer sat talking.

"Excuse me," Mr. Parthi said.

The two men glanced up.

"Greta," Ian said.

When he stood and reached out his arms to hug her, she stepped back. She thought she was going to throw up. A hand squeezed her gently on the shoulder.

"Why don't you put your backpack in your room?" Mr. Parthi said.

She climbed the stairs as he extended his right hand to the officer to introduce himself and, when she returned, they were deep in conversation. Unsure whether they had heard her, she took a deep breath and backtracked to the kitchen. She left the lights off and stepped through the archway. Lost in the shadows, overpowered by the scent of Pinesol, at first she felt nothing.

Someone had cleaned up the blood. It was a substandard effort at best. There was a pink tinge under the table. When her stomach started to churn, she grabbed the back of the kitchen chair to help settle the dizziness, but her legs buckled, and she landed on her butt on the seat. She waited for the nausea to pass and opened her eyes slowly, adjusting to what was around her. Three strands of her mother's long auburn hair hung from the side of the metal table, stuck in the congealed blood. She had no idea why at that moment she needed to blow on them, but she did. Gently. She wanted to be sure they were real. They waved ever so slightly.

She sat stalled. Mr. Parthi and Mr. Katz's story prickled her mind. It didn't make sense, and she hated being the one to point it out. Anger cursed through her as she crossed the kitchen. Unable to contain it, she flung open the oven door. A cold chill hit her, the floor tilted, and she grabbed hold of the kitchen counter. There was nothing in there. She ran around the kitchen in a frenzy.

Not a single crumb on the floor. No dirty bowls. No cookie sheet. No buttered loaf pans. No muffin pans either. No raw, half-baked, or fully baked anything anywhere.

Her world split apart and she sunk to her knees on the floor.

News of Emily's death travelled quickly. The next day, neighbours dropped by the cabin with homemade meals packed in Tupperware and wrapped in words of comfort to help soothe the grief. Their sudden presence with glazed berry tarts and crusted casseroles sickened her. Why did it take her mother's death to meet the neighbours for the first time in ten years? What did they want? And who wrecked butter tarts by mixing shriveled old grapes up into the syrup? Her mother never would've done that. Grateful for the meat and devilled eggs they delivered, she left the desserts untouched.

Upstairs in her room, she perched on the end of her bed with what was left of Bunny. Annoyed by the persistent banging, she drifted towards the window, forehead pressed against the cold glass. Below, the neighbours whispered to each other before climbing back into their cars; parked haphazardly at the bottom of the laneway. Cheap talk and banter. She overheard it all.

"Poor man. What happened?"

"Heard she fell and hit her head right there in the kitchen where we were standing."

"They have a daughter?"

"Tragic, losing your mother at that age. Didn't see her inside, though. She's a track star. A runner."

"Rings a bell. Wasn't it her photo in the *Examiner* last year?"

"This whole thing is awful. Lucky she has her father."

"He's kind. A pillar of our community."

"Horrible for him, too. Widowed at that age."

Greta wanted to gag. When she arrived home the afternoon before, she'd overheard what the officer had asked Ian. *Why were you home today and not at work? What time was it and where were you when the accident occurred? Did you drive to your neighbours' house? Walk? Did you run? Is there anything you'd like to tell me about your marriage?*

Twenty-four hours later, the laneway was flooded with people, and not one was asking the same questions.

***

Night fell, and Ian and Greta sat in the kitchen. Ian shoved a plastic container across the table. "Eat."

She pushed it back. The thought of eating anything made her sick.

He shrugged. "Fine." He pulled the container back. "All the more for me."

"Knock yourself out."

His fork stopped in mid-air.

She glared at him. "I don't give a shit if you eat it all."

Ian's hand shot across the table. He squeezed her wrist hard to show her how it could snap. "Stop sulking," he said, squeezing harder. "I'm warning you."

Her eyes brimmed and tears slid down the sides of her cheeks. She couldn't look at him.

"What?" His jaw dropped and he let go of her wrist. "You think this is *my* fault?"

She didn't know what to say. Wasn't it obvious? Now she'd never have her adoption papers.

Ian picked his fork back up and stabbed at the lasagna. "Your mother wasn't exactly easy to live with, you know."

She lifted her eyes, incredulous.

He stuffed a big piece of pasta in his mouth. "You're a kid." He waved his fork in the air. "You think you know everything but you only saw one side."

"I saw enough," she said flatly. "I'm not stupid."

"Right. You saw your mother throw things?"

"No."

"Punch me?" He paused. "Kick?"

Her whole head flickered. She felt her skin crack from the inside.

"Didn't think so."

He stood from the table and slammed his plate in the sink. She flinched, drew in a quick breath, and shrunk down in her seat. In the archway, he stopped and glared over his shoulder. "That woman gave as good as she got." He turned and walked out of the kitchen.

The day of Emily's funeral, the weather was dull and threatened rain. The mile-high apex and brick exterior of the church, usually glowing bright in the sunlight, was dark and grey. The usually bustling library and senior's centre on either side were Tuesday-morning-in-March quiet. Greta walked through the solid wood entry doors, following the worn red carpet into the nave. It was a trip she'd taken a million times before, but this time everything felt strikingly unfamiliar. On a bench near the front by the altar, she sat and took a deep breath. Her nostrils filled with the smell of furniture polish, old paper, and the dusty brown fabric on the knee stools. When she was younger, she didn't know why she and her mother prayed for peace. When her mother clasped her hands and kneeled, she did too. When she whispered, she did the same. Greta shivered when she remembered her words.

Dear God, Keep our hearts light and safe. Let us be strong enough to offer forgiveness. Amen.

This time, clasping her hands and kneeling down to pray was different. She had no one to look up to. No one to follow. Everything had changed.

She'd never attended a funeral before, but Greta understood mourning. Everything around her was black. Black in her heart for the secrets she kept. Black for the grief of the loss her mother. Black for the look Ian gave her when he put on his suit and black for the car that took them to service. As her mother's casket was lowered to the ground in a wooden box in the graveyard, even the dirt she shoveled on top to say her goodbye was black, black, black. That part felt right, that and the overcast day. She couldn't have shouldered the weight of a sunny one.

Greta walked back through the wet breeze that swept unfettered across the vast expanse of the cemetery. It unnerved her that, with so much death around them, they had to hold a party in the church basement. Murmured greetings and perfumed hugs. She felt ill from the scents. Unable to find a familiar face in the crowd, not even her mom's old friend Colleen, she couldn't help but wonder who all the people were. Her grief was too heavy to circulate among the mourners, to eat the mountains of food set out on white dollies beside plastic cups, paper napkins and lemon-yellow plates. A closer look at the table revealed strange little sandwiches from a different era. Cucumber and cream cheese. Something pink. Tuna. Flakes of ham with—was that relish? Cheese slices and roast beef. All had different fillings but were strangely uniform. Greta peered closer. None had crusts. What? Old people didn't do crusts?

In the buzz of exhaustion, Greta searched for her mother's face across the decorated church basement before she remembered why they were there. Her eyes stung as she looked up to the water-stained ceiling. If she had been there, she would have tugged at her sleeve and reminded her of the conversation they'd had on the back patio two summers ago; the one about the old lady she lived with in Lindsay; about how confused she'd got when her mother said she got spooked and it was just how the elderly were. Now she knew: old people got cranky like three years olds; they didn't like crusts either. She slipped out of the room to the hall so she didn't have to hold it all in.

"Mom," she whispered, taking a deep shuddering breath. Her words came tumbling out. "Where are you? I need to tell you something. I figured the old people out. I finally get your story."

But her mother wasn't there to hear her. Her mother was in a closed casket, deep in the wet dirt of a lonely graveyard.

Back at home in her bedroom, all Greta thought about was her father's meanness. It was like he'd captured it in an IV bag he kept secured under his clothes. Meanness dripped from his veins silently all day long and throughout the evenings, and when the IV bag burst and spilt all over the place, it made things unbearable. She couldn't count the times she'd prayed the bag would burst at the most inconvenient of times, revealing his true self to his friends or to his community—or, better still, to the questioning officer. Or maybe it would have been better if it slipped down below his heart and stopped the flow of his blood. But then she could just as easily wish it had lost the capacity to hold one drop more, backwashing toxins through his body.

She'd prayed for a respite. Just for one night.

"So you made it through the funeral?" Detective Perez asked.

"Just. But I wanted to leave. I didn't want to eat. I wanted to sleep. Everything was pissing me off. All I wanted was to be left alone. To disappear off the face of the earth."

The detective nodded.

"You know the worst thing? Everyone bought his bullshit. When they showed up at the cabin with their stupid food, his boss said he never complained at work. They called him *a pillar of the community*. People talked about how he delivered things from the bakery in town to sick people—"

"A deacon. A family man."

"It was crap. No one had my back. They repulsed me. He repulsed me. I wanted him dead."

Detective Perez looked up sharply.

EIGHTEEN

"Why would you say that, Greta? Again. That you wanted him dead?"

Greta hauled herself to her feet. "Did you not hear a word I said? My dad got away with murder and the cops did nothing about it. Where the fuck were you with your questions and recordings then? And now the asshole dies of cancer and you want to nail *me* for it?"

"Perhaps it wasn't the best choice of words."

"No shit," she shouted.

Detective Perez cocked her head. "You seem very angry right now."

"Because you suck at your job and you've got a big ass communication problem."

She crossed the room and perched up on the ledge of the window. To calm down, she started to count inside her head. *One*. Breathe. A man stood in his office window and stretched, looking at the traffic moving on the street below. *Two*. A crowd milled about out on the pavement on the corner outside a restaurant and a policeman watched them, flicking through his phone. *Three*. A lady walked two little dogs wearing matching coats. Her breaths came slow and steady now. The sound of the clock on the wall filled the room.

Tap, tap.

She turned and glared at Detective Perez holding the pencil. She felt the urge to shove it down her throat.

The detective put it down. "There must've been some sort of—"

"Investigation?" Greta suggested, wide-eyed.

Detective Perez held out an arm, ushering her back to the chair, her smile measured. "Yes. You must've told them something. Everything you've told me?"

She pushed off the ledge, stepped forward, and pounded her fist on the desk. "You know what the cops did?"

"I don't, but I'd like to."

"Same thing as me." Her knees buckled and she fell to her seat, her voice a whisper. "Nothing."

A week after the funeral and the quiet in the cabin was unsettling; it'd been like it all that morning. Greta heard the rumble of a car turn into the end of the laneway outside the cabin.

"Don't move," Ian said. "I'll get it."

She was startled by his sudden appearance at her bedroom doorway. His hair was a mess and his puffy face told her how much he'd drank the night before. He descended the stairs and opened the front door.

"Good morning. Ian Giffen?"

"Yeah."

"Deacon Ian Giffen?"

"That's me."

"Officer Pappas."

Greta sat straight up in bed and sucked in her breath. Had she heard right? Pappas? On the off-chance she was right, she slid off her bed and crept to the top of the stairs; silent and hopeful.

"From the OPP," he said. He extended his hand.

Ian looked at it but didn't take it.

"May I come in, please?"

From the tone of the officer's voice, Greta knew it wasn't a question. Her father stepped back and let him through the door. A crackling sound rang out through the cabin and bounced off the walls, a voice asking to 'Confirm arrival at location'.

Greta slid down four steps to the middle of the staircase where she could see Officer Pappas. He stood in front of her father, but he was at least a full head taller. Wider, too. He looked like he played linebacker for the CFL.

She stared at his uniform. The dark blue shirt, the navy pants, the radio on his left shoulder—they were all identical to what the community officers wore when they visited her school, but she'd never seen the bulky black vest with POLICE emblazoned across the chest in big, yellow letters. Her gaze travelled south and her eyes widened. There was a gun in his holster. A real one.

There was an awkward shuffling between Officer Pappas and her father in the hallway before they squeezed around one other and filed into the kitchen. For a moment, Officer Pappas stood there, motionless. His eyes flitted as he took a good look around. Did he see the stained linoleum and old cupboards scarred with years of use? Greta sat on the step, willing him to look closely at the knife marks in the table and at the scuffmarks on the wall from where her father had thrown the salt and pepper shakers.

Ian gestured him towards a chair. "What can I do for you this morning, Officer?"

"I'd like to talk to you and your daughter about Emily's death."

Greta flinched when she heard her mother's name. At least he hadn't said 'passed', but what she hoped he'd have said was 'murder'.

"Greta, honey," her father's voice rang out, "can you come down here please?"

She didn't move until her father's chair scraped backwards across the kitchen floor. She jumped to the bottom of the staircase as he rounded the archway from the kitchen. He held his hand out.

"There you are, sweetheart."

She wanted to gag as he led her to a chair. Officer Pappas studied them from across the table.

"Let me start by expressing my condolences for Emily's..." he coughed, clearing his throat, and looked directly at Greta "...for your mother's death."

She winced and looked away from his dark brown eyes.

Ian nodded slowly. "Thank you."

He was such a faker.

Ian reached his hand across the kitchen table and rested it on Officer Pappas' forearm. "Death is never easy."

Officer Pappas looked uncomfortable with the sudden gesture. "That's true, Deacon." He cleared his throat again. "I've had the opportunity to review the responding officer's notes back at the precinct and have a few questions."

Ian's covered his surprise well. "Really. How can we help?"

Officer Pappas shifted in his seat. "I'd like to speak to both of you alone. Greta first. Then you."

"Is that really necessary, Officer? My daughter's just lost her mother. She finds it difficult to be away from me. You must understand."

She looked over at her father, gobsmacked by his audacity.

"It is," Pappas told him. "If you can just step out of the kitchen, it will only take a minute."

Ian raised himself out of the kitchen chair and, as he did, he brought his face down to Greta's. He whispered softly in her ear. "I'll be right there in the other room." He straightened and gave her a faint smirk, like he was daring her to do something drastic.

When Ian left the kitchen, Officer Pappas looked right at her. "I know this is hard, Greta, but I need to ask you a question."

She nodded.

"Is there anything you'd like to tell me about your mother's death?"

She shrugged, but wouldn't meet his eye.

"Take all the time you need."

She crossed her arms. Ian could hear every word. She couldn't say it. She couldn't launch into every sordid little detail of their miserable lives that led up to her mother's death. She couldn't just say her father killed her mother. She didn't see it happen.

"You okay?" he asked. Deep grooves appeared across the man's forehead.

She opened her mouth to respond, but her throat was so tight she had to work hard to speak. "I'm fine." She was trying to sound normal, but her head flooded with the image of the three strands of hair left dangling from the table. She forced herself to smile. "Can I ask you a question?"

"Sure, Greta. I'll tell you whatever I can."

"I need to know what happened to my mom. Did she crack her head open?"

Officer Pappas sputtered. "Well, yes. Kind of."

She stared at him. "Which one is it?"

"She cracked her skull and experienced bleeding on her brain."

She thought back to the night before. "Did you see the other injuries?" She knew there must have been.

Officer Pappas tilted his head. "Like what?"

Ian barged into the kitchen. "That's enough," he ordered. "Up to your room now." He pointed to the stairs.

Officer Pappas reached into his top pocket and handed Greta a card. It had his name written on it in fancy letters. "If you change your mind or if there's anything you want to tell me, you can call me at that number." He pointed to the number, making sure she knew where it was.

"Sure," she said, in as convincing a way as possible. But she knew she couldn't call him.

It was Ian's turn next. Greta took her familiar seat at the top of the stairs and shut her eyes tight. Tears seeped out of the corners. She could only hear pieces of the conversation, but her father was doing his best to conceal his emotion. His legs would be jiggling a mile a minute under the table. It was what happened when he was agitated. And she knew he was. He had to be. She hoped Officer Pappas noticed.

Ian sighed heavily. "It's just one of those things," he said, "I'm devastated. *She's* devastated. We all are."

"I understand that, Deacon, but I'm sure you understand I have to investigate when anyone comes forward with new information."

Low mumbling followed. Greta leaned forward, straining to hear what they were saying.

"I do. It's just such a heavy, dark time for me."

She wasn't sure whether Ian meant heavy because of the stress of the funeral or dark because he was hiding his guilt. The sound of chairs as they scraped on the kitchen floor made her wince and, suddenly, her father and Officer Pappas were standing back in the hallway. He'd sweated through his uniform.

"Reach out anytime," he said after he leaned around her father and waved goodbye.

Greta raised her hand.

When the door closed behind him, she was left thinking about what he'd said.

"God damn him," Ian muttered.

Greta's heart lurched, and she folded her hands in her lap to stop them from shaking. From where she sat, she could hear Ian rummage beneath the kitchen sink. When he reappeared in the archway of the kitchen, he was holding a rectangular bottle with a familiar logo. Jack Daniels. He twisted the top and tipped it up to his mouth, taking a good, long drink. Then he wiped the back of his hand across his face and took another. When half the bottle of brown liquid was empty, he lowered it from his lips. This was the father she knew: angry and drunk.

He turned around to face her. "You little shit," he snarled.

Greta's blood ran hot. She felt his rage. But it wasn't *his* rage that frightened her; it was hers. It rang through her ears and pumped through her veins so hard her body quivered. He'd killed her mother and she knew it.

She exploded. "You're a fucking liar," she shouted.

Ian's throat reddened and colour spread up his cheeks. He grasped the bottle by the throat and smashed it to the floor. Shards of glass scattered, but the sounds didn't faze her.

"You killed her. I *know* you did." She jumped off the stairs and snatched a photograph from the wall—the one of her father smiling. She flung the picture straight at him as if it was a baseball. It hit him square in the head. "I hate you."

Face dead calm, he stood motionless.

"And you're *not* my real father. Where are my adoption papers anyway?"

His body tensed; he looked like a caged animal.

"I fucking hate you. Mom said she'd give them to me."

Ian clenched his fists and his eyes narrowed. He looked down, examining the floor. Then he stooped, picking up the biggest piece of glass he could find, and took a step towards her. "Greta," he said. His breathing grew heavier.

"Murderer. You're a murderer. You know it. And I do, too."

He lunged forward, the piece of glass tight in his hand. When it grazed her arm, she gasped. Was he going to slit her throat? Was he going to kill her, too? Was he going to make his promise real when he'd told her mother all those years ago that he'd slit all of their throats? She stepped backwards, regained her footing and veered around him, grateful for her training. As he lunged again, she sidestepped around him, darting down the hallway. She blew through the front door, her feet taking her as far away as they could.

This time she was running for her life.

NINETEEN

It was after one o'clock and Greta knew the drill. "Pappas. P-A-P-P-A-S."

Detective Perez scribbled in her notebook. "Did you get a first name?"

She shook her head.

"I'll look it up when we break. It's important I hear what he has to say."

Break? That was supposed to be an hour ago. Did the detective visit the ladies room? Eat? Drink? Check her phone? "He won't tell you anything different from what I've just said."

"You better hope not." Detective Perez checked her watch. "One last thing before we discuss what occurred between you and your father in that hospital room prior to his death. What did you do when you left the cabin?"

She'd watched the cabin from deep in the bush. Her father's truck was gone, but she didn't trust that he wasn't lying in wait for her. Legs streaked with mud, she snuck up to the front door and took a quick look inside. Pieces of glass were strewn across the hallway, their colours bouncing off the walls in the late-afternoon sun. Purple. Blue. Orange and magenta. The Jack Daniels logo glinted in a thin pool of brown. Inside, the stink of him—his blood, his breath—made her want to hurl. After searching through the cupboards in the kitchen, she found a bucket and gloves, and got down to work.

By mid-evening, when Ian's headlights appeared at the end of the laneway, all evidence of his earlier rage had all but disappeared. She scurried upstairs and locked her bedroom door. The walls shook as the front door banged and steps thundered towards her. Did he know she was there? He'd be drunk and she wasn't sure the knife she'd stolen from the kitchen and hid under her mattress would be enough to keep her safe. If she was forced to use it, could she do it? Could she really imagine herself plunging the blade through his chest? Dragging it across his wrists or up his arms to his elbow? Stabbing him in the top of the leg? She knew she would if she had to.

On her bed, with the sheet wrapped around her, Greta held her breath, biting back the urge to scream. His footsteps receded and his bedroom door closed.

"When I woke up in the morning the cabin was empty," Greta said.

"After you accused him of murder, he ignored you?"

"He never said anything. Didn't acknowledge it."

Detective Perez grazed her teeth over her lower lip. "I find that odd."

"Why? It was the same thing he did to my mom. I heard them fight the night before he killed her. It was ugly. But he acted like none of it ever happened."

The detective glanced up but she didn't respond. She made a note and waited for Greta to continue.

***

Spring turned to summer. Strange women came to the cabin at night as her father strutted like a bull out in pasture, milking his newly single status for all it was worth. Nobody noticed her or even cared. An invisible guest in her own house, occasionally the women waved a perfunctory hello as they stood outside on the front porch, drinking liquor from plastic cups, smoking menthol cigarettes burned down to the filter. One summer night, through a symphony of crickets, she caught part of a conversation.

"How old is she, honey?" a sultry voice purred.

"Just turned eleven," her father said.

She perked up. So, he *did* know it was her birthday last month? Why hadn't he said anything? Why would she expect he would? He didn't so much as acknowledge her existence.

"What are you going to do?" the voice asked.

What? Do about what?

"How does she spend her time?"

He sighed. "Runs up and down the laneway in her flips flops."

Through the wall, from the tone of his voice, Greta knew her father's look. He was smirking, making fun of her. If he cared about anyone but himself, he might have put two and two together. She'd grown out of her running shoes months ago.

"Doesn't it hurt her feet? It's so dangerous; full of ruts and gullies. It nearly took the bottom of my car out."

She read right through that, too. *He won't clean it up, sweetheart. He won't do a damn thing for you.*

"Yeah, I'm worried about her. I don't know what to do. She's obviously in pain, you know, after her mother's death. It's so hard."

She clenched her fists. *Hard? Hard for who?*

"She's all I have left now. I'll do anything for her. I love her so much."

Her eyes widened, repulsed.

"Oh, honey, I'm sure she loves you, too," the smoky voice soothed.

"All I can do is stay close. Let her talk when she needs to." Her father's voice cracked. Then silence. Then crying? Pathetic. "It's what any good father would do."

It was as if the wind had been knocked out of her. The sounds of rustling and tussling made her recoil. Her father's voice, lower, muttering, the box spring across the hallway squeaked. Then moaning and grunting.

The next day, his room would smell of damp, like the earth. She bit her fist and wrapped the corners of the pillow around her head.

Greta twisted in her seat. "I'm telling you: Ian was evil. Cold. Hard. Like stone. Every day that summer I thought he'd bash my skull in."

The pencil stopped writing. "That seems a bit dramatic, don't you think?"

"That's how he killed my mother. Why wouldn't he do the same thing to me?"

"The horrors a child can conjure up in their mind are always way worse than what actually is."

Her heart quickened. "He was dangerous, not stupid. Because of my mom, he got sympathy. Free food. Sex. If he killed me, too, he'd get nothing—nothing except questions, anyway. Officer Pappas would've come back."

"How did he seem to you that summer?"

"Except for the one big fight we had, he controlled himself. He didn't have any more outbursts—none that I can remember, anyway. But he hadn't changed. He was busy. I mean, all those women..."

Detective Perez dismissed the suggestion bluntly. "Perhaps you were worried he was developing a relationship too soon after your mother died?"

She bristled and made a face. "Couldn't have cared less."

"It doesn't sound like it. I think it was a concern."

"No one could replace my mom. I knew he'd do the same thing to me as he did to her. He just needed time to figure out how he could get away with it. Why don't you write that down in your fucking notebook?"

Near the end of the summer, Greta had asked Ian to take her to visit her mother. They hadn't been back to her gravesite—not once after Sunday service—and she wanted to see how she was. She wanted to talk to her, to let her know she still missed her, to tell her how much she loved her. She wanted to remind her she'd had a birthday and was eleven now. More than ever, she wanted to know more about where she came from; who she was.

When she explained why she wanted to go, Ian put his bottle on the floor, lifted his head off the couch and he laughed.

"Are you nuts?"

She stood her ground and waited to see what he would do.

"If you want to go visit, put your shoes on and start walking." The sharp sting of his comment shocked her. He picked up his bottle, polished it off, and threw it onto the ground with a thud. Then he turned to face her. "She's done to me. Pick your mouth up off the floor and get over it."

In the silence that followed, Greta raged. Of all the moments since her mother's death, this was the worst. Her mother would never be done to her. But she was done with him. She stormed upstairs and slammed her bedroom door. Crouched at the side of the bed, she felt her way between the mattress and box spring, wrapping her fingers around the handle of the knife she'd hidden earlier that summer. Smooth in her palm, the blade hovering an inch above the underside of her arm, she slid it directly across her wrist. She drew in a sharp breath. Her fingers worked nervously around the blade as she examined her art, she dug in again deeper, carving an angry red line. Raw, sick and afraid, tears splashed down her cheeks and dripped onto the floorboards. She dropped her head back onto the side of her bed and exhaled.

***

"Do you still have these scars?" Detective Perez asked.

"What?"

"The scars. Are they there?"

"I don't know." She yanked up the sleeve of her sweatshirt and inspected the underside of her wrist. When she found what she was looking for, she thrust her arm in front of her. She pointed. "There."

Detective Perez put on her glasses and leaned forward. She reached out her hand, a finger grazing the skin. Then she sat back, eyebrows furrowed, pencil to her notebook. "Alright," she said, after writing something down. She opened the drawer of her desk and pulled out a leather wallet embossed with her initials. *A.P.* "Let's take a break. Go get something to eat while I track down this Officer Pappas."

TWENTY

Thirty minutes later, Greta sat on the ledge staring out the fifteen-foot tall windows at the buildings around her, with only the buzz of the afternoon rush-hour traffic building up from College Street below. Cars were honking; breaks squealing. The trees shimmering with green. A low pressure throbbed on the sides of her head until she lifted her hands to her temples, rubbed them gently, and turned from the window.

Framed certificates lined a far wall. *Decorated Investigator. Leader of the year.* Detective Perez's job was to gather facts and pass judgement, yet the time they'd spent together, stilted and stiff, felt like she'd only been half-listening. Yes, she'd scribbled some notes, but she'd also nibbled a muffin and only occasionally asked a question. Greta was tired of talking about the whole thing. But the questions still gnawed at her. Did Perez believe what she'd said? Could she see the chink in her armour? Anything was possible. She worried about what Detective Perez was thinking, despite all the ways she'd dissected their conversation so far.

When the bells from The Old City Courthouse rang out three times, Detective Perez walked into the room. Her eyes narrowed. "I'd like to fill in a few holes from this morning, but before we do, tell me, yes or no, did you go back to school?"

The creeping sense of uneasiness rising in her stomach stopped. The detective may not have understood much about her life, but it was clear she was trying hard to understand her account of what happened so many years before. From all the plaques and awards covering the walls, she assumed this wasn't her first rodeo. Her office must have held a thousand sad stories.

"Life moves on," she said as she slipped off the window ledge and took a seat across from the detective.

Detective Perez's smile was more of a grimace. "I hoped we would've, too, by now. I need to close this case. However, if you're not going to come clean about your father's death, go ahead, say what you need to."

The first thing Greta noticed when she was called down to the office on the second day of Grade Six was Principal Parthi's new glasses: they were the same colour as his bulbous nose. What they didn't match were the thick, brown hairs that stuck straight down out of it. They weren't there last year. If they had been, she would've noticed.

"Welcome back, Greta." He led her inside. "It's good to see you."

Her stomach felt queasy. "Sure," she mumbled, not wanting to say more. The last time she'd been in the school office, it was to learn her mother was dead.

"I called you down to let you know I've added your name to the list of students Mr. Katz sees on Thursdays. You remember him, right?"

She hadn't seen that coming. "Really? That's what you're leading with?"

He stared at her, mildly confused. "The guidance counselor."

"Guidance for what?" She'd been alone by herself every day the last five months and she'd done pretty well thank you very much.

"It's not guidance *per se*." He paused. "Think of it more like an opportunity to talk. To share what you're feeling. To get stuff off your chest. You know?"

No. She had no idea what he meant. She didn't have a chest yet and she wasn't feeling anything. She was numb.

"You've been through a lot the last few months. It's a lot to process. A lot to work through. Mr. Katz can help you."

"Thanks for your concern, Mr. Parthi. I appreciate it. But I'm not interested." She paused and half-smiled. "If I feel like I need someone, though, I'll be sure to let you know."

Principal Parthi looked disappointed. She could tell it wasn't how he'd envisioned the conversation unfolding. She felt the need to clarify. "I don't feel comfortable around Mr. Katz."

Mr. Parthi looked puzzled. "Why's that?"

She leaned forward and whispered, "He's kind of weird."

Mr. Parthi shifted awkwardly in his seat. "How so?" A look of concern spread across his face. He was, after all, the official Guardian of School Safety.

She stopped. She'd learned from her previous trips to the office that Mr. Parthi believed in three distinct stages of law enforcement: the warning; the consequence; the execution. As her mother always told her she had an overactive imagination, she chose her next words carefully.

"Don't take this the wrong way." She lifted her eyes to meet his. "Mr. Katz reminds me of a card-carrying member of the Mile High Club." When Mr. Parthi stared back at her in disbelief, she interpreted the look on his face as an invitation to go on. "Except I think he got his membership using his hands. Not pocket pool or the five-knuckle shuffle." She paused for effect, giving him a faint hint of a smile. "You know what I mean? Full. Out. Manual. Override."

Mr. Parthi's jaw tensed. His cheeks turned fire-engine red and the colour spread, past his glasses, up over his ears, and disappeared into his hairline. He looked like he wanted to say something but couldn't form the words. He rose from his desk and stormed out of his office. She sat, watching the walls, and waited for him to return. After what seemed like a lifetime, she stood and left.

"Oh, Greta," the school secretary called, "your appointment with Mr. Katz is set for tomorrow morning." The secretary let out a deep smoker's laugh. "See you at 9:30 AM sharp, dear."

Detective Perez interrupted. "That's reassuring."

She frowned. "It is?"

"Your principal." She glanced at her notebook. "How he got to you in there straight away. Did you benefit from your appointment?"

"Appointments," she said firmly. "Plural." She paused. "And no, not at first."

"That's a shame. The important thing is you went."

"Every week. On time. Every Thursday."

The next morning, Greta sat on a slatted wooden bench, head in her hands, and waited to be called into the office. The school secretary smiled and waved. Mr. Parthi offered a cheery hello. When Mr. Katz arrived dressed casually in a golf shirt and jeans, he shook her hand, led her into a small room with no windows, and welcomed her.

"So, how are we doing?" he asked.

She snorted. *We*. Like they'd bonded or something. "You're kidding me, right?"

"Nope," he said.

"Living the dream, Mr. K., living the dream," she replied sourly. "How do you think?"

"I don't know. I'm not you,' he pointed out. "That's why I asked."

She looked at him, confused. Wasn't he the one who was supposed to be giving her guidance? Telling her how she should be feeling? She blew a huge pink bubble, snapped it loudly, and sucked the whole glob of gum back into her mouth.

"You've been through a heck of a lot," Mr. Katz said.

"That's an understatement," she shot back. If looks could've killed, Mr. K. would've been dead right there on the spot.

"I get it," he said. "I'm here if you want to talk."

She crossed her arms in front of her. "No thanks."

Mr. K. sighed. "Then how can I help you?"

She gritted her teeth. Adults asked the most stupid questions. "You can't. No one can."

"That's okay. It's a lot to deal with. It's going to take time."

"Whatever."

"The only thing I can tell you is you need to give yourself permission to feel whatever you're feeling. That might be hurt. Disappointment. Anger. Fear."

She glared at him. Anger? She wasn't angry. She was pissed. She started counting in her head. *One, two, three.* She jumped up and threw her arms in the air. The chair crashed against the back wall. "The whole world can fuck off right now."

At her next appointment, when Mr. K. prodded, ever so gently, she broke down. "I hurt all over, Mr. K, and I hurt every day." The weight she was carrying was excruciating, and she didn't want to feel quite so broken inside all the time.

"Tell me about the pain, Greta. There are all different types. It would be good to know what it is you're feeling so we can make sense of it."

"It's heavy and it's dark, and it sucks. And it's not just in my head, you know? It's actual physical pain. Like when I wake up in the morning, I feel fine for the first few seconds, and then I remember what happened, and..." She broke off, unable to continue.

"That's normal, Greta."

"I don't care if it's normal. It hurts. I can't make it go away."

"Grief's not easy," he sighed. "And I don't know much about yours. All I can tell you is the only way out of pain is through it."

She looked at him. What the fuck? Words strung together to make him feel smart and her feel stupid weren't going to help. Did he think saying anything was better than watching her cry? Or was he framing her, ready to launch into a history lesson like her mother used to? She felt both comforted and annoyed by the thought of it.

"What I mean is, if you ignore your pain and push it deep inside you, you're robbing yourself of healing. You've got to acknowledge it. Let it out. Work it through."

Her voice trembled. "How am I supposed to do that?"

He shook his head. "I don't know. Everyone's different. Write in a journal? Take up kickboxing?"

Her face flushed. "Aren't you supposed to have some sort of expertise in guidance?"

"I do, but I'm not you. How do *you* want to deal with it?"

"I don't know," she shot back. "My dad drinks Jack Daniels. Should I give *that* a try?"

His eyes met hers. "Maybe not."

"You're the one with the fancy degrees. The one with the answers. So tell me. Tell me how to do this."

Mr. K. smiled like he'd thought he'd made a breakthrough or something. "Talk to me. Talk to your teacher. Talk to Mr. Ennis. Think. Write. Draw. Exercise. Do yoga. Whatever works for you."

"I run."

"Excellent. Then that's it. Pour all your pain into running."

She looked at him. Wow. What a brainiac. That was his big solution? What a fucking tool. She was done with adults. They were useless, the lot of them. She gave him the middle finger and slammed his door behind her.

The phone rang.

Detective Perez held up a finger, picked it up, listened, and looked at her from across the desk. "Give me a sec. It's the OPP detachment, up in Huntsville."

After she tucked her notebook under her arm and disappeared into the hall to take the call, Greta cringed. She'd only been able to recall bits and pieces of everything that had happened after that. She'd floated through the fall, frightened and confused, lashing out. She swore at her classmates, yelled at her teachers, got into fistfights in the back hall. When Mr. Ennis bought her new shoes, she told him she wasn't running unless he increased their deal from a dime to a dollar. At home she scrounged through the food in the cupboards Ian never thought to fill and avoided him.

On warm nights, Greta would venture outside to the back patio to feel her mother's spirit, the pale sliver of the moon the only light for miles. The eerie sounds emanating from the deep brush that had frightened her as a child washed away some of her loneliness. The symphony of crickets, the occasional coyote howl, the distant whistle of a train; it all eased a pain deep inside her. On clear nights, the stars twinkled down on the pine and the spruce in the moonlight, and she imagined all the planets out in the universe, wondering which one she could call home. Some nights she gave into the pain and held her mother's photo to her chest. On other nights, when she felt stronger, she rummaged through her dime box: hair clips; an old elastic, stretched and worn down to a thread; the tarnished gold chain with the little pink bead; an unfinished painting they'd started together; the smallest stone from her mother's collection at the end of the patio; and Bunny's tattered ear. She'd pick it up and turn it over in her hands, lacing it between her fingers. She'd hold it to her face. Though the smell of her mother always brought her comfort, she never managed to feel whole. And so, other times, with her mother's photo beside her, she'd counted the coins in her dime box, hoping there'd be enough money to buy a ticket somewhere—anywhere—far, far away. But she remembered that, in the two years she had it, she'd only saved $56.00—and knew it was enough to go nowhere.

Detective Perez strolled back into the room. "Sorry about that."

"What'd he say?"

"It wasn't Officer Pappas. It was his partner. He confirmed they were the attending officers the day your mother died."

"Of course he was. I already told you."

"He said they were at the funeral and talked to you at the wake."

"He did?" Greta hadn't seen Officer Pappas there.

"They were standing beside you when your father came over to see how you were doing and you stormed out."

"This guy came, too?" She had no recollection.

"Yes. He asked me how you were. Remember him? He was the one who found you when you took off."

"No, I didn't. I sat outside." That she was certain of. She'd been talking to her mother.

"Not at the funeral. In the woods. You were about six? Your mom was away for the weekend, and he told me you got mad at your father, so Sunday afternoon you ran into the woods."

"That's when it happened?"

"You got lost for a few hours."

"Impossible. My dad would never let my mom do that and it wasn't the afternoon. I was alone in the woods in the night."

"That's not what he said, Greta. He remembers it all pretty clearly. Your mom called the detachment late Sunday afternoon."

Greta stared at Detective Perez. She felt sick. How long had she actually been out there that weekend? What had her father done to her? To her mother?

"Anyway, nice man. Retired shortly after the funeral and now volunteers a few hours on the phones. Officer Pappas works evenings so I'll talk to him later."

Greta glanced at the clock and slumped in her chair. "Never getting out of here."

Detective Perez glared at her. "Where were we?"

***

While most of the year was a disaster, track went well. It was the only thing she loved—the feeling she felt when she ran. It soothed her pain and it helped her feel whole, and the new shoes Coach Ennis had bought her earlier in the year allowed her feet to breathe. Like the year before, she swept the regionals and was expected to take the big race. On the day of the championships, the sky started spitting, and the runners huddled together under the trees. She'd sat stretching, her chin on her knee, when someone called out her name. When she glanced up, a girl from a rival school stood in front of her, feet planted wide. Greta rose to hers.

"I'm going to kick your ass today," the girl said.

She looked her up and down. Although she was small and in good shape, she wasn't a threat. She didn't have the stride. "I don't think so, sweetheart."

The girl nodded, smiling, egging her on. "Get ready to go down, loser."

She paused. "Who are you?"

"Emily," she said. "Don't forget it."

Her heart twisted at the mention of her mother's name. Her teammates called her from the starting line, quietly at first, then more desperate. With her blood cold, her stomach churned, and she ran a finger across her cheek, wondering if the wet she felt was sweat or tears. She turned sideways and puked.

Coach Ennis jogged over. "What gives, Giffen? You're going to miss your race."

Her feet wouldn't move. She wiped the sourness from her mouth. Cheers drowned out her words as the starting horn sounded in the distance.

TWENTY-ONE

"**M**ust have been a rough year," Detective Perez said.

Greta's stomach tingled, and she nodded. "The scariest was first thing in the morning. Not night; just before dawn. You know, waking up... There was nowhere to hide."

"From your grief?"

She stopped fidgeting. "From myself. Everything was still so fresh. So real. It was raw."

"I guess a mother's love can swallow you up."

She swiped a hand at her cheek. "I wanted things to be normal. But they weren't. I couldn't move on. I couldn't move past it—or even move at all. She took my courage with her."

One Thursday morning, Mr. K. stared at Greta from across the table. "There's someone here at school that's worried about you," he told her.

No desire to be part of the conversation, she sighed heavily. Deep navy-blue bags circled the underside of her eyes. No friends. Marks in the tank. Fingernails filthy. Her grey sweatpants were torn and stained at the knees, and her faded red Badgers T-shirt had fallen apart. She knew what her mother would've said, but she didn't care; they were comfy. So what if she hadn't washed her hair in a week? Who cared if her black, shiny army boots were second-hand from BFT? Of all the things she'd stolen from that place, they were her best five-finger discount.

"Tell whoever it is to stop." She knew it was him.

"They won't believe me. You look tired. Drawn out. Frankly, I'm concerned, too."

Maybe it wasn't? "I'm fine, Mr. K."

"How can you be? Your complexion's sallow."

"Whatever that means."

"Yellowish. Jaundiced. Pasty."

"We can't all be part of the cast of *Glee*."

The look on his face indicated he didn't understand what she'd said. It took every ounce of her energy not to leap across the table and smack him.

"What's going on, Greta? Are you in trouble?"

She made a noise. "Here? Living out in the boonies?"

Suddenly his eyes widened and he exhaled, fluttering the piece of paper in front of him. "Are you smoking pot?"

The question hung in the air like stink. She stopped picking her nails. "Come again?" Why would she want to wreck her brain? Her body, her temple, was the one and only thing she controlled in her messed-up life. Besides, she was an athlete. They'd discussed running as an 'emotional outlet.' After all the time they'd been forced to spend together, he clearly knew nothing about her.

Mr. Katz blinked. He waited, pointedly, for her confession.

"Hello?" she snapped. "I'm on the track team. And because I don't wear brand names or you don't like my face or I can't seem to 'find myself again',"—she used air quotes for effect—"doesn't mean I'm doing drugs. That's a pretty big leap for you to make."

He looked at her dubiously.

"What's with you people? Always judging."

Mr. K. lifted his palms in the air. "I'm not."

"You are." Her eyes flared as she stood and scanned him up and down. "Look at you. Zero style... It's pathetic." She didn't mention his dandruff. "Are you smoking *crack*, Mr. K?"

"What?"

Her only answer was to slam the door behind her.

Back at home that evening, Greta realized Mr. K. would never have made the comment he had if he'd known what was going on in her life. She hadn't told him her father was never home or that, when he was, he was passed out on the couch or drinking in his room. It wasn't a secret. The only one using was him. She hadn't explained why she was exhausted. Hadn't mentioned money was tight or how humiliated she felt to dig for clothes through the Lost and Found. If she got caught, would he think she liked to steal? Would he offer her help? Or would he believe her when she said her father killed her mother? How *could* she ask for help? It would be like accusing Ian of neglect. And if Mr. K. confronted him, then what? What would she do? Run away so he didn't kill her too? She was sick of hiding the truth. She'd lied because the truth was another trap.

During the winter, Greta worked hard to dial her boil down to a simmer. It took time to find calm in the chaos, and although there were days Mr. K. sounded like the teacher from a *Charlie Brown* episode, she pulled herself slowly back from the brink. She pressed on, sometimes struggling, but found that, over time, things were getting easier. That spring, for the first time since her mother's death, the thick fog that had been squeezing her head in a vice-like grip for so long, started to burn off. Something stirred inside her. She felt herself breathe.

The first day of the new track season, Greta stepped out onto the pavement. She scuffed at the ground with her feet. "Okay. I'm ready to go this year," she said to the team.

The girls stared, guarded, keeping their distance.

"Last year I was off, maybe a bit—"

"Mean?" one of them suggested, whistling through her teeth.

Her throat tightened. If they were anxious, she didn't blame them.

She stumbled on blindly. "Fair enough. An ass." Did they have to make this so hard? It wasn't like any of their mothers had died. To make matters worse, from the corner of her eye, Mr. Ennis had approached from across the field and was within earshot of the conversation. She exhaled, slow and steady. "I'm sorry. I want to move on. With you. With the team. I want us to win the championships."

Her teammates exchanged glances. Unsure what to do, she stood, arms at her side, waiting for their next move. One girl reached out and squeezed her hands, which felt good and stopped them from trembling. When another stepped forward and picked her up in a bear hug, spinning her in circles, the rest of the team broke free and rushed in. No words were spoken; none were needed. She was grateful for the second chance they offered her—and she was ready to prove she deserved it.

"Ladies," Mr. Ennis boomed across the track. "We aren't going to win the championships standing around hugging each other."

The team surged forward and as they circled the backfield together, Greta's heart soared, her mind cleared, and she started to relax.

By the end of the practice, her muscles were screaming. She bent over, hands on her knees. "I don't remember being this winded," she panted, sucking in air. "I'm a slug."

Mr. Ennis laughed. "We've got ninety days. If you want to win it, you'd better up your game."

She knew the mantra. "Show up. Do the work. Repeat tomorrow."

For the next twelve weeks, she increased her training, doubling the length of her runs in the morning and in the evening before she went to bed. Though Ian remained oblivious, Coach Ennis noticed she was dropping weight. He fueled her renewed commitment with snacks he brought for breakfast and after school. She ate everything.

When the season started, the girls won their first meet without much struggle. The second was tough, and when it came to the third, with two girls injured and the long-distance race lengthening to seven kilometers, it posed a challenge for the entire team. By the end, they'd only squeaked into the championships. When the bus pulled up at the park, people crisscrossed the open lot and girls stood warming up in small groups. No one looked at them, and the officials at the marshaling table barely raised their eyes when they registered. After their warm-up, Mr. Ennis gathered the team together to pass out their bibs.

"I'm going to lay this out simple," he said. "Our season was rough, and everyone here knows we're the underdogs."

Greta looked at him. Was that what he truly believed? From her teammates' faces, they weren't feeling it either. The team wasn't a threat. Their confidence had been shaken to the core.

"We've got nothing to lose," he continued, "so go out there, be scrappy, don't give up—and push through the race."

The warning signal ended his pre-race pep talk, and the team ran over to take their places across the starting line. Greta shut her eyes and sucked in a slow, deep breath. She wanted the win, and she wanted it badly. She wanted it for the team who'd stood by her after she abused them—just like Ian had abused her mother.

The horn blasted and a cheer went up. Greta positioned herself at the front with the fastest runners. Her teammates filed in behind her, running in the middle of the pack. For the first two kilometers, her breathing was painful. She couldn't find her zone and was struggling with a nagging cramp in her leg. By the middle of the race, she hit her stride. Her gait was smooth, her arms flailed out less and she inhaled the smell of the spring earth. She looked ahead at the two runners, their breathing ragged, and watched as they lost steam. She checked over her shoulder at the girl closing in and a group of five or six others trailing three or four steps behind her. This was her chance.

With two kilometers left to go, she shot forward and passed the leading girls. The cramp in her leg flared up, but she ignored it and kept up the pace. She focused her thoughts inward, tuning out the sounds from the sidelines. Near the end of the route, one of the girls behind her sped up and started to close the gap. Breathing steady, mind relaxed, she tapped into something deep down inside, and poured on a little more speed. When she tore through the finish line, the screaming exploded around her. She left her challenger in the dust.

Mr. Ennis jumped up and down and reached in to muss up her hair. While the shimmer of cameras should've blinded her, she didn't notice. Folded in half, gasping for air, she kept a look out for her teammates as they crested the hill and tore down the side. She stood and yelled over the heads of the other runners, giving them encouragement to cross the line and finish the race.

Detective Perez crossed her office and opened a small black fridge by the window. She pulled out a couple of bottles and put them on the desk between them. Drink in hand, she sat down. "Sounds like things were finally starting to look up," she said.

"Yep. School, too." Greta reached out to take one.

"And your relationship with your father?"

"About that..." She sipped her soda to buy herself some time. That summer, Ian had been invited to join his friend at his cabin by the lake. Excited to go somewhere, anywhere beyond Ravensworth, she couldn't accept he'd called the trip a 'family vacation' when she'd overheard him on the phone. It didn't feel right. They'd stopped being a family two years ago when he murdered her mother. It hadn't mattered anyway because, after he'd hung up, he told her she hadn't been invited.

Detective Perez put down her drink. "You were twelve?"

"Thirteen that summer."

"He left you by yourself for a week?"

She looked at the detective. "I've told you a thousand times: he wanted nothing to do with me. He only cared about himself."

"And nobody noticed?"

Greta shook her head. The week he was away, she'd woken to the sounds of birds chirping. The air smelled piney and fresh, and she ran every morning to focus her mind on the track season ahead. In the afternoon, she watched TV, a bowl of whatever she could find to eat beside her. Evenings, fireflies glowed brightly as they darted in droves over top of her on the back patio. Their lights, twinkling and bright, held memories of her mother.

With so much her mom never had the chance to tell her—things she was still desperate to know—one night she gave into her fear and stood outside her parents' bedroom door. She pushed it gently, letting it creak open in front of her. Inside, she slipped to the edge of her mother's side of the bed and, with fingers looped through the cold metal hoop of the drawer of the bedside table, pulled it open. There were stacks of folded papers, a receipt for furniture, faded recipes, cuttings from old magazines, a slip with a single phone number—no name; nothing on the back. And at the bottom of the drawer was a novel, earmarked at the corner three-quarters of the way though, as if waiting for her mother's return. Greta knelt down and pressed her fingers in further, fumbling around the rough edges, and found what she'd spent years asking for.

She held the birth certificate up to the light; not a photocopy, it was the size of her palm. It had to be the original. Hopeful her adoption papers were in there too, she tucked the birth certificate into the front pocket of her jeans before digging her fingers back into the drawer. All that remained were the knots in the sides of the wood. She slammed it shut. Where were they? That night, she'd turned the cabin inside and out, but no matter how hard she tried, she couldn't find them.

"I'll assume you didn't ask your father about them after his trip?" Detective Perez said.

Greta took another mouthful of soda. "No point. He got lit as soon as he walked back into the cabin."

TWENTY-TWO

As soon as he pulled into the laneway and parked the truck, Ian charged inside and flopped onto the couch of the main room, bottle in hand. Told to unpack his things, she spent the evening lugging around camping gear. Airing it. Cleaning it. Putting it back in the hallway cupboard, without comment or complaint. On top of a chair, her hand high inside, she pushed the last of many bags flat on the shelf when her wrist brushed a piece of paper. She pulled out a white envelope. Addressed to her, she jumped down and pulled out a kitchen chair.

Dear Greta,

I'm writing to tell you how sorry I am to have heard about your mother's death. I can't imagine the pain you're feeling, and I'm hoping warm memories of your mother sustain you through what I'm sure must be a very difficult time.

I knew your mom from a few years back when we worked together. In fact, you and I have already met. It was years ago and you were pretty young, so I'm not sure if you'd remember.

If there's anything I can do for you or if you have any questions you want to ask about your mom, feel free to get in touch with me.

My deepest sympathies.

Colleen

Greta's stomach lurched and she gulped for air. She hadn't taken a single breath the whole time she'd been reading. Colleen. The lady who wrecked Sundays? Images of her parents and Colleen huddled in the back aisle of the old-fashioned candy store surfaced in her head. The woman had been nothing but trouble. She read the note again. How did Colleen know where she lived? She picked up the envelope and turned it over. The address was right. Her eyes shifted to the top left corner.

Colleen Jones. Bracebridge Women's Shelter.

She gasped. Her mother had never told her where she'd worked when she first came to Bracebridge; this was another piece of her mother's life she could claim. Her mood lifted, but quickly deflated again as she imagined what would happen if Ian found her in the kitchen with the letter. At first, she had no idea how she'd explain it, but then she reconsidered. Why should she have to? Addressed to her, her father had hidden it, so she didn't care if he knew she had it. It belonged to her. She stormed down the hallway to confront him. Her stomach turned. Barely breathing, he'd passed out, sprawled over the length of the couch in his camping clothes.

That week, up in her bedroom, Greta read Colleen's letter a thousand times. Postmarked two years ago, shortly after her mother's death, she'd had a lot of time since then to consider the stories her mother had told her about her life. She didn't believe she'd lied outright; more likely, she'd left the bad stuff out. Now she had Colleen to talk to, she needed to fill in the missing pieces. Maybe she'd know where to find her old adoption papers.

One morning after her father had left for work, she picked up the phone and dialed the number at the bottom of the page.

A woman answered. "Bracebridge Women's Shelter. Can I help you?"

She slammed down the phone. She hadn't thought about what she was going to say if someone answered. She collected her thoughts and dialed again.

"Bracebridge Women's Shelter," the voice said. "How can I help you?"

A chill surged through her veins. She felt hot, and then she felt cold, but this time she didn't hang up. "Hello," she said, her voice a whisper. It was shaking. "Is Colleen there?"

There was a pause. "Colleen who?"

She didn't need to look at the letter; she'd memorized every word. "Colleen Jones."

"Hmm. I'm new on reception and I don't see her on the staff list. Hang on, honey, let me check with the others."

The voice put her on hold. She waited for an eternity until it returned.

"Still there, honey?"

"Yep," she said, slightly annoyed at the pet name. Still, she ignored it. It wasn't the time.

"Colleen's off this week. Vacation. Leave me a number and I'll get her to call when she's back."

Greta didn't hesitate. She rattled off her name and number. She wasn't worried about her father intercepting the call—he was never home anyway.

Waiting for Colleen to come back from vacation was the second longest week of her life. Only the week of her mother's funeral felt longer. When the phone rang, she jumped and took a breath. She answered. She listened. She could barely contain her excitement.

"Yes, I did. I finally got the letter," she said, no thanks to her idiot father. An image of the envelope in her dime box appeared in her head, tucked away safe with the treasures she valued most. She listened again and started to count. *One, two, three.* Then her mind went blank. She'd spent hours poring over every detail of the conversation she wanted to have with Colleen but now had no idea how to ask any of her questions. Her well laid-out plan evaporated into thin air.

She centred herself quickly to steady her voice. "You said if I had anything I wanted to know, I could ask..." She kicked herself for skipping over the small talk she'd so painstakingly worked through.

"Absolutely. I'm so sorry about everything that's happened," Colleen said.

Greta's eyes stung and her mind flashed back two years. It would be too painful to let the conversation go backwards. She was stronger now and she needed to move forward. "So, I guess... First off... How did you know my mom?"

"I met her here at the shelter before you were born."

Her mind swirled. That was where her mother must've worked when she first moved to Bracebridge. Another piece of her mother's past slipped into place.

"I've met you, too," Colleen said, "twice, actually. You were probably too young to remember."

"Try me."

"First time in the hospital. You were maybe about three?"

Greta paused. "Me? Are you sure?"

"Didn't your mom tell you?"

"No." She had no recollection of a hospital visit.

"Your mom said you were an active kid. Went from crawling to walking to running in a blink of an eye."

She grinned. No wonder track had come so naturally. Apparently she'd been running forever.

"You'd taken some type of fall down some hard, wooden stairs," Colleen said.

Greta knew those stairs all too well.

"Cracked your head right open."

An icy chill went down her back. She thought of her mother splayed out on the kitchen floor. She pushed the image of blood out of her mind and focused on Colleen's voice.

"When your parents got you stitched up, the doctors said you were in shock. You wouldn't talk. Wouldn't even respond to your name. Didn't cry. You just sat there. They did a CAT scan and found you had a nasty concussion. You scared your mother to death. She was so glad to get you back home."

Greta knew exactly what her mother would've felt. Home together meant not lonely. Home together meant safe. Except home was where the danger lurked. The feeling of loss weighed heavily on her heart.

"I called your mom a few days later to see how you were doing and she was worried. You still hadn't said a word. The doctors told her it would take time, but she wasn't seeing a difference."

Dots began to connect in her mind. She reached to the back of her head, drawing her fingers along the long-knotted scar. Was that why she had lost so many of her early childhood memories? If it was, what was the big secret? Why hadn't her mother told her? Every kid falls. Every kid has accidents. Unless it hadn't been one...

"Greta," Colleen said, "you there? Still having trouble with your memory?"

Greta laughed. "No. I spaced out for a sec."

"Do you remember the second time I met you? You were about six or seven and—"

"Yep. The old fashioned candy store." Greta blew out air into the phone. "But I thought you'd be at my mom's funeral."

Colleen paused. "Sorry, I couldn't make it. I was out of town."

"I guess that happens sometimes."

"How old are you now?" Colleen asked.

"Thirteen."

"A teenager, huh? That's tough. What to wear. Who to hang out with. It's not easy. And all those models out there looking like they were born perfect..."

"I'm just trying to make it through Grade Eight," Greta said, trying to keep the conversation on track. "Colleen, you know I'm adopted, right?"

"I do."

"Did my mom ever tell you where she put the papers?"

Colleen paused again. "Why would she tell me?"

"You're her friend, right?"

"Yes. What did your father say about that when you asked?"

"Nothing. He won't talk about it."

An uncomfortable silence sat between them until Colleen cleared her throat. "On to high school next?" Greta guessed she wasn't getting an answer. "Your mom spent a lot of time reminiscing about her high school days. So much so she made me feel like I'd been there with her."

She perked up. "What did she say?"

"She went somewhere north of Hamilton. If I remember where, I'll tell you."

Her heart pinched. Almost another piece of new information. Almost.

"She was a big reader, your mother. She told me she was always getting called out for being a nerd."

Greta laughed. Her mother always had a book in her hand. "So she liked it?"

"High school? I guess. Like everyone, she was scared of the older kids, the Grade Thirteens."

She couldn't imagine her mother being scared of anything—only Ian.

"They were half-bearded giants that shoved kids in lockers. You can imagine..."

"What's Grade Thirteen?"

Colleen chuckled. "In the nineties, high school was five years for everyone. Everything's different now. So many ways society can swallow you. If you don't fit the mold. If you aren't a cookie cutter version of somebody's idea of perfection, you're a freak. I'm sure you've picked up on these things by now."

Greta thought back to her conversations with Mr. K.

"Don't get obsessed with that," Colleen said. "It's a trap. It'll snatch the colour from your life, sap the adventure right out of you." She paused and laughed. "Listen to me rambling on. I sound like some sort of nut bar. Be strong is all I'm saying. Do your own thing."

Colleen had no idea how strong she already was, but nonetheless stored her advice away for later.

"Whatever you do, your mom would be proud."

Colleen's comment made her smile. "Thanks."

"Listen, I've got to get back to work. Call me if you need anything else."

Greta had other things she wanted to know, but she knew they'd have to wait for another time. She thanked her and hung up the phone.

Detective Perez rose, dropped their empty bottles in the blue box beside the desk, and placed it by the edge of the door. "I'd like to discuss that scar again," Detective Perez said. "Was it an accident?"

Greta shrugged. "I told you, I can only guess."

The detective looked up over the edge of her glasses. "Don't bother. Guessing in my line of work is as good as a no." She paused. "Can I see it?"

Heat rose up in Greta's cheeks as she stood and leaned across the desk. "Give me your hand."

Detective Perez ran the tip of a finger along the side of Greta's head, then drew it back and wrote in her notebook. "What about this letter? From Colleen?"

"What about it?"

"Do you still have it?"

"No." She fell back in the chair. "Why would I?" She had. It was tucked into her dime box with all her treasures from her mother she valued most. They were none of anyone's business.

"After you connected with this colleague of your mother's—"

"I felt calmer. Ian never mentioned or talked about my mother, so Colleen was the only living link to her that I had."

"Did it change things?"

"My marks went up. I made friends. I kicked ass in track." She thought back to the way the team had dominated the season and how, on the day of the big race, she'd jumped to the front of the pack as soon as the starting horn sounded, hit her stride, and tore through the route she knew by heart. It was no surprise she crossed the finish line two minutes ahead of her competitors. "I won the championships. Even though everyone said they knew I would, to me, it was a big deal."

"I'm sure it was." Detective Perez paused before she sat down. "But what you've told me doesn't make sense, Greta. If you knew so much more about your mother then, that she'd gone to seek help at a woman's shelter before you were even born, why—"

"I hadn't figured that out yet."

"But this Colleen told you she worked with her."

"I thought they were colleagues. My mom called her an old friend."

Detective Perez put her hands on her desk and leaned forward. "You didn't put it together?"

Greta stopped and took a deep breath. Had she? Had she thought of the implications? She'd only been thirteen. "I don't know. No. Maybe. Probably a bit. Maybe I didn't want to face the fact Ian was beating the crap out of my mom before they ever adopted me because that would mean—"

The detective's voice rose. "But why wouldn't you tell someone? It would have corroborated your story that your father killed your mother."

TWENTY-THREE

Greta wanted to strangle the detective with her bare hands. "I did tell someone."

"Who?"

"Who the hell do you think? Officer Pappas." She pulled her coat and purse from the back of the chair and stood. "This whole thing is stupid. Talk to him later. I'm going home."

Detective Perez's voice hardened. "No, you're not. And I'm losing patience. You brought him into all this. Sit back down and explain to me what you told him about your mother."

She'd picked up and dialed the phone in the kitchen.

"You said I could call, right?"

"Yes."

"I have new information."

"Is your father home?"

She pulled up a chair and placed it in front of her. "He's at work."

"Then we've got a bit of a problem."

"What's that?" she said.

"I can't talk to you without him there."

A knot formed in her stomach. She put Officer Pappas' card down on the table. She didn't want Ian anywhere near them. They'd done that once and it had got them nowhere.

"You're kidding me," she said.

"The law's the law," he told her.

"Can you break it?"

"No."

"Ignore it?"

"No. And I can't change the law either."

She put her head in her hands. "Is there any other way?"

"Not that I know," he said.

She hung up the phone and shut her eyes, defeated. There had to be.

During the last day of the school year, Mr. Katz pulled into the Kearney precinct. It was an ancient brown-stoned building, surrounded by dried-out old ferns, squatting low to the ground. The parking lot was to the right. There were four spots; two were taken. He turned into an empty one and shut off the ignition.

"I'm not saying a word," he said from across the front seat.

Greta frowned. "I don't need you to."

Mr. K. got out of the car and made his way along the path. She fell instep beside him, trying to keep up. He stopped at the front door. "I'm standing in *loco parentis*," he said as he swung the glass open.

Greta examined the pavement around them and, seeing nothing, walked by. The moment they stepped inside, her eyes watered and she swallowed the sick from the back of her throat. Was that sweat? Rancid tuna fish? She had no idea. Either way, the place stunk.

Officer Pappas appeared from around a corner. "Greta, Mr. Katz, welcome." He extended his hand and motioned them forward. Dressed in chinos and a long-sleeved collared shirt, there was no sign of a black vest or a gun. They followed behind him through a narrow corridor to the back of the building.

"Sit in there." He pointed to a room on his left. "I'll be back in a minute."

Greta pulled a chair up to the table, her fingers landing in soft gum underneath. She wiped them on her jean shorts and stared out one of three white-framed windows to the depths of the forest. Thick with trees, the leaves drooped, and lost in thought, she wiped the sweat off her forehead. Two minutes later, Officer Pappas strode back in the room with a middle-aged woman wearing a red dress. Her gray hair was wafer-thin, as fine as mist. He introduced her as a child advocate.

"So I hear you've got new information?" Officer Pappas said, smiling after they sat at the table.

Greta nodded. Her hands shook so badly, she kept them tucked down at her sides.

He opened a small-spiraled book. "What have you got?"

She steeled herself and took a deep breath. "My father hit my mother."

"You've seen this happen?" he asked, writing it down.

She nodded. Then she explained he'd hit her, too. The woman looked at her from under hooded eyelids.

"When was the last time?"

Greta thought back. "Maybe three years ago?"

Officer Pappas and the child advocate glanced at each other, saying nothing, but Greta noted she gave him a muddy look. He leaned forward in his chair and put his elbows on the table.

"I've looked into this every which way since Sunday. I've talked to your neighbours. They've got nothing. Neither does Minister Marchello. I've searched for your mom's medical records, and—"

"We don't have a doctor."

"At the hospital—"

"I went. She never did."

He sighed. "I dropped by the walk-in clinics to see if she'd been at one of those."

Greta scoffed. "Ian would never allow it."

"So where did she go?"

She couldn't answer and he didn't ask again.

Officer Pappas put a hand on her forearm and gave it a squeeze. "Greta," he said, "we need evidence."

She pulled her arm free and nodded, but she wasn't sure what that meant. Why wasn't he listening? She'd given him some. What type of evidence could he need?

"Did you talk to someone at her work?" she asked.

Officer Pappas' face dropped. "No one told me she worked."

Greta crossed her arms. "I just did. When she first came to Bracebridge."

"How long ago was that?"

"I dunno." She raised her palms in the air. "At the Bracebridge Women's Shelter. Before I was even born."

Officer Pappas and the child advocate looked at her in unison.

"You're sure about this?" he said.

She nodded.

Officer Pappas leaned in to the woman beside him. Their eyes locked, hers thin yet kind, framed with black-rimmed glasses. "Is that enough?" he asked her.

Greta's heart pounded in her chest.

"Investigate," she told him.

"Finally," Detective Perez sighed. "I knew there had to have been more of an investigation than you first alluded to."

She scowled. "Well, I'm sorry to burst your bubble, but..."

"You said the child advocate approved it."

"But it didn't go anywhere."

The detective lifted her fingers to her temples. "That's impossible."

"You don't know Ian," Greta grumbled.

The summer heat came and three weeks passed since Mr. K. had taken Greta to see Officer Pappas. There was no food in the fridge, but still she ran every day to keep in shape and spent evenings in the main room watching TV or alone out on the patio.

Late one night, Ian burst through the front door. "Where the hell are you?" he shouted.

Greta muted the TV. When she looked up, she froze. He towered over her, his eyes bulging.

"What the hell did you say?" His hair was plastered to his head with sweat. His hand shot out, and he wrenched her arm behind her. "And don't play games with me."

Something popped. Pain flooded her shoulder. She couldn't move. "I don't know what you're talking about."

"You're lying." Spit flew from the sides of his mouth. It landed on her cheek. "You must have said something."

"I didn't. Not to anyone."

Ian let her arm go and stepped backwards. He ran his hands across his cheeks and started to pace. Back and forth, fuming, walking the length of the room over and over again. Then he stopped in his tracks and turned his black eyes on her—eyes all at once full of terror.

"Fucking neighbours got me fired," he screamed.

Her eyes widened. She shifted her butt on the couch.

"And Minister Marcello booted me out of the church. I have nothing now. Nothing. I'm going to kill them..."

Greta sat still, bile in the back of her throat. Nothing? That was rich.

"Get packing," he ordered. "We're outta here." She gazed off into the distance; vacant. He snapped his fingers in the air in front of her. "Earth to Greta. We're moving to Bracebridge."

She shrunk, unable to process the new information.

"8.00 AM Tuesday. If you're not ready, you can walk. All eighty klicks."

The week before they moved, Greta had walked through the cabin to sharpen her memories. The only home she'd ever known—the pitted kitchen cupboards, the rickety staircase where she'd fallen and cracked her head, the large windows in the back room overlooking the back patio, the dresser mirror. Her mother's smell was gone, but her presence lingered everywhere, and she wanted to bring as much of her with her as she could. Mom, barefoot, baking cookies in the kitchen. Sloped to one side, the upstairs hallway, a perfect space to play jacks. The back patio where they'd sat, heads bent over the table, feet touching, reading books. She didn't care they were moving to the city: the thought of leaving her mother behind made her sick.

The next Tuesday, outside the cabin, Ian laid on the horn. It was just past seven and pouring rain. He rolled down the window and yelled. "Get out here, Greta, or I'll drag you out myself."

The air inside the cab was stuffy, and she felt light-headed. Huge raindrops pelted against the truck windows, drowning out her sobs from the back seat. Out the back of the truck, mist rose from the pavement like a ghost, and her desire to get out at the side of the highway was overwhelming. When the truck turned into a crumbling Bracebridge parking lot next to a shabby two-storey building, her need to escape grew. From the back seat, huddled between the boxes, she stared outside. Not a tree on the boulevard... The street was empty. The large black and white sign hung across the front of the first floor read Honey Bee Restaurant. Beneath it, in red scrawled handwriting, *Best Chinese Food Around*. She got out of the truck, and an uneven line of cement patio stones scattered along the left side of the building teetered underfoot. There were four small windows by the back entrance; three boarded up and one splintered like a spider. Between them, the only entry a screened door.

Bang. Bang.

She climbed the stairs. The air was stale and smelled like grease. It looked lived in; it felt dirty. Paint peeled from the woodwork of the doorframes and the floors were blotchy and pocked with stains. A narrow hallway separated the two apartments sitting on top of the restaurant. Ian unlocked the door and pushed it open. She stepped inside. A crocheted afghan perched high across the back of the couch and a ratty blue rug crumpled at the edge of the kitchen were the only spots of colour. The soles of her running shoes stuck to invisible patches of grit. In two short steps, out of the living room and at the door of her bedroom, she stared at the faded brown paneling spreading halfway up the walls; the rest painted winter white. Only the bathroom kept her from screaming and running back out. It was indoors. It had a door with a lock, and not a rusty hook but a strong metal one. Back in the living room, a *Welcome to Bracebridge* brochure had been placed on one end of a small wooden table. Ian sat down at the other.

"Home, sweet home," he smiled.

"Home?" she repeated, hardly able to believe her ears.

"Got something better?"

Tears welled in her eyes, and the threads holding her together unraveled. She picked up the green garbage bag containing everything she owned, turned her back to him, and slammed the door of her bedroom.

***

The Detective's pencil flew across the page. "You lived there for...?"

"Almost two years." Greta waited for her to stop writing. "And it wasn't."

"What?" she said, her face pinched in concentration.

"Living. In the beginning, I only existed."

The first night in the apartment, on top of her bed, she listened to the sounds on the street. Dogs barking. People talking. Tires screeching on wet pavement. Each time a car passed by, the room lit up, and they passed by all night long. In the morning as she dozed, a man's voice barked out orders on the phone through the paper-thin walls. In bed all day, by evening, the pillow wrapped around the sides of her head, overcome by the sweet and sour smells wafting up from the restaurant below, she finally fell asleep.

Within a few days, what was new became more familiar. She tuned out the sound of the bell downstairs announcing new customers. It was considered a local landmark for its savory homemade egg rolls, but from the crushed cardboard boxes tucked into the trash bin at the back of the restaurant, she'd realized that was another lie, too.

"I have no idea what my mother would've said about us living over a grease bowl. For years my father demanded these perfect cooked meals. Beef kabobs. Shepherd's pie.

Soups. All from scratch. Mom would've either been pissed or would have laughed hysterically."

"You missed her."

The thought made a hard lump in her throat. "Still do. Every day."

TWENTY-FOUR

"Jerk."

The words came from outside Greta's bedroom. She got up from the floor and cracked open her bedroom door. Ian was lying on the couch. His cheeks were ruddy, his face bloated, his body swollen. He was getting fat. He slammed down the phone.

"What are you staring at?" he said.

Greta didn't say a word. Another rejection didn't surprise her. He was basically unemployable.

He wagged his finger at her. "Where's the goddamn bread?"

She closed the door behind her, shut her eyes, and pressed her back against the wood. What bread? *She* was hungry. If there had been any, she'd have eaten the whole loaf days ago. "I dunno," she said.

"Stupid bitch. Don't lie to me."

Her stomach felt sick. She'd heard that tone before. Ian got off the sofa and stepped between her and the apartment door.

"I bought it last night," he said. "Brought it home. Stuck it right here." He pointed to the counter.

There was nothing on it.

"Did you take it?" He swiped at his nose, marbled with purple veins spread up to his cheeks.

She held her tongue. From past experience, she knew he wouldn't take no for an answer and that it was unsafe to argue.

"Answer me." He got up in her face. "Are you deaf or stupid?"

"I didn't take it."

He lunged at her.

"Don't touch me," she yelled, scrambling away.

There was a knock on the apartment door that startled them both. A voice drifted through. "Open up. Mr. Giffen? Greta? Everything okay in there?"

For the first time in a week, she didn't regret their move. She raised her eyebrows at her father. He had two choices; what was he going to do? He opened the door.

A woman, her square face lined with worry, stood there. "Oh good. You're alright," she said, her eyes travelling between the two of them.

"We're fine," Ian said, arms folded across his potbelly.

She looked him up and down. "Didn't sound like it." Then she smiled at Greta. "Hi. I'm Mrs. Xiangzi."

Greta mumbled a hello.

"My husband and I own the building."

Greta raised her eyes to meet hers.

"School soon?"

She nodded. "Starts in less than two weeks."

"Which one are you going to?" Mrs. Xiangzi asked.

Her shoulders slumped. All her old friends were going to Almaguin, but she had no idea where she was supposed to go. Her father hadn't told her.

Mrs. Xiangzi glared at Ian. "Don't close that door." She disappeared down the hallway and, when she returned, she passed Greta a beat-up laptop. "You need to look it up."

Greta held the laptop to her chest.

"Go ahead. Open it. I'll show you."

Greta put the laptop on the table and Mrs. Xiangzi sat down beside her.

"There." Mrs. Xiangzi pointed to the screen after she googled *Bracebridge high schools*. "Type in the address of our building in the line. Good. Now click that link. Now download the file and save it to the desktop. Excellent." She stood up. "Now fill out the form. If you want help," she hooked a thumb behind her, "I'm just across the hall. And we've got a printer downstairs you can use."

Greta looked up and smiled at her. "Thank you."

Mrs. Xiangzi turned back around and brushed by her father. "You," she warned him, shaking an index finger in the air, "no more noise."

His face reddened. He slammed the door behind her and slunk to the kitchen.

An hour later, Greta tucked the laptop under her arm and knocked on the door across the hall. Mrs. Xiangzi opened it.

"Greta." She reached out and shook her hand. "Good to see you. All done?"

"Like you showed me."

Mrs. Xiangzi checked the desktop and then led her downstairs, stopping in front of a small table outside the kitchen. "I've heard it's a great school." She picked up the forms from the printer and looked over her shoulder. "And I hope you'll be happy here."

"Thanks," she said sullenly, trying her best.

"Oh-oh. You don't look so good."

Great. A rocket scientist. "I'm not," she said. She kept her tone low key.

Mrs. Xiangzi jutted her finger to her right. "Sit down and talk to me."

Greta followed Mrs. Xiangzi into the kitchen. Navy and white painted cement tiles were set out in a checkerboard pattern. Three industrial sized fridges sat side by side. There were sets of stainless steel bowls on the countertops, and shelves ran floor to ceiling for the dry goods. She sauntered across the room, past three sinks filled to the brim with pots and pans, and a long counter cluttered with chopped vegetables, before perching up high on a stool. Mrs. Xiangzi was mixing some sort of concoction over a low flame on the stove. Steam billowed everywhere. The smell wafting through the space between them made her mouth water.

"Why so glum?" Mrs. Xiangzi lifted a spoonful of the mixture to her lips.

Greta paused, trying to figure out a way to explain the situation. She didn't want Mrs. Xiangzi to think she was rude; they'd just met. She couldn't think of a way to do it, and so she let herself go.

"There's nothing to do here. I don't know anyone. I miss my house. My friends. My old room."

Mrs. Xiangzi didn't look up. "Adjustments are always painful."

"I hate it."

Mrs. Xiangzi added more spice to the sauce. "I felt the same way when we moved. Everything was so different."

"Different? It sucks. It's like being on a totally foreign planet."

"It'll get better with time." She smiled, her voice softening. "I promise."

Greta sighed. "Not for me. I'll be trapped here till I get married or die."

Mrs. Xiangzi cackled out loud. "You have more choices than that."

She didn't laugh. She wanted her preference known. "I'm hoping for death, and I hope it comes fast."

Mrs. Xiangzi moved the sauce from the stove and picked up a knife to chop vegetables. "Greta, Greta... You ought to be thinking bigger than that. It's not a great goal for someone your age. Think further ahead. Long-term. First, a job. Then a career. A career is important for a woman."

She picked her nails. She was fourteen—she hadn't even started high school yet. She wanted a job, but a career? "Aren't they the same thing?"

"Pick something you like to bring in money. You'll need to be independent and take care of yourself one day."

She scoffed. "What type of career would be good for someone like me?"

Mrs. Xiangzi put down the carrot in her hand and stared at her in disbelief. "Anything you want. Anything you set your mind to. Construction? A CEO? A nurse to help people? An astronaut? Own your own business? Maybe have a restaurant? Maybe this one? Not now, but when my husband and I retire."

Greta looked at her shocked.

Mrs. Xiangzi laughed. "You don't have to decide today. Keep your options open and dream big. No more of this death stuff, though. It's bad luck. Now go. Take those forms to the school and register."

With her backpack in one hand and a carton of chocolate milk in the other, Greta climbed the ten steps into the building. Ahead of her was an office. A far door opened and a woman stepped out from behind the counter. Stocky, with red hair scraped back tight behind her ears and dressed all in white, she looked like a martial arts instructor.

"Grade?" the woman said.

"Nine." Greta handed her the papers. "Can I ask—"

But the lady raised her hand. She turned and passed through the door of the inner office, which closed behind her. Greta waited. And waited. And waited. The lady finally returned with a stack of paper.

"Greta Giffen?"

The red-haired martial arts instructor handed Greta her class schedule.

"Seven of eight courses are mandatory," she explained, "but because you're late, Introductory Business is all that's left."

It wasn't the worst alternative. Greta thought back to the conversation she'd had with Mrs. Xiangzi about owning her own. She'd thanked her, and on her way out of the office, noticed a letter-sized envelope stapled to the top of the documents. On a bench outside in the hallway, she held it out in front of her. The top-left insignia was the school's, but underneath it was missing the Latin motto. It was replaced with one word. Blues. She sliced open the envelope and pulled out a typed note.

Dear Greta,

Welcome.

I watched you run last year at the cross-country championships.

A shiver ran up her spine. Someone out there was watching her?

Congratulations on winning the race. We have a track team here at the school—The Blues. We could use you on it.

She stopped reading. Was this an invitation to try out?

Practices are Tuesday and Thursday mornings, and Fridays after school. We'll be starting the second week of September.

Greta mentally checked her calendar for availability. Yep, free as a bird.

To be clear, I'm not asking you to try out: I'm offering a full spot on the Junior Varsity team. Consider it.

I hope you can join us.

Sincerely, Coach Dewson.

Greta read the note a second time, then a third. Her feet tingled. Forty-five minutes after walking into the building, she strolled back out with a reputation that preceded her and a track team of potential new friends. She blew a kiss skyward.

***

"So this woman—Mrs. Xiangzi, you say—can verify what you've told me about your father?"

Greta nodded. "Greta nodded. She helped me register for high school in Bracebridge."

As Detective Perez jotted it down, Greta remembered feeling at the time that her mother had sent her a little nudge of luck. "It was fifteen minutes from the apartment. No way he planned that."

"Then your records must still be there," Detective Perez said.

"How do you mean?"

"By law, schools are required to keep them."

"Whatever."

"Listen Greta. A lot of people sitting in this chair would have trouble with the story you're telling me. I want to see what's in them. Official documents from Social Services. Correspondence from the police."

"Knock yourself out. All you'll find are my crappy marks."

The detective frowned. "I'll have the file sent down. Maybe there's something from Officer Pappas. Sometimes we crack a case from the strangest things."

She sighed. "What's to crack? My dad died of cancer and you're still trying to pin it on me."

Detective Perez leaned forward and spoke slowly. "So why don't you get to what happened at the hospital and we'll clear it all up?"

With her fists at her sides, Greta's face flushed. "Him. Him. *Him.* Why don't you shut up and listen?"

She'd been out of her depth. The first day, the school was a maze. She was late for her classes and no familiar faces smiled back in the halls. Cliques she knew nothing of sprung up and spread out, claiming turf in all parts of the building. She had nowhere to go, and so she sat outside the front of the school and ate lunch alone, vowing to herself she wouldn't panic. Every day, she slumped home after school, unlocked the door to the apartment, and dropped her backpack on the floor, with no idea how she was going to make it through another week.

Hot and sweaty, she stood in front of the fridge, looking for something to eat. Someone banged on the apartment door.

"Open up."

"Okay, okay," she said irritably, recognising the voice on the other side. But she didn't move; instead, she continued scanning the top three shelves for food.

Mrs. Xiangzi kept knocking, and then the apartment door rattled. "Hurry up in there," she said louder. "I need help in the restaurant."

Greta closed the refrigerator and unlocked the front door. "Mrs. Xiangzi, the most I can do is toast or scrambled eggs. Maybe French toast on a good day. And I very much doubt any of those things are on your menu."

Mrs. Xiangzi laughed. "Not cooking. Too many people. I need help serving."

"What?"

"Give people their tables. Clear up the dishes. That kind of help."

A knot formed in Greta's stomach. "I guess I could do that." She looked down at her sweaty track clothes. Her nose told her everything she needed to know. "When?"

"There's a line up out the door. Why do you think I'm knocking?"

Greta sighed and followed Mrs. Xiangzi downstairs. Eighteen tables covered with red and white tablecloths were overflowing. Families and couples were sat talking, laughing, shoveling Mr. Xiangzi's delicacies into their mouths. There were plates everywhere. Glasses empty. Through the large glass window next to the front door, a line-up of people flooded out onto the street.

Greta quickly got to work. While Mrs. Xiangzi brought out steaming dishes on big white platters, Greta cleared the empty ones from the tables and refilled the customers' drinks. She brought them soy sauce, serviettes, soft drinks, crayons for the children to colour in their menus, and cutlery when they gave up on the chopsticks. When they left, she wiped down the tables, re-set them as fast as she could, and after she'd sat new families, started all over again.

"When the dinner shift finally slowed, Mrs. Xiangzi made me supper. She hated that I wanted sweet and sour chicken balls and French fries over her famous Almond Soo Ga. And then, after the place cleared out, she gave me the thirty dollars left on the tables. But I passed it back."

"Why would you do that?" Detective Perez asked.

"It didn't feel right. Ian treated me like a slave and never gave me a dime. But Mrs. Xiangzi insisted. She said

I seated and bussed, so the tips were mine. She told me to save them for something, and I had thousands of things I wanted. Food. Clothes. A phone. New running shoes. She told me if I showed up again, I'd earn more."

"She gave you a job?"

Greta laughed. "Only if I showered first. On weekends, it was packed. Weeknights were slower, so sometimes we'd sit in the kitchen and talk or I did my homework. Mrs. Xiangzi helped me out. After about a month, I had earned enough that I managed to buy myself a phone. I wish my mother had seen it. The first thing I did was take a picture of her photo that I'd hidden behind my bedroom mirror. I uploaded it to the home screen. Then I got in touch with my old friends."

"They must have been happy to hear from you."

"Yep. But it was hard. I wasn't with them anymore. And I hadn't made any new ones. I'd searched the other kids up on social, been creeping them for days, but their posts were shallow. Nasty. Some were mean. I don't know what they were thinking. They shared stuff I'd never share."

Detective Perez sighed. "I know all about sexting."

She shook her head. "No. Not that. Stupid pranks. Parties. Stuff I didn't need. So I decided I was good alone and kept to myself, kept busy. I discovered I loved making my own money. I went to school, ran track and worked. No drama."

TWENTY-FIVE

One Saturday evening after the restaurant closed, Mrs. Xiangzi picked up her new phone. She pointed to the home screen.

"Who's that?"

"My mom."

"You must miss her."

Greta swallowed hard.

"Where is she?" she asked, gesturing for her to sit down.

Greta punched in her password and scrolled through the images of her life before her mother died. Mrs. Xiangzi flipped through them with her thumb. She stopped to examine some more closely and pushed others aside. When she described the day her mother died, Mrs. Xiangzi's grasped Greta's hands across the table.

"I'm going to tell you an ancient proverb," Mrs. Xiangzi said. "Our ancestors were wise, my dear. Long ago, they passed along insights in stories and sayings so we could learn from them," she said.

Greta had never heard an ancient Chinese secret. She perked up. "Like what?"

Mrs. Xiangzi paused. "Mr. Xiangzi always reminds me aged ginger is more pungent than fresh."

That was true; Greta knew that, at least. He'd said it in the kitchen before, but she thought he'd been talking about the beef dish. "So what's the lesson?"

Mrs. Xiangzi laughed. All four-foot-ten of her shook to the core. "It means the older, the wiser."

She shook her head. Ian wasn't.

"Let me put it another way," Mrs. Xiangzi said. "Young people need to listen to their elders because some of them have life experience and can give good advice."

She thought of her mother. That made sense.

"Not everyone uses proverbs correctly, though," Mrs. Xiangzi explained. "Mr. Xiangzi is two months older than me, so when he wants something I don't, he reminds me not to close my ears to my elders or I may suffer loss."

Greta looked at her startled.

"No, dear, he's not serious," she laughed. "He's using the proverb to try and get his own way."

"You don't give in, do you?"

"It depends," she said, her shiny black hair sliding sideways. "Compromise is the seed of longevity."

What? She tucked that expression away for later. "So, what would you say is *my* proverb?"

Mrs. Xiangzi squeezed her hands. "If my great-great grandmother had met you, I bet this is what she would have said. She would have told you: if you work hard enough, you can grind even an iron rod down to a needle."

"What? You lost me in the translation, Mrs. X."

"Miss G.," she smiled, "let me try again."

Greta liked the sound of that—both trying again and the new spin on her name. *G.* It had a nice feel to it; like sliding on a new pair of pants. Which reminded her... God, she needed new clothes.

Mrs. Xiangzi folded her hands on the table. "It means constant work can grind down big problems, like wearing away a stone."

She crossed her legs under the table. "Come again?"

Mrs. Xiangzi grinned. "One more time, Miss G. We need to be patient with issues we're dealt with because persistence and effort helps solve them."

Greta tilted her head, waiting for Mrs. Xiangzi to go on, but she sat there, rested her chin in the palm of her hands, and left the explanation in the open between them, untouched and simmering. She shifted in her chair and, after she nibbled on her almond cookie to avoid the awkward silence, she stood and said goodnight. Mrs. Xiangzi clasped her hands warmly and gently cuffed her on the cheek.

Back in her bedroom that night, Greta tried to decipher the proverb. The iron rod was her current situation, and she wasn't scared of the hard work required to push her way through. But the details were light. How could she whittle the rod down? Turn things around? Make sure there was money to pay the rent? Eat? And how could she focus in school to get a career when she was bored out of her skull?

All night that night, she tossed and turned, weighing the possibilities.

"You became close with the Xiangzis?" Detective Perez asked.

Greta smiled. "Without my mom, they were my family."

"What about your coach?"

"Dewson? It wasn't like elementary school. Running varsity's big, you know."

"I gather. Hundreds of runners. I'm sure all of them hungry—"

"To win? Every single one of them. But he helped me make the leap."

The warning signal sounded at the Blues' first meet, and Greta edged up to the front of the line. She looked left. She looked right. Then she froze. She knew that face. There, ten feet away, stood Latoya. When the horned sounded and the runners shot forward, it took the first two kilometers to clear her head. By the third, she'd found her zone and followed the fastest runners behind a hundred meters. By the fifth, she'd narrowed the gap and was on her competitor's tail. As the finish line approached, she put on a burst for the final two hundred meters, but her rival did the same and won. After she'd circled back to the finish line, hands on her knees to steady her breath, she felt a tap on the shoulder.

"Never had to run that fast to catch you."

She looked up at black shorts and a white T-shirt. She looked higher. Latoya still had the gap between her front teeth. She was beautiful.

"Oh my God, how are you?" Latoya said as she pulled Greta into an embrace.

"Good." She stepped back and pulled off her bib, and pointed to Latoya's. Orillia Secondary School. "Still there, huh?"

Latoya wiped a line of sweat from her forehead. "Yeah. My mom had an affair with some guy so my parents split."

An awkward silence descended; Greta didn't know what to tell her. She shifted her left foot to her right. Latoya's parents weren't the only ones who'd split—but at least she knew what happened.

"And," Latoya rolled her eyes, "now he's my step-dad. But I'm guessing it won't be for long." She leaned in. "My mom has a bit of a wandering heart." She laughed.

Greta took her comment in. There was so much she wanted to say but she couldn't form the words.

Latoya looked over her shoulder toward the bus. "I've gotta bounce. DM me. On Snapchat or Instagram or something."

"Sure."

"Or text. Here's my number." Latoya reeled off the details. She then placed her hands firmly on Greta's shoulders. "So stoked we reconnected again."

Greta laughed. "You're stuck with me now. You won't get away."

Latoya's face lit up and she smiled a mile-wide smile. "We've kinda been stuck together since the water table in Kindergarten." She gave her one last hug. "I missed ya."

Three months passed and the Blues made it to the spring championships. In the marshaling area, Greta found the roster; her adrenaline pumping, her stomach a bundled knot of nerves. Her eyes followed her finger to the bottom of the page, and then more slowly back up to the top. Her heart sank. No Orillia Nighthawks. No Latoya McCeighan.

At the starting line, with runners on either side, Greta's stomach tightened. One made eye contact, mouthing words. Another flipped her the finger. Smack talk. She ignored it and focused. The course coordinator shouted across the field and the girls shuffled forward. When the horn sounded, the fastest leapt out in front to set the pace. The first part of the course was the easiest; two kilometers over flat, smooth ground, and Greta hit her stride near the front of the pack. Spectators stood along each side, their mouths open, their arms up in the air, but in her head, they were silent. At one point, a thin woman with long auburn hair looked straight at her, but when Greta blinked, she was gone.

In the middle of the course, the runners faced rolling hills full of ragged pits and mud. Jostling for space, they bumped into one another and pushed each other out of the way. Greta's foot caught in a hole, turning her ankle. She yelped. The runners beside her glanced her way. Smiling? Sneering? Smirking? Their reaction didn't faze her. Instead, their looks spurred her on. She wanted to win and she wanted the other runners to feel pain like she did.

The pace picked up through the last stretch. She lagged behind the fastest runner by ten feet. The pain in her ankle flared, but she worked through it, swinging her arms loosely. Then, when the time was right, she exploded forward with a renewed burst of speed, pumping her legs hard. The closer she got to her opponent, the more certain she was she could take her. During the last kilometer, she cleared her mind. Three minutes later, she had passed the finish line, winning the junior varsity championships.

That night, after the dinner shift slowed, Greta lay on her bed. Her phone lit up. Texts. Instagram. Snapchat.

She couldn't scroll through fast enough to read the messages pouring in.

G., you're amazing.

Kudos, G..

Someone had posted a video of her crossing the finish line on YouTube. Underneath they'd added a caption: *Blues Rock.* She smiled, wishing her mom could have been there.

Her phone pinged again at midnight. Half-asleep, she glanced over at the screen. She sat up.

Latoya: *Hey!*

She picked up her phone.

Greta: *Hey!*

Latoya: *Saw u on YouTube! (Heart Heart)*

Her fingers flew across the screen. *I know, right! (Smiley face).* Then she changed it to *Really?* and pressed Send.

Latoya: *Ur smtg. U kicked ass 2day.*

Greta: *(Smiley face puking green puke)*

Latoya: *So what's up?*

Greta: *idk*

Latoya: *lmk*

Greta: *Where to start...*

Latoya: *First day of Grade Three.*

Greta texted back and forth with Latoya late into the night and, by early morning, she'd lost steam. Phone back in the charger, she turned out the light. With her arms around her pillow, she stretched down the length of the bed, smiling, her dreams giving way to her forever best friend and her mother.

***

"That sounds like it was a pretty impressive year for a rookie," Detective Perez said.

Greta sighed and looked down at her shoes.

"Uh-oh. What? Did you get an injury?"

"No. More like trouble in class. I said..."

"Something you shouldn't have? *Quelle surprise*."

She glared. She'd taken French. She thought back to the words that had slipped out of her mouth. What felt sweet at the time wasn't. Sour? Maybe more salty.

"It wasn't my best moment," she said.

"Did you apologize?"

Sweat beaded the top of her lip. "No. The problem was my marks sucked."

Detective Perez put her chin in her hand. "Which you need for varsity."

She'd been gobsmacked the day it had happened.

After Coach Dewson cut her from the team, she sat hunched over on the floor in her bedroom. Her reflection shone back from the window a couple of feet above the head of her bed. She looked around her room; stale and white and barren. The medal she'd won hanging over the side of the mirror was the only decoration. It was a reminder of her greatest victory—the result of persistence and effort. That all-too-familiar pain built up in the middle of her chest as she picked up her phone.

Greta: *Hey... Got the axe today.*

Latoya: *ur the star of the team*

Greta: *not anymore*

Latoya: *OMG what r u gonna do?*
Greta: *tbh dunno but screw school*
Latoya: *?*
Greta: *Im done w it*
Latoya: *?*
Greta:
Latoya: *lmk. Here for u. Ily*

"I'm not sure why but I guess those rules are in place for a reason," Detective Perez said.

Greta swiped her cheeks with the back of her hand. "It was the one thing that cleared my mind, that kept me calm, that made me feel part of things, a part of something. *Poof.* Taken away. Gone in an instant."

Detective Perez reached into a drawer and passed over a box of tissues. "How'd you fill your free time? School? Pick up more shifts at work?"

"My past." She blew her nose.

"Pardon?"

"There was only person who could tell me about it."

The detective sighed. "Ahh. Right. This elusive Colleen."

TWENTY-SIX

Greta googled directions for the Bracebridge Women's Shelter, grabbed her jacket, and headed downtown. After a brisk twenty-minute walk in the fresh air, with her hands shoved in her pockets and jacket collar turned up against the springtime chill, she found the building. With knots in her stomach, she swung open the red front door.

Beyond the reception desk, a dim-lit hallway gave way to a series of closed offices down to the end. Up front, a large man with tattoos across his forearms sat at the desk. Dressed in a T-shirt, he had shaggy hair and thick sideburns. He needed a haircut. On the phone as she approached him, she noticed he had a very large forehead that bobbed up and down, his bushy mustache twisting as he talked. He directed her to a seat in the waiting area, offering only a few chairs and a low coffee table with magazines. She perched on the end of a seat and waited.

"Can I help you?" he asked after hanging up.

She put the magazine down on the cluttered table beside her and stepped forward. She examined the glass between them and lowered her face to speak through the hole in the partition. "I'm looking for Colleen," she said.

"Colleen who?"

"Colleen Jones."

"I'm new. Hang on. Let me check the list."

It was *deja vu*. The same exchange as before. Except the last time, it was a woman's voice, and his was soft and low. His eyes darted up and down a piece of paper. "There's no Colleen Jones on here."

She rolled her eyes.

"Hang on, let me check with the others."

She sat back down in the chair she'd first perched on when she'd arrived. At least he hadn't called her *honey*. He picked up the phone. She straightened, straining to hear, but the glass between them garbled his voice. When he hung up, he leaned over the countertop and looked through the glass.

"I spoke to our supervisor. There used to be a Colleen here, but she left six months ago."

A wave of fear washed over her. She hauled herself up from the chair. "That's not possible," she stammered. "I spoke to her."

"Really? When was that?"

Her mind raced. It had been about a year ago. Or was it over a year? She thought back but she couldn't remember. The room spun and she grabbed the counter. She was going to be ill.

"You look like a ghost. Let me get you a glass of water."

The receptionist buzzed his way out of the office. She sat down, shaking, and pushed the glass of water he brought away.

"I need to talk to her. It's important."

The man raised his hands in the air. "I don't know her. Never met her."

"Can you find someone who did?" she said. "Where'd she go?"

"I don't know. And if I did, I couldn't tell you anyway. It's against our privacy policy."

Her face turned red, and angry blotches rose up on her cheeks. Colleen was the only link she had to her mother. She did her best to smooth her voice. "Can I speak to anyone who worked with her? Or someone who worked with my mom?"

The man looked puzzled. "Your mother worked here?"

She nodded. "Yes. About fifteen years ago. With Colleen. That's why I need to speak to her."

The receptionist smiled. "Let me call the supervisor back. She was here. Maybe she can sort this out."

He buzzed himself back into the front office area and picked up the phone. A tall woman with a bright teal crew cut and hoop earrings appeared from a back room, and peered out through the glass. Relieved she had a file in her hand, a laptop in the other, Greta gave her a little wave.

The woman nodded and pointed to a door at her left. "Come on in. I'm sure I can help."

Greta stood, crossed the room and followed the woman down the dim-lit corridor into a small room that smelled like old cheese. As the outside door to the reception area slammed shut behind her, she jumped.

"Sorry about that," the woman said, after they sat down at the table. "I've worked here so long I forget they can be intimidating."

"Why's it so locked up?"

The woman jabbed a thumb over her shoulder. "Our clients live in the residence at the back of the building.

They've had the courage to get themselves out of some pretty difficult situations."

"So you lock them in?" It sounded like an accusation.

The lady shook her head. "No. We keep them safe from anything they might be fearful of. If their partners come looking for them, they can't get in."

A lump formed in Greta's throat. She tried hard to blur the memories that came rushing back. "I guess that's good. Considering what they might've been through."

"So, I understand you're looking for Colleen?"

She nodded. As her story tumbled out, the woman sat and listened, tapping, taking notes on her laptop.

"What was your mother's name?"

"Emily. Emily Giffen."

The woman scanned a database angled in a way Greta couldn't see it. She stopped, peered into the screen, and then typed in another password. A two-finger hunter, Greta held her breath, waiting. Adrenaline pumped through her veins. The woman pushed her thick-framed glasses up onto the top of her head.

"I'm not sure what to say. I don't remember your mother, even though I was here, too. To complicate things, I can't find her name in our system."

She felt like she'd been kicked in the stomach. How could that be? How could the computer not show any of her mother's details? Details she knew were true and had to be there. It took every ounce of her energy not to jump over the table and check the laptop herself. Her lips trembled. "Please. I know she was here. Colleen confirmed it about a year ago."

The lady sighed and went back to the database. "There's no record."

"There has to be. Colleen told me she worked with her." She took out her phone and held it up in the air. The woman slipped her reading glasses back down her head and studied the screen. Her expression changed.

"Do you remember her?"

"I might." She pulled the laptop closer, her fingers tapping the keys.

"Is she in there?"

"Hang on. I need to pick something up from the printer."

The woman stepped out of the room and, when she returned, she handed her a photo. Greta stared at the image—an image of her mother. A wide-open grin, she was a younger, her hair longer, her clothes artsy; she looked almost retro.

Greta laughed. "I thought I was going crazy."

The woman sat down. "You're sure this is her?"

She snorted. "I know my own mother."

The woman's face became brittle.

"What?" she said.

Knees nearly touching in the space between them, the woman pulled hers back. As she did, Greta could tell she was arranging words in her head. Her heart sank. If her mother had been there but hadn't worked there, there was only one other possible answer. She narrowed her eyes. It couldn't be.

"Your mother was here with Colleen and I," the woman said.

"I know. I told you," she said pointedly.

"Her name was Emily Strachan."

Her mom's maiden name: Emily Strachan. She filed away the new information. "What's the *but* I can hear there?"

"She didn't work with us." The woman paused. "Your mother was a client."

Greta shook her head. She didn't believe it. She scrambled to recall her phone call with Colleen, replaying each word of the conversation in her head. It'd been a year, but she was certain she never mentioned a thing. Had Colleen lied? Underestimated her? Had she misunderstood? She thought back to the day she stood alone in the kitchen the afternoon her mother died and mentally reconstructed the murder. At that point, she'd had no sense of the extent of her mom's full story. No idea how far back the violence went. All she knew was that her mother was dead.

She sat across from the woman and started counting. *One, two, three.* But she could feel her anxiety creeping, and counting wasn't working. *Four, five, six.* She could not and did not want to lose control. *Seven, eight, nine.*

"Where's Colleen now?" she asked.

"Gone," the woman said. "She got another job. Somewhere down in Toronto."

Greta exploded. She screamed, reached across the table, ripped the laptop from the woman's hand, and threw it against the wall. It shattered; black pieces flew across the floor. Then she stood, picked up the chair over her head, and slammed in down hard on the carpet. "I'll never find her now."

The woman sat, visibly upset. "I'm so sorry about all this, Greta. I'm sorry you had to find out this way. Your mother was a strong and brave woman. She got away from her abuser. As for Colleen, she left the shelter about six months ago."

Greta punched the wall with her fist. "Emily Strachan didn't get away from her abuser. She married him."

"I'd like to hear more about this," Detective Perez said. "I find it odd it hadn't dawned on you your mother was a client."

"From the woman's tone, I knew something was up. But I—"

"Frankly, it was obvious."

"To *you*. You're old. I was fifteen. Up until then, how would I know? I hadn't put it together. My mom only dropped hints about her life. Bits and pieces."

"But, Greta, you said yourself your father beat your mother and terrorized you. You said your father killed your mother one morning when you were at school. How could you not think your mother went to a women's shelter to get help?"

"You trying to pin this on me, too? I could ask the same thing. How could the woman who worked with her not know she was murdered?"

"What did she say when you told her?"

"Nothing. She stood there."

"Shocked?"

"Who knows. I left."

"And then what?"

"I went home. Numb. Pissed off. I'd had it."

"Because of Colleen?"

She looked at Detective Perez. "No. Because of my mother. My whole life was built on secrets. Lies. I didn't know who I was. I didn't know if anything my mom had ever told me was true. What kind of woman seeks shelter from her abuser and then marries him *and* adopts a kid to raise?"

Detective Perez raised her hands in the air. "More to the point, what kind of adoption agency places in a kid in a violent home?"

Greta looked at her strangely. "Ian was a deacon and a very good liar. Apparently, my mom was, too. The initials carved into the bottom said DS. She'd even lied about that."

"She hadn't bought it"—she flipped back through her notebook—"in Bracebridge?"

"At a stupid antique fair? No. It was hers. The *S* stood for Strachan. Her maiden name. I didn't know what the D stood for. Maybe Emily wasn't even her real name. All I knew was that she'd lied to me and left me alone with Ian."

She'd curled up on her bed that afternoon and sobbed. In less than a heartbeat, the woman who'd made up half of her whole had not been who she'd thought she was. Crumpled in the sheets, she hadn't noticed the shadow that swept cross the doorway. When she finally did, she'd jumped, scattering the contents of the dime box across the bedroom floor.

Mrs. Xiangzi stared down at her. "Don't remember giving you Saturday night off, G."

She shook her head, the lump in her throat as hard as a pebble.

"Do you need an invitation? We're packed downstairs."

"Sorry. I lost track of the time. Give me five."

When she didn't move, Mrs. X frowned. "Five seconds or fired."

Greta pushed herself up and waited for the head rush to pass. She couldn't wake up; her mind was in the throes of a nightmare.

For the next week, Greta worked and slept with a churning stomach. She was rudderless. Though she missed her mother every day, she no longer felt sure who the woman she so desperately missed actually was. She gave up. No icy chill of panic overcame her. She shut her eyes and traced the knotty scars on her wrists. It was a simple and sweet surrender.

TWENTY-SEVEN

Detective Perez's eyes darted in the direction of the door as the same narrow faced woman who turned up earlier that morning peered around the corner. As the woman stepped forward, a file in her hand, she glanced at Greta quickly before passing it over.

"Sorry to disturb you, Detective, but we have a problem."

All Greta could hear of their scattered conversation was urgent and hushed, clipped tones.

Her mouth a hard line, the detective leafed through the pages and then stopped, running her finger down one of the notes crammed inside. For a full five seconds, the room fell silent. "That's quite the story, Greta," she said.

Eyes straightforward, Greta wiped her palms on her sweatshirt. "It was a long couple of years."

Detective Perez made her way back across the room and smacked a hand down on the desk. From the other, she dangled a yellow note from the file, finger and thumb pinching the corner. "You lied to me."

"No, I didn't."

"You said when saw your father Saturday night, you didn't touch anything."

"That's right."

"And you're lying now." She waved the yellow note in the air. "I've got your fingerprints."

Heat prickled along her hairline as she stared at the inky smudges at the bottom of the page. "I said I was in the room. I told you I might have held the bedrail."

"Or touching your father's respirator?"

Her head spun. She couldn't breathe. She knew exactly what she was talking about. Shit. The bloody green button.

Detective Perez leaned forward. "This doesn't look good. Anything else you've lied about?"

Greta swallowed. She had no idea what had possessed her to touch it. But how had they found out? She searched around the room. Her eyes fell on the blue box beside the door. It was empty. They'd lifted her prints from the bottle.

"Okay, okay. I did."

"Would you like to explain it?"

"I don't know. I can't. But I didn't kill him."

"I'm going to need more than that."

From the corner of her eye, there was a rustle of movement. Officer Sanchez and Officer Hatten stepped into the office, blocking the doorway. Her heart leapt into her throat, and she braced her feet against the chair.

"You're lucky I'm not arresting you right now," Detective Perez said. A muscle jumped in her jaw as she tacked the note to the bottom of her screen. She turned her attention to the officers. "In fact, I will." She looked back at her. "Maybe it'll help you remember."

She leapt from the chair. "Are you fucking serious?"

Officer Hatten's mouth tightened. He took a step toward her. "Nice language."

She spun around and, when she did, her arms flew in the air. Then a thud and someone grunted. Officer Hatten pulled his hands from his face. Red trickled down from his nose. His partner lunged forward and clapped a hand to her shoulder, slamming her down in the chair.

"I'm arresting you for assaulting a police officer, too," Detective Perez said.

"It was an accident."

"It's my duty to inform you—"

She screamed. "No one's listening."

"You have the right to retain and instruct counsel without delay. You have the right to telephone any lawyer you wish."

"Like I can pay for that."

"You also have the right to free advice from a legal aid lawyer." Detective Perez rattled off a phone number. "Do you understand? Do you wish to call a lawyer now?"

Officer Sanchez bent down and spoke slowly, her breath warm on her neck. "You are not obliged to say anything unless you wish to do so, but whatever you say may be given in evidence. Do you understand? Do you wish to say anything in answer to the charge?"

Jerked off the chair, arms wrenched behind her, a loud snapping sound rang out, and she felt the bite of cool metal against her wrists. She turned to Detective Perez. "This is total bullshit," she yelled.

Her face red and tight with anger, Detective Perez's voice rose in disbelief. "Assaulting an officer should be the least of your worries right now."

Officer Sanchez patted her down, pushed her toward the door, fingers digging deep into the flesh of her forearm with every step. As she staggered from the room, Detective Perez's voice faded behind her.

Greta was directed out the front doors three floors below, and a hand pushed down the top of her head as she stumbled into the back seat of the cruiser. Cheek on the ripped seat, she gagged from the smell. Sweat? Old coffee and cigarettes? Plexiglas spread in front of her, and a sign below read *NOTICE. This vehicle is fitted with recording equipment. Your words and actions are being recorded.* Beside it, someone had scratched the word *smile.* Before she could sit up, the door banged closed and the car sped through the downtown core.

Early spring, still light out, she watched the bustle on the streets from the window. Shoppers, bags overflowing. Men and women, stern-faced in suits, scurrying their way home. A drunken couple bickered beside a stop sign, dead leaves and empty liquor bottles scattered around them. Behind, a group of teens, fingers pressed hard to the glass outside the front of a restaurant, examined a greasy menu. She felt ill. A sharp pain vibrated through the side of her head as the cruiser jerked around the corner. She couldn't make heads or tails of the squawking and static coming from the police scanner. With her body hugged to the door, she closed her eyes and wished she were home.

Five minutes later, they were in a parking lot outside a two-storey station; red brick with glass front doors. Were they all built the same way? Save for the sign outside that read '52 Division', it reminded her of the day she and Mr. K. had visited Officer Pappas up in Ravensworth.

They veered to the left, and she followed the edge of building as the car bumped through the lane, wretched with potholes and rusty pop cans, and stopped at a small entrance located near the back. When the door of the car swung open, cold air slapped her in the face.

"Let's go," Officer Sanchez said.

Greta hopped out. Escorted through the opening, along a corridor and past a garbage can overflowing with empty coffee cups, Officer Sanchez held a hand at her back, her fingers tight to her spine. Doorways on either side led to offices, with a small sign duct-taped to one reading *Out of order.* She hoped there was another washroom somewhere in the building. At the end of the hall, they turned right, and she was steered toward a dark room. The door, swollen with age, its glass riddled with cracks, groaned as it opened.

Officer Sanchez flipped on the lights and shoved her elbow forward. "Don't say a word."

Greta collapsed into a metal chair. As Officer Sanchez spoke into the radio perched on the top of her shoulder, she stared at the freckling across her nose and forehead. How could this be the same woman she'd met at her apartment just twenty-four hours earlier?

"Suspect secured," she said, and then turned to her. "Wait here."

She didn't move. Was there any other choice?

"They're on the way to do a fingerprint and search."

"For what?" All she could picture were the movies she'd watched the summer after her mother was murdered.

Officer Sanchez smirked. "That's the point." She slammed the door and left.

Half an hour later, two officers shuffled into the room and removed her handcuffs. Skin tender and raw, she massaged the red marks on her wrists. They emptied a large blue tub and scattered a camera, a file of loose-leaf paper, a white container, and a box of plastic gloves across the table. Her stomach churned. One of the two twisted a head in the direction of the wall.

"Stand there, look forward," she said, hands planted on ample hips.

Greta gritted her teeth. After being photographed, fingerprinted and searched, her purse and phone taken away, two hours had somehow slipped by. She didn't care. Dressed by the time Officer Sanchez reappeared, she had the one thing she wanted: her dime, tucked deep into the front pocket of her jeans, undetected.

"You can make one call before we head downstairs," she said. She pulled a phone from her front pocket and passed it over.

"Thank you."

She squinted at the poster across the room stuck up on the wall with scotch tape between the cheap, framed photos of dogs and yellow bins for safe syringe disposal. Though she promised to connect with Latoya by the end of the day, she punched in a different number. After two rings, a man's voice answered.

"Legal Aid, Phil Robinson, Duty Counsel."

Her eyes watered. "I need help."

She explained who she was, where she was, and the situation she was in. "Bottom line," she said, when she finished her recap, "it was all an accident. I did nothing and no one's listening." Over the course of the next few minutes, her shoulders dropped and her stomach relaxed a little as she answered his questions. "Why?" she asked, near the end of the call. She sat straight up. "The whole interview?" She paused. "Why would I stay silent?" She paused again. "I don't care if it's my right." She clenched the phone to her cheek. "If I did that," she shouted into it, "how can I tell my side of the story?" She listened again and scowled. "Fine. I'll see you tomorrow." Red-faced, she hung up.

"Let's go," Officer Sanchez rapped the doorframe with her knuckles and turned away.

Greta followed her out of the room. She grasped the railing to keep from stumbling as she followed Officer Sanchez in front of her down the concrete stairs. At the bottom, in a small glassed-in office, multiple screens showed every cell, each one a constant stream of activity. She pinched her eyes shut as the heavy bolt clunked and a gray door swung open.

Calm down.

She opened her eyes and inched inside. The corridor was thin, the light dim, and on either side sat what looked like a mile of metal bars. White hands, black hands, yellow hands, young and old and hairy rested outside. Laughter and an occasional shout drifted through the cells. Panic rose in her throat when the door clanged shut behind her.

Breathe, breathe.

With her eyes locked straight ahead, she moved forward, soles squeaking on the tiles, so tired she could barely walk in a straight line. Officer Sanchez stopped halfway down, swiped a card to the wall and a door slid open. She reached out to steady herself and stepped inside.

The cement of the wall was cold on her hand and the floor sticky underfoot. The room was small—scarcely big enough to contain the single bed. A stainless steel toilet was bolted to the wall with no windows. From where she sat on the bed's metal frame, she could see the other cells. She rubbed her eyes. Recently painted, the fumes burned her nose and the place reeked of sweat. How many unwashed bodies had sat where she was sitting?

"Girlie," a voice called out, interrupting her. "Yeah, you in the cage."

She looked over into the drunken eyes of a woman standing across the way. She eased herself off the bed, took three steps, and pressed her forehead to the bars.

"Whatcha in for?" the thin woman asked through a spit lip. She stretched out her arms.

Greta held hers stiff at her sides. "It's all a mistake."

The woman cackled. "Fish." She batted a hand in the air. "It's what y'all say."

Greta opened her mouth and shut it again.

"Who'd ya got in the box?" Like a dirty rag, the woman's sour breath wafted across the space.

She stared at her for a moment.

The drunk woman clarified. "The cops? Tomorrow?"

"Detective Sergeant..."

"Perez? That old geezer's still around? Lady, you're screwed."

Tightness wrapped across her back and around her chest. "Why do you say that?"

"Don't blame no one for not listenin', but I been around the block. A few times, you know? That one? She's all changed." She muttered something under her breath.

Greta shifted her weight against the bars. "How do you mean?"

"Not like when she was undercover. Playing hard and fast with the rules. Did what she wanted, they told me."

Greta thought back to the conversation they'd had earlier in her office about regrets in life. Was there something more to what she'd told her? "What do you mean?"

"Ugly things. Made shit up? Used the product? Got cozy with the boss? Now that's all gossip, ya hear, but gossip's always got a grain a truth. Whatever it was don't matter now. Heard she lost her job. Her husband. Her family."

"She has a job. She's been grilling me all day."

"A different one. She's chi-chi now. Pushing paper. Has to dot her i's and cross her t's, ya know. But it don't mean nothing. She's still all balls and ambition." She turned away, muttering, her words almost indistinguishable. "Hope for a bullet, but you'll get all day. Good luck to ya."

The drunk woman withdrew to the back of her cell, and Greta did the same. She sat down on the bed and drew her knees to her chest. She found the pillow at one end of the metal frame and pulled the thin blanket up over her head. It scratched at her face and she couldn't breathe. The knot in her chest, every noise coming from outside the bars, every story the prisoners tossed out, set her heart racing. Longing for home, she wanted to scream, but instead she choked back any sounds. Soaked in sweat, she shivered, her teeth chattering. She searched for a prayer, but couldn't remember the words, so instead she turned her face into the pillow and sobbed.

TWENTY-EIGHT

Greta shifted out of the metal bed. It was just after 6:00 AM. Eyes unfocused, her back ached, her head pounded, memories of the last time she woke up in a strange place.

A shadow fell over her cell. "Breakfast." An officer opened the door and passed her a discoloured tray. "Probably not what you're used to."

She took it from his hands and stared at the clump of lumpy oatmeal smeared into a paper cup. Like most people she met, the officer had no idea of the irony of what he'd said. She poked at the raisins on top. Black and shriveled, they reminded her of the meals she'd been forced to make when Ian passed out at the cabin or forgot to buy groceries. After her mother died, the soups she'd made from the berries and plants scavenged in the bush behind the cabin were the best, and though she'd never told him, Mr. K. would've been impressed with how she'd mixed in bugs to add protein to the broth.

She picked up the plastic spoon on the edge of the tray and gulped down the lukewarm mess, followed by a waxy apple and a carton of milk, and then, back to the wall, she sat on her bed and waited. At seven-thirty, the officer reappeared at the bars.

"Your legal's here." He unlocked the door. "Better get moving."

She flattened the wrinkles from her clothes, stepped out of the cell, and followed him upstairs. When he opened the door to a room halfway down the hall, a tall man with ebony skin sat reading at a table.

"Greta," he said as she walked in, "I'm Phil Robinson."

Sinewy and lean, a wide, full mouth, he stood and gestured to a chair. Dark jeans belted around his hips, she knew instantly he was a runner. He sat back down and passed her a white paper bag. "Bet you're hungry."

She opened it and sucked in the smell. An egg and peameal bacon sandwich... She unwrapped the waxed paper as quickly as she could and stuffed it in her mouth. Sweet smoke and salt danced across her tongue. She'd never tasted a sandwich so damn good. She'd never been more grateful.

For the next hour, Phil led them through a thick file and they discussed her case. He answered her questions, she answered his, and when the knock at the door came to let them know Detective Perez had arrived, for the first time in two days, Greta felt more hopeful. Phil pushed his chair back, collected the papers, and put them in the folder.

"Time to go." He jerked his head in the direction of the door. "We're in Number Two."

The box.

Greta stood, shoulders tense, her stomach now unsettled. She took a deep breath, pushed her hair from her forehead, and followed him down the hallway. Before she stepped into Number Two, she felt him set his hand gently on her shoulder.

Her eyes skirted the room. A scratched, rectangular table, a mirrored window, a camera high on the wall. She pulled out a plastic chair that looked like it was from high school. The room was stuffy and there was no air, yet it had a sharp smell. Rotten fruit? The urinal pucks in the park bathrooms from her running days? Antiseptic at the dentist's office? Three glasses and a pitcher of sweaty water had been placed in the centre of the table.

A tap on the door came. Face solemn, Detective Perez strode into the room. "Good morning."

"Astra." Phil pushed back his chair back and extended his hand across the table.

"We ready?" she asked.

He nodded.

"Greta?"

She kept her mouth shut but nodded too.

Detective Perez read out the date and time, stated the reason for the interview, and declared the people present in the room. "Now, let's get started. I've read this over twice," she informed them, tapping a thick file of papers in front of her. "And let's just say: there are gaps."

Greta shifted uncomfortably. The detective wasn't the only one who'd read it. In preparation for the interview, she and Phil had reviewed it, too. They'd studied it, discussed and dissected every document. Besides her fingerprint, the doctor's report was the most problematic. While he confirmed her father was dying, it was his word choice that landed them all there. He'd used the term *close to death*.

Detective Perez opened the file and flicked through it. "You were with your father the evening he died?"

Despite the detective's inflection, Greta knew she wasn't asking a question. They'd been through it all the day before and this morning she'd seen the surveillance tape. The camera had caught her coming through the hospital's revolving front doors at 8:02 PM and then running out again an hour later.

"I needed answers," she said.

"About what?"

"You know. My mother. He killed her."

The detective peered over from across the top of red plastic reading glasses. She nodded slowly. "Right. When I spoke to Officer Pappas last night, he shared your thoughts with me."

Her face reddened. Thoughts? Was that how Officer Pappas described them? They weren't thoughts. Was that what the detective now believed?

"It's the truth," she said.

"Which is what we're here to get to the bottom of."

The truth was all she'd thought about the last nine years. Hopeful, she edged forward.

"So, did you see the autopsy report? Her broken bones? Old fractures?"

"I'm not here to get to the bottom of your mother's truth, Greta. I discussed that for quite some time last night with Officer Pappas."

"And?"

"There are spots in his notes that differ from your early recollections."

"Yeah? Like what?"

"For starters, the day your mother died. He found baking sheets in the sink and there were crumbs all over the floor."

Greta looked at her. Some days her memories surfaced, other days they didn't. There were times, trapped by walls of darkness, that they refused to surface at all; on those days, they simply vanished. "That means nothing. I probably didn't see them. Who wouldn't expect a mess from a fight?"

"His recollection of your conversation at the cabin after your mother's death and then again three years later with the child advocate are different."

"That's bullshit."

"Greta." Phil turned to face her.

She didn't look at him.

"And despite you insisting it wasn't, the investigation surrounding your mother's death was re-opened. These discrepancies are alarming Greta; however, that's not why we're here today."

"You said you wanted the truth."

"I do. But as I just explained, I'm here for your father's truth."

Greta barked a bitter laugh. Her father's death from cancer was still more suspicious than her mother getting brained on the kitchen table and her father conveniently forgetting to call for help? The unfairness of the whole situation made her want to weep.

Detective Perez reached into the file, shuffled through the documents, and held up a black and white photo. She pointed to the date stamp. "So you were with him—"

Three days ago. She stared at Ian's image; his every inch ravaged by cancer. On his back, hands gnarled into fists at his sides, his chest and face so pale they bled into the sheets. His neck extended, she could see the sinews tight in the straight. His open eyes stared up at the ceiling and his mouth gaped.

She swallowed her smile. "To confront him," she said firmly after she pulled her eyes away, "about my mom's murder."

Detective Perez looked at her coldly. "It's highly unusual a conversation ends up with someone dead."

She paused to consider what the detective said. She knew about the other documents in the file. The coroner's report. The nurse's affidavit. The recording of his 911 call. It still echoed through her head.

911, what's your emergency?

A man just died on my ward.

That can't be that unusual, sir.

Well, this one is. His estranged daughter was with him before he passed. They were alone, and then she just tore out of here, like a bat out of hell. No tears. A big smile on her face. It was crazy.

She grimaced. "Wouldn't you want to do the same? Get answers before he croaked?"

Detective Perez was silent with disapproval.

She glared at her. "He messed my whole life up."

When Phil laid his hand on her forearm, she jerked it away again. "You know I left Bracebridge three years ago to get away from him. I needed to know."

"Know what?" the detective asked.

"Everything. How he got away with it. How he could live with himself. After Grade Nine, I couldn't live with him anymore, either."

Detective Perez said nothing. She opened her notebook on the table.

"I couldn't take his abuse," Greta continued. "There was no nasty incident. No ugly drama. I just shut down."

"So, you ran away, is what you're saying?" the detective asked.

Greta shrunk. Escape was what she'd done. Avoided her own death was even more likely. She took a deep breath and tried to calm her nerves. "No, I dropped out of school. I read somewhere—I don't know where now—that Steve Jobs dropped out, too. I thought that, if he'd done it and still made it big, it wasn't impossible for me to make something of myself... You know, live a better life."

"In what area did you think you'd do that?" The detective asked with a sour look. "He dropped out of college, not high school. Did you talk through this decision with any adults before you made it?"

"Like who? My dad? The man who couldn't have cared less?"

"So that's a no then?"

She sighed. "It's not what I said. When Mr. and Mrs. Xiangzi found out, they didn't say anything."

"Really?"

"They didn't need to. I could see the disappointment in their eyes."

"Then you didn't talk to them before you decided?"

She blushed deep red. "After I decided was when I talked to them. Mrs. Xiangzi worked hard with me each night on my homework, so I knew she'd be mad and want to try to stop me."

It had been almost four years, and she still felt guilty about the grief she'd caused them. She looked down at the floor, ashamed. "I wasn't their child but they treated me like a daughter."

The detective nodded. "You're lucky you still have them in your life."

She made a mental note to call them as soon as they'd finished. She hoped it wouldn't be much longer. Not like yesterday. It wouldn't be. It couldn't be.

"I am. And they were clear. If I wasn't in school, I had to be in the restaurant. All day. Every day. On time."

Greta worked at New Haven for the next six months of the long, cold Ontario winter. While the days were flat and never seemed to brighten, the half-year passed quickly. They were a little family because, by that time, her father had all but disappeared. He only used the apartment as a place to crash between the women and the forty-ounce bottles that had taken over his life. Although there were days Greta wished it, she knew he wouldn't take off forever. He was never able to sell the cabin, so the nest egg he'd sunk into it was stuck there. The thing that weighed most heavily on her mind was all the times he had driven back to visit in the dead of night, navigating the dark windy country roads, with his good friend Jack Daniels open on his lap. Happy if he died in an accident, she didn't want him killing someone else.

The detective put her pencil on the table. "At fifteen? You worked full-time? Day and night?"

She bit her lip. "I gave up running."

"That's a shame."

"I couldn't do it anymore. Everything was too dark. Too heavy. I had so many questions about my mom. About her life, our life together. I didn't know who I was anymore."

"Do you know now?"

She shrugged. "Kind of, I guess."

The detective turned her clear green eyes on her. "Which is it? Either you do or you don't."

"Yes, I do. Mostly."

The detective leaned back in her chair and folded her arms across her chest. Her look didn't change.

When the spring weather arrived, the warmth lifted the thaw from the ground, but the ache in Greta's heart and stomach remained. Then, one Saturday afternoon while on Skype with Latoya, what in the past had seemed insurmountable became crystal clear. She googled a map of Ontario and calculated it was a little over a two-hour drive to Toronto. For fun—or out of boredom, she had no idea of which—they'd also figured out that, if someone were crazy enough to walk, it would take six or seven days. She wasn't an idiot.

Detective Perez took notes and, when her pencil stopped, she forged on.

"The woman with the answers lived here," she said.

"In Toronto?"

"Colleen."

Detective Perez looked up. "This Colleen Jones?"

She nodded. "So I packed up my things and left."

The detective's eyes widened. "By yourself at fifteen? Pretty bold."

"My birthday's in July and I left in May. So, technically, I was nearly sixteen."

Detective Perez's eyebrows rose unnaturally high, right into the top of her forehead. "It's still young to be— what did you say?—striking out on your own... Down to a city you'd never been to before."

"Back in the pioneer days, by the time women were fifteen they were married and had probably popped out a kid or two."

"Thank you, Greta. I'm aware of history. I'm grateful women have been empowered since then."

Greta frowned. Empowered? Odd choice of words. Had *all* women? *Some* maybe. Others, not so much. She wanted to dig into the conversation, but it wasn't the most suitable time to get into a debate.

She thought of her mother. She would have jumped at the chance. Maybe there was more of her mother in her than she realized.

TWENTY-NINE

May 2015. Greta stood in the Greyhound Station at the Riverside Inn in Bracebridge, alone and elated. Dressed in jeans, a T-shirt and a light jacket, she had everything she valued, everything she loved, folded up and stuffed into a backpack. As the bus pulled up beside her, she took one last look around before she stepped on-board. "You can do it," she'd whispered to herself. "You've got this." She scanned the aisles, found a window seat, and put her backpack beside her. The bus pulled out, and the rocks and twisted pines of Muskoka turned slowly to snow-capped fields around Barrie. She wasn't hungry, but she dug into her backpack anyway, wanting to make sure the lunch Mr. and Mrs. Xiangzi had packed for her was still there. She sniffed and wiped her eyes, turning her face to the window.

There were three fortune cookies nestled on the top of the bag. Greta took them out and unwrapped them one at a time. *You inspire others with your principles.* She squirmed; she hadn't inspired anyone by dropping out of school. She turned over the thin slip of white paper. *Vous inspirez la confiance rien qu'avec vos principes.* It sounded a lot better in French, but it still wasn't true. She cracked open the second. *Keep your ideas flexible, and don't ignore the details.*

"*Restez soupies,*" she pronounced out loud, laughing. She had no idea what it meant, but it sounded hilarious. "*Dans vos idees et ne negligez pas les details.*"

She stopped. Her mouth tightened, and she felt her pulse in the base of her throat. She hadn't spent a lot of time working out exactly what she was going to do when she reached Toronto. The last fortune cookie provided a jolt of inspiration. *You are about to receive a big compliment.* She smiled. That would be nice. She copied down the numbers on the back. 1 21 26 41 42 49. For Lotto Max Friday. Maybe luck would take care of the pesky details she'd neglected before she left. She'd need to find somebody to buy her one for her when she got off the bus; she wasn't old enough to buy one herself. But if she won, she decided, she'd give them a cut—a good one.

The bus slowed, Greta dozed, and when she woke, it was pulling into the terminal downtown. With the five hundred dollars she'd saved up from working at New Haven all rolled tightly and stashed in her backpack, she stepped off the bus and into a diesel cloud of idling coaches.

When the bus pulled away, for one long excruciating minute, Greta simply stood there. It was midafternoon on a bright, sunny day, but she had no idea where she was. She strolled down Bay Street to the bottom of the city. Facing a strong breeze off the harbor, she sat on a white bench beside Lake Ontario.

After sitting and watching the boats and windsurfers for a while, she walked back up Yonge Street, excited and terrified of the sights and sounds. There were horns blasting and music blaring through the open front doors of the stores. There were happy families and strange faces. Every restaurant was packed. She'd never seen so many people rushing everywhere and in every direction. She estimated there were probably more people on a hot Saturday afternoon in one square block of Toronto than in the whole of downtown Bracebridge on a summer weekend.

By early evening, the sun faded. Greta felt her stomach growl, and so she dropped into Taco Bell to quell her hunger. While she chewed slowly to make the burrito last longer, it struck her she had nowhere to go.

Night fell and the streetlights switched on. She searched around and found a small, parkette south of Yonge and College, full of people, littered with dirty fast food wrappers and empty Starbucks cups. Couples strolled by, hand-in-hand, and others gathered in small groups. Some people sat by themselves. She wondered whether they were there in an effort to be alone.

With her eyes growing heavy, Greta parked herself on a bench tucked into the back. When exhaustion took hold, she tried to fight it, but she'd run out of steam.

Suddenly, a garbled voice roused her. "Yo, lady."

She didn't understand who was speaking at first. It sounded like the voice was coming through a wind tunnel. *It's just a dream,* she told herself. Just a dream she'd forget when she woke up.

"Hey, miss," she heard the deep voice grumble.

Then something poked her. She shot up. Her head wheeled around. A strange man stood in front of her.

"Hi."

She looked at him and said nothing. Scruffy and unshaven, he had a series of colorful tattoos inked up the side of his neck. He wore a long beat-up black leather coat.

"New here?"

She pulled her backpack up as tightly as she could to her chest. As if that would save her.

The man stuck out his hand. "The name's Max."

She didn't take it; his fingers were filthy.

"This here's my hood," he told her, pointing around the square. "I take care of the newbies."

How did he know she had just arrived? Was it that obvious?

"Need anything?"

A strong whiff of alcohol pulsated off him like cheap cologne.

"Nope."

He jabbed a thumb towards a group of girls across the square. "Those're mine."

She craned her head in their direction. "They *belong* to you?"

"I give them a place to stay. Something to eat."

She stared at the girls at the edge of the parkette, their pinched faces pale as they shivered in the night air. They had red-lacquered nails and pretty dresses, but they all looked really skinny.

"No, thanks." She rolled off the bench and stood to her full height.

He looked her up and down. "Once you've been here a few days, you may change your mind."

Her nerves jangled; something didn't feel right. She smiled and tried to keep her voice from shaking. "See you around."

He didn't smile. Instead, he reached out to touch her face. She shrunk back. There was no chance of that. Then he stepped away, walked across the parkette, and disappeared into the shadows.

Greta exhaled. She hadn't realized she'd been holding her breath for most of the conversation. She shut her eyes to focus. *Slow, steady breaths.* Then a sudden thought struck her. She dug deep in her backpack to make sure everything was still there. Money? Check. Clothes? Check. Library card? Check. She felt down to the bottom for her dime box and ran her hand along the grooves carved into the wood. She rubbed all four sides, taking in every crack, the familiar feeling under her fingers calming her. She looked out into the darkness, feeling safer, but the parkette was pitch black and the quiet she'd craved earlier was now giving her the creeps. She squinted at her watch. It read 2:00 AM. With nowhere to go, her only option was another bench across the parkette; one that was out in the open, flooded by the light of a streetlamp. There was one no one had claimed. She looked around, stood, shouldered her bag, and ran over. She took it for her own and fell fast asleep.

Detective Perez's notebook slipped off her lap and fell onto the floor with a thud. "Lucky break."

Greta saw the detective's face had paled a little since they'd first sat down that morning. She understood why. It was only later she'd realized how narrowly she'd escaped being trafficked or pimped out.

"I took precautions. Slept in wide-open spaces. Kept my money tucked inside in my backpack. Kept to myself, too."

The detective stretched her arm down, felt around the floor, and put her notebook on the table. "How long were you out there?" she asked.

Greta ignored her grating voice. She looked at her reflection in the one-way mirror and sighed. "Longer than I'd hoped for."

After two weeks of sleeping rough, forced by hunger and tenants in the parkette who wanted to share her bench, she relinquished it. With her clothes wet and chilled to the bone, she walked to Queen Street, past St. Michael's Hospital, through Moss Park and Corktown, and over the bridge into Riverside. Further along, she reached Leslieville, a gritty pocket in the east, gentrifying in spots. She slept in a brown cardboard box in an alley behind a restaurant. It became her comfort, her prison, her home.

Over the summer, the heat reminded her of the cabin in Ravensworth. A sad, comfortable familiarity crept in. Everyone who passed her on the street fought the suffocating air in slow motion, their eyes fixed to the ground, their shoulders slumped. She was never alone, but she felt alone. She guessed it was a city thing.

The detective's face lost whatever colour it still had. "You panhandled?"

"Yeah." What did she think she did?

"Better than the alternative, I guess."

Slouched in her seat, she startled at the mention of what the detective was insinuating. She hadn't even considered it. "Queen and Carlaw was a jackpot," she said.

"Really."

Was she shocked? Or judging? Either way, she clearly did not agree with her definition.

"How much could you pull in?" the detective asked.

"Twenty—"

"Dollars?"

"Why are you whispering? That's more than enough for Tim's or Wendy's."

"You ate it every day?"

"On slow ones I made two or three, but I packed away loose change to cover those off."

The detective folded her arms across her chest. "Where did you learn to be so financially prudent?"

"Grade Nine Business didn't cover hunger as a motivation for saving." She stuck her hands under her thighs. "It might be a good addition to the course."

On one night, Greta woke to unfamiliar sounds that startled her. Scrabbling, chattering noises. A cantankerous family of well-fed raccoons were making their way down the edge of the alley, rummaging in and out of the trash bins in search of a midnight feast. After they'd gone, the moon, luminous in the sky, shone down into her damp cardboard castle and wouldn't let her sleep. She reached for her backpack. The one she'd bought before she'd left was built for people like her; people who needed to keep papers and documents safe from the changing seasons. She unzipped the mid-sized waterproof pouch. Birth certificate. Library card. A few toonies. A tarnished loonie. Two damp fivers with Sir Wilfrid Laurier on the front peaked up from the bottom of the pack. She dug past the stern, blue face of Canada's seventh Prime Minister, felt around inside, and pulled out her dime box.

She dug through it. At the bottom was her Kindergarten class photo, creased deeply in quarters. It was yellowish and had cracked with age. She unfolded it and smoothed it out on her lap with care, then stared at the little girl standing to the right of Latoya. Who was she? A small pale face looked directly into the camera. Not petulant, not confident either. A full head taller than any of her classmates, bony and sinewy, but not malnourished. Children sat on the bench in front of them, palms on their knees. While most clutched Beyblades, Hot Wheels, Transformers or Strawberry Shortcake dolls, her hands were tight-fisted at her sides.

Greta stroked the photograph. She was pretty; large blue eyes under unnaturally long lashes, like college girls around her pasted on for weekend parties in miniskirts and stilettos. A fringe of black bangs unevenly cut lay halfway down her forehead. Two hasty knit braids, tied with beige ribbons, hung either side of her face. There had to have been some thought put into those ribbons because they matched the colour of the pants and the shirt she was wearing. Greta peered more closely. Hers wasn't a big wide-open smile like the other kids on the bench beside her. It was less pronounced. Understated. Uncertain. Tears slipped down her cheeks and splashed onto the photo.

Weeks turned to months, and Greta's cardboard box grew wafer-thin, its dank, earthy smell overpowering. Cold to the bone and hungry, she sold her watch at the local pawnshop. When the first snowflakes fell, she was convinced it was time.

THIRTY

"Time for what?" Detective Perez said.

"To get off the streets."

The detective puffed out her cheeks to the size of balloons, and then blew warm air slowly straight out of her mouth. The whole thing looked kind of awkward; almost painful.

"I remember the exact day," Greta said.

"You went to…" the detective rummaged through the papers in the file.

"Penn House." She studied the detective's face. Her eyes looked tired, but even with her fully packed bags of exhaustion, she was visibly relieved.

"With the street worker?" the detective asked.

She nodded. "In her car. Not hers—the city's. I thought it was funny she was driving a white Ford Escape. You know those ones built for active lifestyles? But there she was, stuck in traffic, succumbing to road rage."

The detective said nothing.

Greta guessed cars weren't her thing. She smiled. "I can still feel that first blast of heat."

"You must have been nervous."

"At first, but when we walked in, a dark-haired intake worker winked at me. I remember walking two scenarios through in my mind."

The detective's pencil stopped.

"One: he was a friendly guy; two: he thought I was a catch."

Detective Perez looked up. Her mouth dropped.

"Hey, with my mismatched clothes caked in dirt and my greasy hair, why wouldn't he?"

Detective Perez laughed; not a chuckle—a full out laugh. "How did you keep your sense of humour?"

She shrugged. "After the mountain of paperwork, he explained the rules. No drugs. No alcohol."

The detective's smile vanished. "Reasonable."

She snorted. "I was the ninja of rules."

"Did you tell them that?"

She balked. "I'd known them for, like, five minutes."

The corners of the detective's mouth tipped downward. "Fair enough."

"They had no idea about *consequences dealt*. Besides, I was an athlete."

"You've never done drugs?"

"Haven't you been listening?" Greta's jaw clamped shut. Her outburst with Mr. K. in elementary school hadn't gone over well. He'd looked so hurt and she'd felt badly. She wasn't going to make that same mistake again. "Sorry. No," she said politely, "I don't and never did."

As the detective wrote in her notebook, Phil reached for the pitcher of water. Ice tinkled against the sides as he filled the three glasses and passed them around the table. She picked one up and took a sip. "Penn was great—an old rambling brick house. It was indoors with a full roof. It wasn't damp. And there were showers, which we were encouraged to use regularly. I think I sunk Lake Ontario two inches every time."

"No doubt a welcome change."

"The bathroom was stocked with miniature bottles filled with soaps and lotions and shampoos and creams.

The smell gave me flashbacks to when I played with my mom's make-up."

The detective smiled.

"And we didn't have to steal them. More just magically reappeared every day."

The detective avoided eye contact. "How long did you stay?"

"I was part of the residential program so I got my own bedroom. Penn's not like those adult shelters; you know, the ones with line-ups for a bed every day. Sometimes people get in. Sometimes they don't. It's like gambling. You take a chance."

The detective pursed her lips. Greta could tell she knew exactly what she meant, and she didn't look happy about it.

"I had three meals a day. Pasta. Meat. Vegetables. Washed and cut fruit. I'd forgotten how they tasted. They were nothing like the jello molds with the shredded carrots and canned crap the ladies made for us after church on Sundays."

The detective shook her head. "People still make those things?"

"Penn had free Wi-Fi, too. *Unlimited*, they told me. All the better, I'd thought. Connecting with the world again was great. Empowering, you know?"

"Did you jump right online?"

"No, I slept for two days." She thought back. A doze? A catnap? No, it'd been a full-out coma, the first deep sleep she'd had in months. And, better yet, not a single dream she could remember. It had been a full-on blackout.

"You probably needed it," the detective said.

Greta stared across the table. Detective Perez was wearing a trim, navy blue two-piece suit and a pink blouse with a soft, ruffled collar. A strand of pearls graced her neck. Could the detective imagine the bone-deep ache that came from the stress of living on the street? She guessed not. But from what she'd heard the night before in the cells, she must have had other stresses.

"I woke up once, probably for no more than ten minutes. I went to the washroom and made a phone call to the Xiangzis in the hall."

"Free long-distance too?" the detective asked.

Greta gave her a relaxed nod. "They were happy to hear from me."

Her next connection wasn't as easy.

Greta: *hey.*

Latoya: *do I know u?*

Greta:

Latoya: *u ghosting me or smthg?*

Greta: *not me*

Latoya: *it's been 6 months*

Greta: *ikr*

Latoya: *so what then?*

Greta: *sorry*

Latoya: *where've u been?*

Greta: *it's a long story*

Latoya: *listening*

After she'd filled in every last detail, she'd crawled back to bed. The stupor lasted another twenty-four hours. When she finally woke—not fully awake, only alert enough to be semi-conscious—she'd quickly discerned things were going to be different from what she'd expected. It was mandatory to attend the clients' residence council. She had to help prepare supper once a week. When she was told, she laughed. That was easy. She knew her way around a kitchen from working at Honey Bee with the Xiangzis. Then the bomb dropped.

"What's up?" she asked after she sat down in the office.

The man from the front desk the day she'd arrived sat across from her. "It's time to consider your future," he said.

Greta scoffed. 'What future?" She'd been on the streets for six months. She hadn't had the chance to think beyond the next day.

"A short-term plan?"

She crossed her arms and looked at the ceiling. "Sleep?"

He laughed.

"And watch TV." Except that wasn't true. She'd been doing that the past few days and was already bored out of her mind. Either TV was getting stupider or she was growing up.

"Rules are rules for a reason," he said.

Her stomach dropped.

"So what'll it be?" He waited. "What about school? It's right on site."

"Can I wear pajamas?" She reached over and got an apple from the bowl on his desk and took a big bite.

"Yep. But you can't be late." He paused. "And you'll get counseling."

"For what?" she said, her mouth full.

"For whatever drove you to the streets in the first place. And to allow you to support yourself."

Mr. K. nightmares filled her head. "Been there and done that," she denounced. She put the apple down and started counting. *One, two, three.*

"This is different," he told her. "Trust us."

Trust? Was he kidding? Except for Latoya and the Xiangzis, who'd had her back from day one? She didn't trust anybody. All the adults in her life had let her down. Her mother, her father, Colleen, Mr. Parthi, Officer Pappas. Even Coach Dewson. There was no trust, and the last thing she wanted was to sit down and talk about her feelings.

She tried to stay calm. *Four, five, six.* Cheeks burning, she rallied, and then lost it.

"I don't need it. I'm the only one who has ever got me. I've been abandoned too many times to *want* support from you."

She stormed up to her room and locked herself in, tears flowing freely—and she let them. After a good half-hour, she wiped her face with the back of her hand and checked the hall, relieved the staff hadn't tried to find her. Good. See? Pissing people off works. The conversation was over.

Detective Perez stood, waggling her cup. She pressed the button on the recorder and reached for the empty pitcher on the table. "Give me a sec," she said.

After she stepped out of the room, Phil leaned over and said, "You're doing fine. Keep the heat in check."

When the detective returned, she slid the pitcher of water across the table and pressed the button on the recorder. "Let's pick up from where we left off." She looked down at her notes to refresh her memory. "If I recall, you weren't happy about the counseling."

Greta's shoulders sagged. She got an odd sensation. The detective was right—and the Penn staff too—but she hadn't been ready to acknowledge it.

"Can we fast forward through that?" she said.

Detective Perez shook her head. "It's important I hear what you have to say."

The lump that had been stuck in her throat since she'd arrived that morning grew bigger. How could she explain what happened? How could the detective understand? She felt guilty. Uneasy was a better word. She twisted in her chair. "That whole counseling thing got delayed." Then she remembered what Phil had said. She looked up and smiled. "I found Colleen."

The look on Detective's face said she didn't believe her.

She'd started by googling Colleen Jones, Toronto. Hundreds of names came up in the search. She refined it. Colleen Jones Toronto Counselor. The results narrowed to less than a hundred. Still not helpful. Next she tried Twitter. If Colleen tweeted, she was doing it anonymously. She hated when people did that. Creepers and trolls without the courage to post their name had zero credibility. There was only one word for them. Blocked. She logged onto Instagram. No luck there either.

The last place she looked was Facebook. It wasn't a platform she used. It was more a space for an older crowd. Not the elderly, like at church, but middle-aged types, like her mother and housewives and aunties. But, Greta had reasoned, as Colleen was older, maybe she used that instead.

Bingo. Persistence paid off, like Mrs. Xiangzi said it would. Colleen's picture came up on the feed. Greta double-checked her profile to see if she'd mentioned anything about living in Bracebridge. She scrolled through the pictures. The waterfall. The main street. Greta posted a message and waited.

Detective Perez held up her hand and cleared her throat. "Hang on. How did you find this Colleen Jones?"

"On social."

"There are over three million people in this city."

Greta looked at her. Do not laugh.

"My grandchildren have been trying to get me on Instagram and Snapchat for years now."

"Did you set it up?"

"I tried. Wasn't for me."

She had no idea what to tell her. If she didn't take the plunge, she'd miss whole chapters of her grandchildren's lives. Social was how they communicated, how they kept in touch. She smiled, trying to encourage her. When Detective Perez scratched something on the page, circling it twice and jotted in the margin, for the first time in two days she wasn't worried about her notebook.

***

Greta worked hard to fill the empty hours waiting for Colleen to message back. At first, she was wired, bouncing off the walls in her room. She checked her phone obsessively and wolfed down every snack laid out in the house. Unwilling to go anywhere, she was restless. Then she needed to get out. She slipped on her sneakers to go for a run, but the air felt so cold in her lungs she was winded after only a few steps. Deflated, it appeared her running days were over and walking was now more her speed. When she returned to her room, she found a message from Colleen in her feed.

Greta: *hey*

Latoya: *get it?*

Greta: *yep*

Latoya: *and?*

Greta: *meeting her tmrrw*

Latoya: *that's gr8*

Greta: *smiley face*

Latoya: *u good?*

Greta: *been waiting my whole life*

Latoya: *questions?*

Greta: *they're ready*

Latoya: *you go girl. good luck*

THIRTY-ONE

Greta felt her blood pulsate in her temples. She was waiting in the coffee shop at a table by the window, eyes glued to the front door. If she hadn't been sitting somewhere so public, she'd have taken the brown paper bag holding the cookie she'd bought and hyperventilated into it, right then and there. Her stomach muscles loosened a little when Colleen brushed through the front door. She sized her up: trench coat, inky jeans, boxy purse slung over a shoulder. Her sand-brown hair was shorter than she had remembered, but her fashion sense hadn't waned. She moved lightly on her feet, and Greta could feel her positive energy. She reached up a hand and waved her over.

"Sorry," Colleen said, giving her a short hug, "the subway was a mess."

"No problem, just got here myself," she said. A lie. She'd been sitting there patiently for over an hour. At one point, Greta had wondered if she was even going to show.

Colleen grabbed a latte from the barista, dropped her purse on the table, and sat down. "What are you doing in Toronto?"

"Long story."

"You're not here with your dad, right?"

"No, he's still in Bracebridge."

Colleen smiled. "Then school or something?"

Greta smiled back. Perfect. The question meant she didn't have to lie again, but she didn't have to tell the whole truth either. Her mood lifted.

"Taking courses. Just finished Grade Ten." 'Cause that was the truth.

"Your mom would've been excited to hear all about high school."

The knot in her stomach grew. "That's why I'm here, Colleen. I'm hoping you can answer some questions. There's stuff about my mom I'd really like to know."

"Like what she was like when she was your age?"

She hadn't thought about that. "Okay. Let's start there."

"Your mom told me Grade 10 was her favourite year, too, except for French and Phys Ed. She had some big argument with her parents and they made her take those."

Her heart skipped a beat. She didn't hear anything Colleen said, save for the fact her mother fought with her parents—which surely meant she had grandparents. Somewhere out there... But where?

"Why was it her favourite year?"

Colleen laughed. "Did she ever tell you about History?"

She snorted. She'd spent most of her childhood trying to stop her mother from playing Trivial Pursuit with her mind—to no avail. If she were still with her now, she'd play it with her day and night, for as long as she wanted.

Colleen took a sip of her latte. "She liked English, too. She told me about this huge project she did on World War Two and all the stuff they read. It was the year of her big dreams."

Greta thought back to the conversation they'd had on the back patio at the cabin the summer she'd turned eight. She'd told her she was her big dream. Everything she'd wanted, she'd said. Was her mother already thinking about her then?

"Which were what?" she asked.

Colleen laid her hands in her lap. "First she thought she'd be a historian. Go to Western, get her PhD, maybe even teach at a university; somewhere romantic; somewhere far away. Like UBC or Dalhousie."

Greta shook her head. That couldn't be true. Her mother had told her she hadn't gone to university.

"If that didn't pan out, she wanted to get a job in the community. She had this elaborate plan laid out. She'd get so excited whenever she talked about it. Start locally, in a recreation centre. Assist a city councillor as a means of gaining credibility. And then, if it all worked, consider running for MPP—that's a Member of Provincial Parliament."

Greta nodded. She'd taken Civics.

"Her world opened up wider when her class took a trip to Queen's Park. It was a big deal for a kid from Brantford travelling to The Big Smoke for the first time."

Greta shot her hand out across the table. "She was from Brantford?"

Colleen stared at her. "You didn't know that?"

"You said north of Hamilton the last time we talked."

"Guess I forgot to get back on that. Yes."

Brantford. Greta pulled out her phone to access her Notes app.

"Anyway, she described her trip in great detail." Colleen laughed. "Too much detail, actually. How the rolling fields and two-lane roads gave way to a six-lane highway in the thick of the cement jungle. How everything got bigger—brighter, faster, louder."

Greta nodded. That part was true. She pictured her mother going on and on about details she'd never notice. She was definitely like that.

"That tour mesmerized her. There was so much history in the stones and the paintings in the halls. When their tour guide said Canada was just over a hundred years old, she thought that was ancient."

Greta thought about the time she'd thought sixteen was pyramid ancient, too. Wasn't that the time her mom had met her father? Something about sixteen rang a bell.

"Because of that trip, your mom's dreams got bigger."

Greta's attention snapped back to Colleen's story. "Bigger how?"

"She wanted to make a difference. Maybe be Premier."

"Of Ontario?" She couldn't believe it. "What did her friends say?"

"They laughed. Obviously. Thought the whole thing was a joke and—"

"Nice friends," Greta interjected.

Colleen took another sip of her latte. "It was a different time. Females in politics weren't common then. It wasn't what people expected. It was Kim Campbell, whose real name was Avril... She was our first female Prime Minister. In 1993. But she only lasted six months."

"How come?"

"Her party lost the next election."

Though Greta couldn't see her mother as ever being a politician, she disagreed. "A woman could be Premier—*and* Prime Minister." Mrs. Xiangzi had been certain she understood that.

"You're just like your mom."

"So what happened?"

Colleen's face clouded over. "I guess that doesn't matter now, does it? Things weren't meant to be."

Greta stared at her from across the table. None of her mother's big dreams had materialized.

"Why hadn't you told me my mom was a client at the Women's Shelter in Bracebridge?"

Colleen looked up sharply. "I told you I worked with her."

"I thought you meant co-workers... You know, colleagues. I was really screwed up when I found out she was your client."

"Honey, I'm sorry. I didn't mean to mislead you."

"Why didn't you help her?"

Colleen's lips pressed into a thin line. "I did everything I could."

"I don't think so," Greta said curtly. "Maybe if you'd tried harder, she'd be alive now."

Colleen stared back in disbelief.

"Well, she obviously trusted you to tell you all this stuff." Greta held her gaze until Colleen lowered her eyes.

"Do you know Hannah?" Greta pressed.

"Your mom's sister?"

"Tell me something about her," she said.

Colleen perked back up a little. "Emily said they were thick as thieves."

Greta felt a pang of envy.

"Hannah was a few years older so, truth be told, it probably wasn't always like that."

"Go on."

"Your mom told me that, when they were growing up, Hannah drove her nuts. She had all sorts of stories about the things she did to her."

"Like?"

"Let me think. Okay... When your mom was maybe seven, Hannah had to babysit when her parents were working. The last thing Hannah and her friends wanted was a whiny kid hanging around then, so they ditched her."

Greta frowned. "That was mean."

"They left her sitting on the toilet all day. She'd accidentally swallowed an ice cube at lunch, and Hannah convinced her that if she didn't poop it out, her insides would freeze and she'd die."

Greta laughed. It wasn't funny; it was hilarious.

"Your mom said she was so scared when her mom got home from work, she was still sitting there, asleep, with her head on the toilet paper roll."

Greta's eyes widened.

"And her father took a picture."

"Seriously?"

"Emily said they kept the photo up on the fridge for years. It was a running joke in their house."

Greta was still laughing. "What else did Aunt Hannah do to my mom?"

"Oh, she was horrible. When your mom was about nine, her friends were all taller than her. Hannah convinced her she'd sprout up an inch overnight if she lay down on her bed and rubbed her tummy with both hands—in opposite directions, of course." She laughed. "Then she took off."

Greta groaned and rolled her eyes. "My mom believed her?"

"Yes, but she laughed it off. She said it wasn't as easy as it sounded, and took her a half an hour just to get the pattern right. By that time, Hannah was long gone."

Greta wasn't so sure about her Auntie Hannah. She didn't sound like the type of person she wanted to meet.

"Hey, don't worry. Everyone's got those types of stories from their childhood."

She looked down at the table. Not *everyone* had them.

"At least your mom didn't have brothers. The stuff they pull is way worse, trust me."

Greta thought back to what her mother had told her about boys. It hadn't been all bad.

"Anyway, those were early days. By the time your mom hit her teens, she and Hannah became pretty tight. They used to sneak out and go to bars... Bet she never told you that."

"Never said a thing." Greta grinned. She had no idea her mother had ever had that kind of side to her.

"One night, she told me about when they went to The Hammer."

Wait. That's where her mom said she'd met Ian for the first time. She wanted to hear *this* story. She *needed* to hear it. She leaned in.

"It wasn't your mom's first time with her older sister and her fake ID."

She gasped. "*My* mother?"

Colleen laughed. "Your mom was a lot of fun. A wild one. They'd gone to bars before."

Greta started to piece together the reason Grade 10 had been her favourite year. It was nothing to do with History class at all... It had everything to do with the fake ID. What had it said?

"Hannah drove. I remember her telling me she felt so free because they were going about 120 km/h down the highway singing at the top of their lungs."

"That would be speeding—not driving," Greta informed her.

Colleen agreed.

"What songs?"

"Probably classics."

"Classic what?"

"I don't know."

"Which ones?" She took out her playlist, preparing to scroll through and mark them.

"*I'll Be There for You* by the Rembrandts?"

"What?"

"Do you know *I Wish You Well*? Tom Cochrane."

She shook her head.

"You have to know *Only Wanna Be With You*? Hootie and the Blowfish."

"Never heard of it."

Colleen put her hands on her hips. "Are you kidding me? How about Seal? *Kiss from a Rose*?"

She shook her head again. She'd never heard of any of them, but the last thing she wanted to explain was that they didn't have music in the cabin when she'd grown up. Rules were rules for a reason—or consequences dealt. She shuddered.

"What was her favourite song?"

"*Insensitive*. Jann Arden"

She smiled. Hallelujah. She was one for five.

"Go back to the night they snuck out," she said.

"They went to some bar called Joey's. It was a run-down watering hole. Cheap draught. Perfect for college crowds."

"Which she wasn't."

"They had a great time and then, a few months later, when Hannah suggested a repeat, your mom jumped at it."

Again? Greta wasn't sure how she felt about it.

Colleen leaned across the table and held onto Greta's wrist, sadness sweeping across her face. "I doubt she ever would have imagined that, at about the same age you are now, her perfect life would have shattered."

THIRTY-TWO

Greta's hands flew up to her mouth and knocked Colleen's half-finished latte across the table. The barista came over and surveyed the mess. As he wiped up the table, he said, "Next time, you may want to stick with decaf."

Colleen shot him a look. "I'll take a refill."

He looked at Greta. "And for yourself?"

Heat rose up through her cheeks. "Hot chocolate."

"Whip and sprinkles?"

"Load it on," she mumbled.

He walked off again behind the counter to prepare the order.

"What happened that night?" Greta whispered. Colleen stared back at her, arranging her words in her head, as she considered the options. "I'm seventeen. The truth is better expressed than suppressed."

Her sharp tone didn't go unnoticed. When Colleen shifted in her seat and put her elbows on the table, pressing her fingertips together, she could see the tension radiating between them.

"You sound like an old lady when you say stuff like that," Colleen said.

Was she? She'd had a lot of life experience in the past few years alone, but nothing she was ready to tell Colleen. Was the whole idea of suppressing the truth a family gene she'd inherited? Maybe she needed to consider taking her own advice.

Colleen cleared her throat. "You're right. You're nearly an adult and you deserve to know."

Greta leaned in. "That night, two things happened." She paused. "And I don't know which was worse."

She didn't like the sound of that. She gripped the side of the table to stop her hands from trembling.

"First, Ian Giffen."

Greta nodded for her to continue.

"Your father had a reputation back then. He was outgoing. Good looking. A bit of a ladies' man."

"Gross, but okay." She'd never considered her father good looking. In fact, she'd never considered his looks at all. He was her father. He certainly wasn't what she thought of as outgoing either.

"Most people have to work hard to get what they want. And even when they *do* work hard, they can't always get what they want."

Greta looked at Colleen perplexed.

"Unless you're Ian, that is. He took what he wanted when he wanted it. So, when he walked into Joey's and saw your mother, he took her."

"What do you mean? Took her where?" Greta's imagination was taking her places, too.

"He took her heart," Colleen said.

Greta sighed with relief. She was aware of that. Her mother and father had fallen head over heels in love the first time they met. She knew that for a fact because it was what her mother had said—that first night in The Hammer.

"Your mom said Hannah warned her; told her it'd end in an ugly way. But, when you're sixteen, who's thinking past a week into the future?"

Greta wasn't thinking past a second. "What happened next? To my mom, I mean?"

The barista returned with their drinks. Colleen thanked him and waited until he was out of earshot. "They were drinking, dancing. The music was pounding, and your mom told me she was giddy with being grown up. By last call, your Auntie Hannah had faded. She was ready to go home and your mom was still wired up."

"But it was late," Greta said.

"She told Hannah she wanted to stay out, that your dad would drive her home. She walked Hannah out, hugged her goodbye, and Hannah promised she'd cover for her if she had to. Then your mom went back in, got Ian, and they left."

Greta frowned and took a sip of her hot chocolate. "She dumped Aunt Hannah? At one in the morning?"

Colleen nodded.

"Where'd my mom and dad go?"

"I don't know. But when your dad dropped her off in the morning, the cops were there; blue lights flashing. They thought they were coming home to a crime scene."

Greta froze.

"Hannah never made it home. Her car was found mangled in a ditch on the road. When they found it, there was nothing they could do. The coroner guessed she died a couple of hours earlier."

Greta's stomach lurched. She thought she was going to be sick.

"Your mom was hysterical. She didn't believe what the officers said. She didn't believe it when her parents told her either."

Greta took a deep breath. "Was she in shock?"

"She collapsed on the sidewalk. Had a total breakdown."

The lump in her throat grew. She knew exactly how her mother felt. The guilt, the self-loathing, the fear. She'd felt them all the day Mr. Parthi had pulled her out of class to tell her that her mother was dead.

"She couldn't eat. Sleep. She told me the worst part of it, besides missing her sister, was that, while everyone mourned her death, it felt like the two of them had died that night."

Tears flowed down the sides of Greta's cheeks. No wonder it was too painful for her mother to talk about Aunt Hannah. It made so much more sense. She wanted to reach out and hug her; hold her close and tell her everything would be okay. But she couldn't. And never would be able to again.

"Her parents said they didn't blame her, but she figured they did. Your mother certainly blamed herself."

Greta sat silent.

"Hannah's death turned your mom's life upside-down."

Afraid to ask her next question, Greta dropped her chin to her chest. "She dropped out of school, didn't she?"

"Not right away. But her marks slid. And her friends' parents weren't keen on her hanging out with them anymore. Near the end of first semester, nothing was normal anymore."

Greta wondered what normal even meant then. And who decided? *Normal* was such an elusive term—normal for who?

"Ian was all she had so she ran away with him."

Greta didn't know what to say. Actually, she did, but she didn't want to say it. Her heart ached for her mother. Now she understood. By the time her mother realized her life would never be her own, it was too late. Sixteen years old, already with her Ian, she must have become trapped. With him. And *by* him. Greta wrapped her fingers around her cup. Cold, a greasy film floated on top where the whip had gathered and melted. It looked like a petroleum spill.

"You okay?" Colleen asked. "It's a lot to take in."

"I need some time to process." What she wanted was to be alone.

Colleen smiled gently. "I'll text you to see if you want to meet up again in a couple of days."

Even though her head was spinning and her stomach was a pit of acid, she already knew that she did. She still had so many questions—more now than when she'd first arrived. But she couldn't handle any more answers—not today.

The walk back to Penn House was a struggle. Her legs felt rubbery and heavier than her head. When she strode through the front door and the staff waved hello, she ignored them; she didn't even look up. She didn't talk. She didn't want to. She needed to be alone.

***

Detective Perez tapped her pencil on the table. "Tell me more about wanting to be by yourself when you're stressed. Is it a strategy you use to calm down?"

Greta's face burned. Her mouth was dry, her tongue thick. The question was not one she'd anticipated. "What?"

Tap, tap.

"You heard me. Do you have problems with your self-control?"

She reached into the pocket of her jeans, fingers pressed to the coin, and counted. *One. Two. Three.* Then she exploded. "Are you fucking kidding me?"

"Greta," Phil said sharply.

She grabbed the arms of the chair. "That's what you're investigating? *My* control?"

Detective Perez's face flattened. "Answer my question."

"What about my father? What about *his*?" she shouted.

"He's not the one under investigation."

Greta leapt up and slammed her fist on the table. Detective Perez coiled backwards, eyes wide open.

"We need a break," Phil said calmly, "while I speak privately with my client."

Red-faced, Greta shot back, "No, I don't." The bottom of her sweatshirt was pulled sharply from behind.

Her lawyer interjected. "Yes, we do."

Greta's eyes travelled between her lawyer and Detective Perez. Neither moved. Neither said a word. She pulled away from the table until her back hit the door. "Screw you both."

Someone banged on the ladies' washroom door.

"I know you're in there." Phil's voice bounced off the dingy walls. "You need to come out."

Greta sucked in a cold breath from the window she'd managed to wedge open, then she turned to the tap, splashed water on her face, and ran a finger over the length of her teeth. With her head in her hands, she slunk down the tile beside the sink.

"Now, Greta. Come out."

She pulled herself up and cracked the door open. Phil's eyes were wide.

"What?" She half-smiled.

He frowned. "What? No, *why*?" he said. "You need to chill out in there or you'll make things worse."

"She's not human. After everything I've just told her, she's interested in *my* ability to control myself?"

He held his hand up. "Don't say that. She's listening to you."

"She's *not* listening. I already know."

"I understand how frustrated you are, but—"

"She told me. The lady in the cell last night. She told me all about her." Her lips trembled. "She's made up her mind about me."

Phil paused. "Meredith's in again?"

"Who?"

"Meredith. She spends most nights in the cells."

"You know her?"

"Paranoid. Drunk and disorderly. She's a shoplifter. One of our regulars."

Her chin dropped. "You knew about Perez's reputation and didn't tell me?"

Phil sighed and pushed open the door. "Let's get two things straight. First, you need to control that temper. You've got a short fuse and you're being investigated for murder. Don't make a case for them. Second, I don't know what you heard last night and I don't care if it's true or not, but right now, Detective Perez is giving you a lot of rope to tell your side of the story. Don't hang yourself with it."

She swallowed, a lump thick in her throat.

Phil pointed to the investigation room. "Get in there. You owe her an apology. And answer her questions. If you don't, Greta, I can't help you."

She retraced her steps to the room, sat down in her chair, and took a deep breath.

"Now," Phil said as he resumed his seat beside her at the table.

"Sorry about that."

Detective Perez rustled her papers, ready to resume. She flicked the button on the recorder. "Do I need to remind you of the question?"

Greta's stomach knotted as her thoughts turned back to the afternoon she'd spent with Colleen in the coffee shop. "It gives me time to think. To mull stuff over. Weigh my options. Maybe all three."

"Were you wondering whether to meet up with Colleen again?"

"No. I already knew. That wasn't the issue."

"What was?"

She paused. "I don't want you to take this the wrong way..."

Detective Perez stopped writing. "I'm listening."

Was she? Was she really listening? Greta took another deep breath. "I know you're a mom and a grandmother..."

Detective Perez smiled oddly, encouraging her to continue.

"My mom died when I was ten years old. She was always just my mom. I mean, not *just* my mom—that's not what I mean, exactly. I loved my mom. And I still love her. But she was my mother." She looked up, embarrassed. She was rambling. Her words weren't coming out the way she wanted them to, and she knew how ridiculous she sounded. "What I'm trying to say is, what Colleen told me made my mom a *person*."

The detective's eyebrows lifted.

"Not a person-person. Someone more than my mom. She had this whole life I didn't know about. Dreams. Goals. A sister. A family. It was all news to me. I never thought of her that way before. That day in the coffee shop, I started to see her as so much more than my mother. It was—what's a good word for it? Overwhelming."

"I can imagine," Detective Perez said.

The comment made Greta nervous. She needed her to understand, not to judge. "I'm not sure you do," she blurted out before her brain could stop her.

Phil's eyes darted in her direction. A bead of sweat trickled down her neck and pooled in the small of her back. She chose her next words carefully. "I needed to know more because, if I knew more about my mother, I'd know more about *me*. It was the only way I could move forward. To be whole again."

There. She'd said it; out loud for the first time in her life.

Detective Perez picked up her pencil and jotted in her notebook. Whatever she wrote, Greta thought it had to be good. She prayed it was. "What did you find out?" Detective Perez asked.

The next part came easily. She explained how she googled *Hannah Strachan Brantford car accident* to learn more about it. The excerpt she'd read was short and provided no additional information.

The Brantford Examiner:

Last night, 20-year-old Hannah Strachan, of Brantford, Ontario, was tragically killed in a single vehicle rollover on a dark stretch of the old 403. Details of the funeral arrangements have not yet been announced.

Next, she googled *Brantford high schools*. Only one came up in the search, and so Greta had reasoned it had to have been the one her mother and Hannah attended. On the school website, she scrolled through the pages, looking for pictures. The alumnae section was password-protected and, while she didn't think her mother's photo would be there because she was in high school before everything went digital, she still sent the link to save in her Notes app for reference. The last thing she did was google *411 Brantford* and, with her dime box in front of her, typed *D Strachan* into the search bar. Three listings came up. She took a screenshot and saved the image in her photos.

The detective interrupted her. "That must have been nerve-wracking. If you were overwhelmed earlier, I can only guess how scared you must have been then."

She thought about it; she hadn't felt either of those things. "I can see why you might think that," she said kindly. "But I wasn't." The detective's eyes narrowed and, for a second, Greta thought she'd blown it. "For the first time I was happy. Relieved. I don't know why, but I felt grounded."

"From a picture in a phonebook?"

"A screenshot."

The V between the detective's eyebrows turned into a crater. "That's hard to believe."

"I know, right, but it's true. I knew that screenshot was going to mean something. I wanted to believe it so badly."

Detective Perez sat silent for a moment. "And...?"

"And I met up with Colleen again."

THIRTY-THREE

Greta slid across the bumpy slats of the wooden bench and dug the toes of her running shoes into the cement.

"So, you came back for more?" Colleen said.

"Can't get my mom out of my mind."

"Won't be easy, what I'm about to say... This is the stuff that came up at our deepest counseling sessions."

"Hearing about it won't be harder than worrying all the time. Wondering about someone the same age I am now."

Greta looked around the parkette. The seat felt familiar. It was *her* bench. Except this time, she wasn't sleeping on it. Not that she was sharing any of her history with Colleen. She wasn't quite ready.

Colleen passed her a cup. "Hot chocolate."

She took it, her face lighting up. "Thanks."

"With a lid."

"Whip?"

Colleen groaned. "Forgot about that."

Greta smirked. The last time she'd left Colleen she'd been out of breath. It could have been because of what they'd talked about. It could have been because she was out of shape. Maybe it was a little of both. Either way, she was done putting anything that remotely resembled a petroleum by-product in her mouth.

"Where should we start?" Colleen crossed her ankles and ran a finger down the crease of her pant legs.

"After Hannah's accident?"

"Your mom and I discussed your Aunt's death at length in counseling, but not a lot about what came next."

"How about after she ran off with my Dad?"

"I don't have those details either. I met your mom in Bracebridge four years later and some details she just wouldn't share with me."

Greta sighed. Four years was a huge block of unanswered time. How could Colleen not know? Surely her mother would've said something. What about the places she'd told her she'd lived the evening they'd sat on the back patio together at the cabin. She perked up.

"How about Lindsay? Peterborough? Either ring a bell?"

"That's pretty vague. The night your mom came to the shelter, I was on intake."

"Intake?"

"It's what happens when clients first arrive. We sit down and talk."

Greta leaned forward, eager to hear.

"Not questions from a list. More a conversation to get their story."

Greta imagined what her mom must have been through—and not just her mom, but any woman in the same situation. The last thing they'd want to go through was an inquisition.

"What'd she say?"

Colleen pressed her fist to her forehead. "She was pale. Thin. Her face was strained."

"Like how?"

"She looked older than she was."

Greta imagined her mother would have felt defeated.

"I got the sense she knew leaving Brantford with your father had been the beginning of the end."

"Did she say that?"

Colleen shook her head. "Not in so many words. But I could tell everything in between then and her sitting there proved it."

Greta's heart hurt.

"She mentioned Lindsay. I remember it because it was the last place she'd lived where she felt safe. Something about an old lady upstairs?"

Greta thought back to what her mother had told her. She'd definitely said she'd liked her. "There's gotta be more."

"Nothing else that night."

Greta slumped back on the bench.

"These things take time, you know."

"How much?"

"There's no recipe. It takes what it takes." Colleen gazed out across the parkette. "Your mom and I only got to know each other after she started to trust me."

Greta leaned forward, her head in her hands. "So, once she did—trust you, I mean—what'd she say?"

"She told me more about Lindsay. How she was grateful for being separated only by floorboards."

"The old lady heard them fight?"

"When she found out how bad it was, she kicked them out."

Greta sat up. Dots in her mind connected. The lady wasn't frightened by something. She wasn't spooked, as her mother had said. She was frightened by her father. Her *own* father. That made so much more sense.

"That's why they moved to Peterborough..." she said.

"It didn't matter. The abuse didn't stop. But that's where your mom told me she was done. She'd waited for your dad to go to work and then packed up and walked out."

Greta exhaled. "Brave, huh?" She'd never assumed strong was loud and quiet was weak. Her mother, and everything about her, had always made that quite clear. Quiet people, thinking people, could actually be stronger than the louder ones.

Colleen smiled. "She was. But he found her a few days later."

"At the shelter?"

Colleen nodded.

"How'd he do that?"

"No idea. He begged her to come back to him. He said he'd manned up, would you believe."

She scoffed.

"It happens all the time, Greta. Empty promises..."

"Broken ones."

Colleen nodded. "Mostly broken. They seem to have a certain power. But anyway, she did—go back to him, that is—and, within a few days, he was beating her up again. Even the curtains couldn't hide it."

Curtains? They had no curtains in Ravensworth. Her mother had told her that her father said they didn't need them living out there in the boonies. Again, that wasn't true. It was her mother who hated them. And now she understood why. It was her choice not to have them. Yet her choice had everything to do with him. Why did everything have to come back to him every time? She pressed her hands into the bench and tried not to scream. He infuriated her.

"When she left him the second time," Colleen went on, "Ian knew he'd found her before, so she needed a clean break. They called us in Bracebridge and we took her in."

Greta sat on her bench dazed. Another secret or another lie? She wasn't sure which, but it was now apparent her father's job hadn't moved them to Bracebridge. Her stomach lurched. He'd found her there. Her father had stalked her mother. Across the province? But he didn't fool her: Greta knew he'd never manned up. He was a monster.

Colleen read the look on her face. She reached across the bench and gently squeezed Greta's shoulder. "I felt sick, too, when he showed up."

"How'd he do it?"

"I've no idea. But it took him a few months."

"Did you meet him?"

"A couple of times."

"Before she left?"

"When she was trying to figure out what she wanted to do."

Bile rose in Greta's throat. It was no wonder he'd reacted so violently when he saw Colleen in the candy store. Colleen wasn't someone they needed to avoid, as she remembered she was led to believe. Colleen was her mother's mentor. Her friend. The one who knew all her secrets and all of Ian's, too. Colleen didn't wreck Sunday. Her father did. And he'd wrecked everything.

Any tiny fragment of doubt, any sliver of hope that had lingered in her mind about what might have happened in the kitchen seven years ago, evaporated. Her father was a murderer; she knew it like she knew how to breathe. Instinctively.

Tears flowed down her cheeks. Were they her way of expressing her anger? Disappointment? Futility? More tears of rage followed. Her father had snuffed the light on their days, and the life right out of her mother.

"I tried, Greta. I really tried." Colleen was crying, too. "Nothing was ever right about that man. Nothing was ever enough. When he and your mother moved out to that cabin in Ravensworth... Well, I was scared. It was so remote. Right off the grid."

Greta nodded. She knew all too well. It had been her home, too. "My mom must have felt sick," she said.

"More than that. I think at twenty years old she felt owned. Maybe she thought it was a peaceful place to live for an end she knew would be coming? I don't know. I'm sure she didn't know when that end would come, but I'm guessing she may've resigned herself to the fact it was inevitable."

Greta shuddered. "Then why adopt a baby? Why bring me into that?"

Colleen looked into her eyes and took her hand. "I don't know. Only she did."

Detective Perez flapped a hand at Greta. "Are you saying that on that day you asked Colleen the same question I asked you yesterday?"

"Which one?"

"When you'd gone to the shelter, Colleen wasn't there. You found out your mom was a client. You were questioning all the lies. I said I was, too, because—"

"An adoption place wouldn't put me in a violent home?"

The detective nodded. "And you ignored me."

Red-faced, Greta sat up. "Because you accused me of lying."

Phil interrupted. "I'm sure no one was accusing anyone of anything at that point."

Greta pointed a finger across the table. "*She* was."

Phil's jaw tensed. He looked across the table to Astra for confirmation, who smiled awkwardly.

"And you carried on about your...' Detective Perez flipped through her notebook, "dime box."

Greta took what felt like her first breath in minutes. "I told you yesterday. My mom lied about it, too. But that lie was a good one—one she said to make me feel better."

THIRTY-FOUR

Greta pulled her phone out of her pocket and showed Colleen the screenshot.

"What's that?"

"My family," she told her. "Or at least the ones I think I have left."

Colleen stared at the three *D Strachan*s on the screen. "And you know this how?"

"It's what's carved into the side of my dime box."

"Your what box?"

Greta laughed and explained its whole history, with some of her own history spilling out, too. The timing was right. It was finally right.

"I think one of these Strachans might be my grandparents."

"Wow." Colleen squinted into the setting sun. "I've underestimated you. You're quiet but there's a lot more going on in that head of yours than I'd realized."

Greta wasn't sure whether to be annoyed or pleased. What was Colleen trying to say? She wasn't a child. She was seventeen.

"So what's the plan?" Colleen asked.

Greta had spent more time considering the best way to contact the people she thought may be her grandparents than the time she'd spent pre-planning what she was going to do when she first stepped off the bus in Toronto two years before. What had she been thinking? It all could have gone so much more badly than it did. She realized then how lucky she'd been. "We've come up with three options."

"*We*?"

"Latoya and me. We've been talking it through and figured it out."

"Is that so?" Colleen said.

"Write. Call. Or you can drive me to Brantford and I'll knock on their doors."

Colleen's eyes widened. "Don't you think a first meeting face-to-face might be a little intense? For you? For them? If they really are your grandparents?"

Greta ignored her comment. Something told her that they were—one of the three anyway.

"Maybe. I guess so. Probably," she mumbled. "Then that only leaves call. Because if they're anything like my mother, they definitely don't do social media. They may not even own a computer."

Colleen looked puzzled. "What happened to the letter?"

"I'm not writing on dead trees," said Greta, "or using snail mail. I could be twenty by the time they get it."

"Have you talked to anyone at Penn about this? Asked them to help you out?"

Greta looked down at her shoes, humiliated. "That counseling thing? They set me up with a counselor, somebody named Kanza, but I don't have anything to talk about." Then she corrected herself. "Nothing I *want* to talk to her about anyway."

Colleen smiled brightly. "Now you do."

***

Detective Perez stared at Phil. "You've got to be kidding me."

He shook his head. "I called Colleen last night."

"She's real?"

"Confirmed it all. She sat in with Greta and Kanza on the planning meeting."

"I need her contact details."

Greta watched them closely. After they exchanged information, the detective reached for her phone on the table. "Give me a minute, please."

Her eyebrows furrowed, Detective Perez tapped at the keys. After a series of *pings* and a *whoosh*, she dropped her phone back on the table, reached for her glass, and took a long sip of her drink. Then another *ping*. Her arm shot out, but not before Greta snuck a look at the words on the screen.

Bringing her in now.

Her heart pounded. The one person to vouch for her and who knew Ian's violent history. She prayed the message referred to Colleen.

Over the next few weeks, Greta, Kanza, and Colleen put together a plan. It took forever talking about the details, and Greta tried to be patient as they worked it all through. Her efforts paid off in a single phone call.

The following weekend, she and Colleen set out for Brantford. Slouched down in the front seat of her car,

Greta's legs jiggled as her mind flooded with the possibilities of what was to come. What if they'd moved since they'd spoken earlier that week? What if, when they met, they saw images of her mother? What if that conjured up painful memories and then decided they didn't like her? If it was all too much? Maybe they'd never want to see her again. Everything made sense when they'd planned it out, but now everything felt muddled. What on earth had she been thinking?

Colleen's GPS led them to a driveway of a small bungalow at the end of a quiet street. Greta didn't have to look past the two-car garage, the manicured flowerbeds or up to the red wood front door to find what she was looking for: an older couple was already standing, arm in arm, at the bottom of the pathway. She opened the car door. As she heaved herself from the front seat, her knees gave way and she pitched forward, head-first, and stumbled out and onto the driveway. She glanced up at her grandparents to check if they'd seen. Then time froze. Not just froze; it reeled backwards. It was like staring into her mother's face. But in two different faces at the same time.

Her grandfather burst into laughter. "How was your trip?"

Her grandmother looked at him in disbelief. "Are you serious, Daniel? That wasn't funny when the kids were younger and it's not funny now."

The small-boned woman with a gray braided bun perched on top of her head walked over and extended her hand.

"Come on, love. Ignore him," she said softly.

Greta couldn't believe what she was hearing. *Come on, love.* That felt good; deep-down-in-her-bones good. She'd waited years to meet her grandparents.

Her grandfather shrugged and tucked his hands in his pockets. "Sorry about that, Polly."

"Don't apologize to me," Polly said curtly. "Apologize to your granddaughter."

"Sorry, Greta."

Her grandfather, a good foot taller than her grandmother, looked embarrassed. He didn't need to; she could already tell he had a zany sense of humour. She liked him immediately.

Colleen, Greta and her grandparents walked up the flagstone pathway to the front door. Polly took Greta on a tour of the house. It was bigger than most houses she'd ever seen. It felt homey, and was decorated with a sense of subtle warmth. There were blankets in the living room, rugs underfoot and large, framed paintings and photographs on every wall. As Greta followed along behind her grandmother, she provided a running historical commentary through every room.

"This table is where your mother and her sister used to do their homework, when I could get them to sit and do it. And this is the finger painting your mother came home with in elementary school. Oh, and this bathroom used to have one sink, but we blew out the room beside it to make it bigger so now it has two".

Greta laughed inside. Now she knew where her mother got her tendency for history recaps.

When they reached her mother's old bedroom, her grandmother pulled open the door. A double bed covered with a red and yellow quilt and a sea of stuffed animals sat to the left. Beside it was a double closet, and a full-length mirror hung on the wall. A huge window looked out onto the backyard. Beneath it, books and perfume bottles and pencils and pens were scattered across the top of a wooden desk. She hovered in the doorway and thought about her childhood, and how different her mother's had been. She took her time studying the posters on the walls and the photos on the dresser before eventually summoning up the courage to step inside and sit down on the side of her bed. She picked up one of the pillows and drew in a deep breath. Nothing. Had she'd missed it? Forgotten it? She breathed in again. She looked up at her grandmother, sniffed and wiped her eyes. Polly's eyes glazed over, too, as she held her in a soft hug.

They spent the rest of the day catching up in the living room. They had lunch; turkey sandwiches with crusts. Most of the conversation was easy, yet there were times it ebbed and flowed. Some questions triggered difficult memories and not everything was straightforward.

Yes, she was adopted, which surprised them, but they said it didn't matter. And since they brushed it off so quickly, she didn't tell them she thought it did.

No, she didn't like living in the cabin where she'd grown up.

Was the isolation difficult? Greta nodded and felt the bump in her throat grow larger. The location felt far out.

Her father? She wasn't close to him. They had a relationship, but it was strained.

Her mother? They had questions about her, too; about the daughter they'd lost years before.

"How far did that conversation go?" Detective Perez said.

"I took my time explaining the best I could."

"The first time you met them? Everything?"

"Almost. The way she looked. What she did. How much fun we had. What she'd taught me and how she was so much a part of me both then and when I was little."

"Did you explain—"

"I said it was an accident."

"So they don't know about your parents' history."

"A little more now."

"Do you know you're here?"

Eyes to the floor, Greta shrugged. "No."

Near the end of the afternoon that first day, she'd met her grandparents, her grandfather hitched up the sleeves of his plaid buttondown shirt to the elbows, and reached out his hand. "Let me see it."

Greta sighed. The sight of her dime box would remind him of the daughter he no longer had, but she pulled it out of her backpack and put it gently in his palm anyway. A dark shadow crossed his face as he held it, struggling, staring, a piece of his life from a long time ago—a piece of their family history. It was Hannah. It was Emily. It was her grandparents, too. He coughed and leaned back in his chair, tapping his fingers on the sides.

"My father carved this from a piece of wood he found in the ravine behind our house," he told her.

"*This* house?"

"No, the one I grew up in. A few streets from here. I watched him do it. He spent hours sanding it down. Making it smooth so I wouldn't get splinters."

After all the times she'd traced the lines in the dime box, Greta knew her great-grandfather had done a great job.

"He asked what colour I wanted it painted."

"You said red."

He winked. "That was my favourite as a boy." He passed her back the dime box and Greta turned it over. "My initials," he told her. "My father carved them in there because he wanted to be sure I remembered where I came from."

Greta traced them gently with her finger, and then passed her grandfather the dime box. He stopped for a moment and wiped his eyes on his sleeve.

"Our family collected dimes in it for the pay phone. When the price of a call went up way back, we collected quarters. But the name stuck. We never could call it a quarter box; it was always a dime box to us."

With his eyes still moist, Daniel put it on the coffee table in front of him. "I never knew where the damn thing went."

"Language," Polly said sharply, reaching down and smoothing out the creases in her skirt.

Greta smiled. She was looking forward to spending more time with her grandparents and observing their relationship. Daniel and Pauline Strachan. Or Daniel and Polly. It had a nice ring to it. And they were adorable together; kind, gentle and funny. They finished each other's sentences, like two halves of a whole. Like she and her mother had been.

"I couldn't be happier you've brought it home to us, Greta. Not because I've missed it. Not because I've wondered where it's been all these years. But because it brought you with it." Greta looked up and smiled. "It's brought our family back together," he said. "We were four. Then we were two. And now we're three."

THIRTY-FIVE

Greta put her head in her hands and groaned as the car pulled out of her grandparents' driveway.

"Is now a good time to ask what you're thinking?" Colleen probed.

She peered through the cracks of her fingers. "I'm so messed up."

Colleen grinned. "It was pretty surreal. You going to be okay?"

Greta laughed; the sound mixed with the sound of her sniffled sobs and helped to release the pent-up energy bouncing around inside her. She thumbed through the pictures on her phone. "Look at this. My mom's eyes are the same as my grandmothers. And she has my grandad's smile. It was like I was looking right at her again."

"There's definitely a resemblance."

"Nothing makes sense. I was so scared to meet them... But they're so nice and I didn't want to leave."

Colleen looked sideways and changed lanes.

"And while we were there, I missed my mom less. Which is freaking me out because if, I see them again, I don't want my memories fading."

The traffic slowed. Colleen slowed with it. "Not *if*. *When*. Did the good ones fade today?"

She shook her head.

Colleen pointed to her head and her heart. "That's where you'll keep them."

She caught her breath. "I still have so many questions."

"Shoot."

"I wish I'd met them before. Why didn't my mom reach out to them?"

The traffic came to a standstill. "Seeing you today, I'm sure they're heartbroken they didn't have you in their life as a child."

She smiled, pleased to hear Colleen acknowledge her as an adult. She'd grown up ten years in one day alone.

"Maybe one day you'll all discuss it. Your mom's situation was complicated. You know that. Nothing you caused, of course. I bet your grandparents had a tough time when your mom took off with your dad."

Greta thought of their kind faces; their warmth and their smiles; and how much they accepted her unconditionally. "Yeah. They'd already lost one child."

"I'm sure they wanted to keep in contact and never stopped trying. But as her life spun out of control and her life became your father's, well, things will have changed."

She balked. "That's an understatement."

"Your mom might've shut them out at first. Maybe she didn't want them to see her like that, especially if she believed she already caused them a ton of grief."

She nodded. "The guilt would be huge." Her mother must've been going through hell.

"By the time I met Emily at the shelter, she couldn't have reached out even if she'd wanted to."

"Ian forced her to cut them off?"

Colleen nodded. "You know what he would've said. Rules are rules to be followed."

"Or consequences dealt."

The traffic moved forward and Greta yanked her seatbelt from around her waist. "Why were my parents allowed to adopt me?"

Colleen looked over her left shoulder and changed lanes. Smooth and silent.

"I mean, didn't anyone in Parry Sound know about Ian's history?"

With one hand on the wheel, the other draped on the back of her seat. Colleen blew her breath out slowly.

"Come on." She turned to face her. "Someone must've known."

"I did. But with your dad so involved in the church, no one else questioned it."

Greta's nose twitched. It filled with the smell of the nave. She crossed her arms and stretched her legs in front of her.

"It all happened so fast. I didn't share my concerns with anyone, but, yes, I should've. I'd never heard of an adoption going through that quick."

Greta glanced sideways. Her mother had told her it shocked her father, too, when they'd got the news in less than a month.

"I'm sorry, Greta," Colleen said. "It haunts me, and if I could go back in time, I'd deal with it differently. I'm going to regret this for the rest of my life."

Greta reached across the front seat of the car and squeezed her hand. Colleen squeezed hers back. They sat in the car in the silence, lost in their own thoughts.

"I still don't understand why my mom would bring me into the picture in the first place? I mean, what if she died when I was really little and I was left with him alone when I was even younger?" The thought made her anxious. It actually sickened her.

"That's a tough one," Colleen said. "When your dad moved them out to the cabin, I think she felt he owed her."

"A baby?"

"You were what she wanted. You think he had it in him to think of kids?"

Maybe that was a good thing. Except, if he hadn't, she wouldn't have had her mother. She pushed those thoughts aside; they were too painful to think about.

"She wanted to be happy. *You* made her happy," Colleen said. "As your father was all appearances, she went at him from that angle. She knew how to work him." ·

"He's pathetic."

"And she was smart. She loved you more than anything."

Blood rushed to her temples as she thought of their days together. They had a lot of fun those first ten years when it was just the two of them. They had plans, she and her mother. They'd move to the city one day. Which city, she didn't know. But they talked about how there'd be bathrooms and bathtubs and neighbours and noise. Parks. And pets everywhere. She longed for times they'd spent with each other, back when she didn't understand. Home together meant not lonely. Home together meant safe. With everything she'd found out the last few months, the phrase that tormented her childhood took on a whole new meaning.

"Your mother lived day by day. In the present. She never thought about what might happen when—."

***

Detective Perez frowned and folded her hands on the table. "Officer Pappas didn't mention anything about this last night. How much Colleen appears to be aware of..."

"He wouldn't," she said confidently. "It was all after I left for Toronto."

"And if Colleen knew about your father's history, why didn't she share her concerns with someone at the time? She could have and should have contacted the adoption agency."

Greta shrugged. She wanted to tell Detective Perez to ask her herself, but if she did, the detective would know she'd read her screen.

Detective Perez raised her eyebrows at Phil and looked over the top of her glasses. Her expression was cautious. "Let me explain something to you, Greta."

Was the room getting stuffy? It was getting hot. Sahara Desert hot. The burn in her cheeks confirmed it.

"I'm not saying it didn't happen, but there's a big difference between accusing someone of committing a serious crime and actually proving it."

Greta rolled her eyes. Did Detective Perez think she was stupid? She'd figured that out a long time ago. She thought back to the kitchen in Ravensworth, to the three auburn hairs stuck on the edge of the table.

"You might think your father murdered your mother—"

"He did." Greta glared at her. Sometimes it was necessary to state the obvious. At ten years old, she knew her mother had been murdered, but when Officer Pappas visited the cabin the day after the funeral, she couldn't give him what he needed even if she'd wanted. Her father was sitting in the next room listening to every word she said.

The heat in the room was unbearable, the air between them tense. Greta wiped the sweat from her upper lip as Detective Perez took off her glasses and put them on the table.

"Proof"—her voice tightened—"requires evidence."

Greta's whole body trembled. She'd just provided more evidence of her mother's murder—a witness who could corroborate her father's abuse. The irony of the whole situation made her sick. "Why are you more concerned with my father than with me? My mother was the one murdered and you're saying the responsibility to prove it was on me? Quite the justice system you've got here."

Detective Perez shrugged. "I'm aware of your allegations against him and I want you to know I take them seriously. Listen, Officer Pappas couriered down an evidence box to my office last night. I'll have my ETs send it over and take a look through it."

"ETs?"

"Evidence Techs."

Greta relaxed in her seat. Good. She felt part of the conversation.

"Until then," the detective directed her attention back to the file, "we've got evidence here we need to deal with."

"Are you for real?" Greta jabbed a finger at the papers. "*That* shit?"

Detective Perez's lips pressed into a thin, bloodless line. "You've got motive means—"

"I didn't do it."

"...and opportunity."

Greta crossed her arms, sucked in a slow breath and clenched her jaw shut. Detective Perez looked to her lawyer. All she got back was a shrug.

"Okay," the detective said, wearily. "Lunchtime. Let's shut it down here."

Detective Perez sat down heavily in her leather chair and pressed the record button. She half smiled, leaving an uncomfortable impression. "So, you met up with Colleen again. You met your grandparents—which, by the way, I think is wonderful. And you got answers to some of your questions."

Greta nodded. The comment about her grandparents made her feel more at ease. But before lunch, the detective had suddenly switched tactics, and she wasn't going to let her guard down. She knew what was coming. What she didn't know was when.

"So, take me through what happened after that." The detective straightened her face and added, "Briefly please. We need to get on to the evening your father died."

There. Detective Perez confirmed it. Greta's stomach tightened. She shut her eyes and tried to pull herself together. Before the inevitable. She paused. "I started counseling."

She'd travelled the recesses of her mind, the pitch-black corners, all the dead-end alleys, with Kanza beside her, as they dragged out demons one at a time, putting each one on full, ugly display. They'd named them. They'd explained them. They'd taunted them. They'd teased them. They'd trapped every one of them when they tried to retreat.

"Did it work?" the detective prodded.

"Kanza helped me pull myself together."

"You're sure?"

She looked the detective straight in the eye. "Excuse me?"

The detective held her gaze. "How would I know?"

Her comment was like a slap across the face. Years of emotion had formed a hard wall inside of her, and getting past it had been so difficult. Very few had done it; her mother, Latoya, Mrs. Xiangzi and Colleen. That was it. She preferred to go it alone. Until Kanza had come along and done it, too.

Heat crawled up her cheeks. Words stagnated in her mouth. How could she prove it? Her mind relaxed; she'd earned her credits and had graduated from high school. She'd started doing yoga and meditating, which, although was painful at first, she liked it now. Wait. She'd started running again. What difference was it if it was only a few blocks? She'd built up to an easy 5K. That she'd overlooked how running purged her insides, like a diuretic for her pain, she vowed she'd never forget again. How could she explain all that—and do so *briefly*?

How could she fit eighteen months into a sentence? She couldn't meet Detective Perez's eye. "I focused on my goals. Passed school. Spent weekends with my grandparents."

"Right. You expect me to believe everything fell naturally back into place?"

She didn't know whether what Detective Perez had said was a matter of fact or an accusation. Maybe both? Everything was a stretch. *Most things* was more accurate. No, that wasn't true. *Some* things. For the first time, she questioned whether she and Kanza should have pushed harder. She drew a deep breath, and picked her words carefully. "I've come a long way." And then, as if to reassure herself, she said it again. "Considering what I've had to deal with."

"Meaning?"

"I still might have had a couple blind spots."

"No doubt."

Greta searched her face, her blue eyes still and cold. Words bounced around her head, but she needed to continue. She sat up straighter. "Kanza suggested facing the past might be a good way to bring closure," she said.

"To put it all to bed?"

"Yeah. If you want to word it like that."

"Did you question that?"

"Up till then, it'd all gone well."

Detective Perez leaned forward. "So you did or you didn't?"

Greta shook her head. "No," she said softly.

THIRTY-SIX

"I don't understand," her grandmother puffed, rosy-faced, as she struggled to carry an oversized suitcase from the elevator. "Why pay so much to live in a shoebox when you can live free in a house?"

Greta took the bag from her hands. She loved her new studio in Riverside. It was hers and hers alone. Floor to ceiling windows graced the living room and led to a balcony overlooking the east side of the city. A modern kitchen and hardwood floors gave it a comfortable, lived-in feel. The only reason she could afford it was because Penn had access to a grant to help with the rent as she transitioned to independent living.

"Looking after myself will be good for me, and besides, I'm still coming to stay with you and Gramps every weekend," she said.

"You trying to kill me?" Daniel said with a wink.

Polly shot him the death look.

Her grandfather leaned in and gave her a hug. "Don't let me down, G. I can't wait."

There was no chance of it. She'd never fail her grandparents. They adored her, yet sometimes she wondered if they realized she needed them more than they needed her. They were her bridge from her past, her bridge to her present, and, she hoped, to her future—whatever that future would be.

As she unpacked her suitcase and hung her clothes in the closet, Polly, a tech whiz, busied herself in the living room, setting up the TV. Daniel unpacked the plates, utensils and pots and pans, arranging them in neat rows in the drawers in the kitchen. When everything was done, Greta walked them along the carpeted hallway to the elevator, grateful they'd helped move her in yet counting the days until she'd see them again.

Detective Perez stopped writing. "Did you want to move out of Penn?"

She shrugged. The detective wasn't buying her story, and she understood why. She hadn't quite come clean. "No choice," she told her. "I'd aged-out of the system."

"How did you pay for this apartment?"

"It's part of the outpatient program. Penn finds the place and their grant pays the rent."

"So you would have stayed?"

"At Penn?"

Detective Perez ran her fingers through her hair, looking flustered. "Here's why I'm asking," she said, without raising her voice. "Is there any chance you wouldn't be in the situation you're in right now if you'd stayed there a year or two longer?"

Greta thought it for less than a nanosecond. "I'd be sitting here no matter what."

She fell silent, giving Detective Perez a moment to digest what she'd said. In case she hadn't heard her, she repeated it. The detective's eyebrows furrowed as she scribbled on the page in front of her. Her decisiveness made her uneasy. She waited for her to look up, but she kept writing at a furious pace. Had she said the wrong thing? Did she need to correct herself? Would it be wise to circle back? Nope. There was no point. She knew in her heart if she had the power to turn back the time, she'd do the same thing all over again.

The tension in the room was stifling. She reached down to the pocket of her jeans again and felt around for the dime she had hidden just for times like these. It was a coin Daniel had given her to keep in her dime box. Not one from years ago, but a symbolic one to remind them how they had been brought back together; a coin she hoped would keep them together in the future, too. Now, she carried it everywhere. She rubbed it slowly, back and forth.

"Just to be clear," she said, breaking the silence, "I like my apartment."

The pencil stopped writing.

"By the time I'd moved in, I passed high school and got my driver's license. I failed the first time, but Kanza said it was important to build my independence so I tried again. And then I applied for college."

The detective looked up briefly. Her eyes gave nothing away.

"I'm telling you this for a reason, right?"

"Enlighten me."

"I may not have been totally ready to transition to independent living, but I was turning things around. My life was good."

Detective Perez stared back at her from across the table. Unable to read her body language, Greta knew something still wasn't sitting well. She didn't blame the detective; she hadn't been fully convinced, either, the first day her grandparents had left her standing alone in the apartment.

The first week had been tough. The silence was eerie and the days felt empty. She didn't have the Penn staff around her, her classmates beside her, or Kanza there to root her on. The silence was scary, but the TV helped—the blare, the repetition—so she kept it on day and night. When her show broke for the local news, the CP24 news anchor announced the most prolific northern lights show in years was anticipated for later on that same week. It reminded her of her childhood when she and her mother would watch the northern lights on their back patio. She recalled wondering—maybe more hoping at the time—if it was her mother's subtle way of saying hello; wishing her a happy eighteenth birthday.

The first five sleeps in the apartment felt like a whole year. Desperate to see her grandparents, to hear their laughter fill the void of the apartment's stifling quiet, she'd talked to Latoya on Skype every evening. Late Friday afternoon, her sprint down the stairwell took less time than a ride to the ground floor in the elevator. She wasn't sure whether it was because she missed them so much or the training regime she'd adopted had started to pay off.

"Did things settle after a while?" Detective Perez asked, her brow furrowed.

Greta's face went still. She started to fidget, and so she sat on her hands as inconspicuously as she could. The detective put her pencil down and waited.

"I kept busy. Introduced myself to the neighbours. Went out. Ran. Visited my grandparents on the weekends."

Downplay. Downplay.

Running was the only true thing in what she'd said. In fact, it was what she spent most of her time doing. Running to mask her loneliness. Running to ease her pain. Everything else was a lie. And the detective was having none of it.

"Want to try again?" she said.

Her comment came as a blow. Though she'd been forced to deal with transitions her whole life, she still found change difficult. Too many changes to count, there was no getting used to them. Even the easy ones were hard. Who was she trying to fool? She hated transitions. She stretched, trying to keep the blood flow in her legs. She knew instantly she needed to back pedal. She decided to fess up.

"It took a little time."

The detective eyes bore into her.

"Okay, a lot," she admitted. "But all that changed in September."

The building intercom broke the silence in her apartment.

"G, you've got guests," a voice said.

She looked at the wall. "No one knows where I am."

"Someone does."

She took the elevator fourteen floors down to the street. The metal doors slid open and she peered into the lobby. Her face lit up. She ran straight into the arms of Latoya, who greeted her a squeeze.

"Didn't you say next week?"

"I was too excited."

She laughed. "Come on." She grabbed her arm and pushed her into the elevator, and when they got upstairs, she swung open the door to the apartment. "Ta-da."

Latoya's face crumbled.

Greta took her hand, pulled her through the front door, and led her to the living room. They sat side by side on the couch, and Greta wrapped her arms around her.

"I hate it here." Latoya cried.

"Your school?"

"Already lost."

"Classes?"

"Start next week."

"What about residence. Your roommate?"

"The food sucks. I can't stand it."

"But she's good?"

Latoya held her hand up to stem the questions. Greta held her in her arms, and her sobs eventually slowed to soft weeping. Latoya wiped her cheeks with the back of her hands. "Good ugly cry, huh?"

Greta passed her a tissue. "We've all done it."

Latoya wiped the snot from her nose and laughed. "Look at me. I couldn't wait to get to the city and now I'm down here I just wanna go home. How messed up is that?"

Greta shook her head. Had things been different, she might've felt the same way. But there was nothing for her to go back to.

After a short break, Detective Perez walked back into the room, cell phone in hand, and sat down in her chair. Under her arm were two blue files: a thin one labeled *Giffen, I., Investigation*, and a thicker one stamped with the outline of a trillium. She opened the first and held up a document.

"How do you explain this?" she asked, sliding the piece of paper across the desk, swift and efficient.

Phil paled as he scanned it, wincing as he read. "This wasn't in the case file you shared yesterday," he said.

Detective Perez nodded. "The document just arrived." She looked at Greta. "It was what my officers said they found when they called my office yesterday."

"How did you get it?" His tone was more inquisitive than condemning.

"Search warrant. From your client's phone."

Detective Perez stood back up and passed Greta her purse. As she started for the door, she stopped in the frame and turned around. "I assume you'll need some time," and walked out.

Silence filled the room. Greta noticed she was holding her breath. Finally, Phil slapped the paper down in front of her. "Did you not think to mention this?"

Her heart sank and she turned on her chair, curled her feet under her butt, and dropped her head.

"Sorry," she mumbled.

"You knew they'd find it, right?"

She picked at the material of her sweatshirt. "It's not real."

"You can't be serious." He held up her finger and thumb to mark an inch. "You're about this close to being charged with murder."

Greta cursed under her breath.

Phil leaned back and raked her fingers across his head. "Holy crap, Greta. I've got to make a call and figure this out." He pulled out his cell phone and turned away.

"Thanks." She was about to say more when he looked over her shoulder, red-faced.

"Don't thank me yet."

She wiped her eyes on the sleeve of her sweatshirt. Though she didn't need to, she reached forward and picked up the sheet. As she read, her hands trembled.

Latoya: *Hey u*

Greta: *Hey*

Latoya: *Thanks for having me over last night*

Greta: *Feeling better?*

Latoya: *Yeah. Gonna stay*

Greta: *Like me*

Latoya: *Would u ever go back?*

Greta: *Only one reason*

Latoya: *??*

Greta: *To kill the fucker*

Latoya: *Wtf?*

Greta: *Smiley face*

Latoya: *Girl, I wouldn't blame you but seriously, no way*

Greta: *He ruined everything*

Latoya: *ik but ain't nobody helping no one meet their maker*

Greta: *KK*

Latoya: *We're here together now. I've got your back*

Greta: *smiley face*

Latoya: *Talk tmrrw. Heart u*

Greta: *Heart u2 Night*

She stood, leaned forward, and pressed her hands against her thighs. She felt everything unravel, pulling apart one thread at a time. Eyes closed, she breathed in and counted.

One, two, three. Collect yourself, damn it. Four, five.

When her nausea eased, she opened her eyes slowly, straightened her back, and sat back down. Detective Perez's footsteps echoed off the walls and, seconds later, she strolled back into the room.

"We ready?" she said, her tone matter-of-fact. The air shifted and Phil nodded. The detective sat at the table and made herself comfortable. "So," she turned Greta, "how would you like to explain this exchange?"

Greta considered her question a long time before she answered. "I get what this looks like"—the detective leaned forward—"but Latoya's my best friend. We were just yapping, having fun..."

"That's it?" she replied with a wry look. "That's your explanation?" She narrowed her gaze.

"It was a joke," she blurted.

Detective Perez's eyes widened. The colour drained from her face. "About killing your father?"

Greta rolled her eyes and flashed a satisfied smile. "Come on. Get serious for a minute. If I'd really wanted to, I would've done it at the cabin."

THIRTY-SEVEN

Greta's bag had been packed for more than two days. It was sitting by the door, waiting for the trip that would take care of unfinished business. The notion of facing it terrified her—and she wasn't alone.

"This is crazy," Daniel told her, drumming his fingers on the table. "Why see him now?"

She didn't know how to explain it. She needed him to admit he murdered her mother, and while having her grandparents in her life now meant the gaping hole no longer felt as wide, she still wanted those adoptions papers her mother had promised her.

Polly looked on. "From everything you've told us, your father is unpredictable. He sounds dangerous, God damn it."

Greta looked at her grandfather, who sat shocked at his wife's language, but neither dared to share their thoughts out loud. Polly abhorred cussing. She didn't withdraw the rest of her comment either.

"Why don't I come with you," Daniel suggested.

She shook her head. "I'll be fine."

She hadn't shared the full truth about her childhood or what had happened to her mother. Not yet, at least. She shivered at the recollection, doing her best to wipe the picture from her mind, and instead pulled her sweatshirt around her. Maybe one day. But today was not that day.

Polly rearranged herself in the chair. "You've got to be vigilant."

"And call us every couple of hours," Daniel added, "and we'll call you, too."

She knew her grandfather's suggestion wasn't negotiable. It was the only compromise that would keep her grandmother from sitting in Brantford worrying all day. She stuck out her hand in front of her. "Deal," she said. It would be an easy one to keep. She'd made the same one with Latoya.

Greta woke up early on the Saturday morning. Her mouth felt dry, her stomach unsettled. There was no way she could sleep. She got up, puttered around the kitchen, and made breakfast. She couldn't eat. Her heart raced so fast she thought it was going to burst out of her chest, and she wasn't even out of the apartment yet. How would she make it all the way up to Ravensworth? She folded herself into the couch in the living room and stared far off through the window. She anticipated she'd feel her mother all around her when she arrived.

Laptop in front of her, she picked at the keys. Her mother liked history, so the least she could do was share some with her. She googled *Route to Ravensworth* and tapped some notes into her phone.

The official name of Highway 401 is the King's Highway.

Ravensworth used to be part of the township of Bethune.

Whatever.

A bunch of artists came up on the feed. Seven of them; Canadians, famous for painting trees. She peered into the screen. Weren't those the same ones in the woods behind the cabin north of where she'd grown up? Where she ran? Her mother was likely aware of them, but she felt certain she'd have smiled anyway and let her ramble on uninterrupted, just happy to be together again and to learn what she'd discovered.

Before she left, she double-checked her phone. As a graduate of Penn, part of the Connect Program gave her access to Kanza twenty-four seven. The fact that she was a text away—no questions asked, no reason required— made her feel braver.

The last thing she did was pick up her dime box from the coffee table. She cradled it in her hands, her fingers following the gentle lines her great-grandfather had carved so long ago; lovingly, tenderly. She closed her eyes.

It was time to go. In the car her grandparents had lent her, Greta travelled north up the highway, past Canada's Wonderland, where the gray cement turned into rolling green fields and the pungent smell of the Holland Marsh filled her nose. She stopped in Barrie for gas. The slim fellow in his early forties who filled the tank turned his nose at her crumpled twenties. When she was younger, it would have embarrassed her, perhaps even made her mad, but not anymore. Now she imagined him some old man, close to retirement, wearing a fanny pack and returning his latte at Starbucks because he asked for light foam. He'd be telling long-winded stories of his glory days to anyone who would listen. That was all he had left. She'd moved on.

She dropped the car into gear and headed to Muskoka. Salmon-coloured veins weaved and sparkled through the slabs of rock sitting on either side of the road. It was like they were decorated for a party—a celebration welcoming her back to her roots. There was a sign on the side of the road, reflective white letters on blue paint. *Bracebridge*. The cut off came quickly. She'd called Mr. and Mrs. Xiangzi to let them she was coming, so they weren't surprised when she pulled in. Though they'd explained her father had moved out a couple of months earlier—some type of cancer, they'd said—the restaurant was her first stop. Family was family.

Back in the car after lunch, she set off again. The clouds spat and the gray sky hung dangerously close to the ground. The ride to the old cabin felt both quick and slow, but the GPS found it easily, where Lake Rain Road and the north end of Aholas Drive met. It was so isolated. She was surprised that her father had moved all the way back out there... but didn't they say criminals always returned to the scene of the crime?

She pulled into the laneway, careful to navigate the scarred pits and rutted potholes swelled to the size of mammoth craters. Overgrown branches scraped the sides of her grandparents' car the whole way down. It annoyed her. Her father hadn't bothered to cut them back, as she remembered from years before.

At the end of the laneway, Greta turned the corner into what had once been a grassy patch; but now it had deteriorated into a sandy path at the front of the cabin. She turned the ignition off. Her heart pounded. She gave it a quick up and down, but she couldn't believe what she saw: it didn't feel possible. Rotting logs, streaked green with moss. Windows dark with grime, encased in weathered plastic and duct tape. Was this all it had been? Where had their brown log cabin gone? What she remembered had been so much larger. She pulled herself out of the car and up to the front porch where a swarm of blackflies circled in a cloud. The door hung loosely; she opened it slowly.

Debris crunched underfoot as she walked through the door. The first thing to hit her was the lack of sound. The cabin was nothing more than a deep, distant void that guarded past secrets, keeping them safe. The smell hit her next. The hot odor of death, stale dust, and her mother's perfume were thick in the air. Woozy, she grabbed hold of the handle on the closet to steady herself, careful not to turn it. She didn't want the door opening, giving the bad spirits any chance to wake up and escape.

In the front hall, Greta stood, feet cemented to the floor. Sweat ran in rivers, making her T-shirt wet against the length of her back. She looked right to the tiny kitchen. Cups and plates and forks encrusted with foot sat stacked on the counter. Grit clung to the walls and floated in the air. Back in the hall, the familiar soaring wooden statue—the one overflowing with jackets that came alive and chased her in dreams as a child—was missing. Where had it gone? Surely it wasn't the worn out four-foot upright with the rusty hooks straight in front of her.

She gulped a deep breath and called out her father's name. The silence was deafening. The hallway, narrow and dark, creaked with every step she took. Another. Then another. She stopped to look at the pictures that hung on the wall—feeling nothing, mostly—and tore herself away. Eyes to the dark at the top of the stairs, she shivered and then pushed towards the back room. Six more easy steps that felt anything but easy.

By the entrance to the back room, she stood silent. Filled with the furniture she remembered as a child—the couch and chair, caked in dust, plastic covers removed—looked like they'd been sitting there for thousands of years. Something about the room was off. While the TV flickered, she didn't recall it being so dark. She waited a moment for her eyes to adjust. Why was it taking so long? Curtains. Long, flowing curtains covered the back windows. Those were new. And now she knew why. While her mother tried to bring light to their world, her father had snuffed it out. The thought of it made her sick. When her eyes acclimatized, his outline materialized in the darkness. He was across the room, sitting in a patched leather chair, with his back to her. Who watched TV with no sound on?

He turned his head and looked up at her. No surprise. No sense of wonder.

She inched forward. "Dad," she said, trying to keep her voice from shaking, "we need to talk."

THIRTY-EIGHT

Ian nursed his drink for a couple of seconds before turning his attention back to the television; his response a rumbling grunt.

"Dad," she repeated, louder this time; a little firmer.

He turned his head and gave her a cold, hard look. "Whaddaya want?"

She was taken aback. The sound came out more like a rattling wheeze. His voice sounded terrible, and now she could see in the pale light of the television, his skin was the colour of tapioca.

"There is a time and place for discussing this," he said, as if reading her mind. "That would be never and nowhere."

Blood raced to her face and roared in her ears. Beads of moisture ran down her forehead, stinging her eyes. She dropped them to the filthy carpet. She needed her moment of truth—and that moment would be *now*, whether he liked it or not. Her mouth tightened and she took a step forward. "We need to have this talk," she said, arms crossed. "*I* need it."

His eyes rolled all over her, top to bottom, looking for any signs of weakness, but when he found none, he shifted his gaze. He shook his head. "What you need is not important. I have cancer," he rasped. "I'm dying."

The words were meant to pierce, and they did. Two emotions consumed her. The first was shame. He wanted nothing to do with her and time hadn't dulled his contempt. But the feelings of rejection passed quickly and transformed into rage. Overwhelmed by the negative thoughts suddenly surfacing in her mind, she gritted her teeth. Nasty, untamed thoughts. Where had they come from? Had they been lurking in her head the whole time? Deep down in her subconscious? Under the impression she and Kanza had already dealt with them, her heart lurched. Maybe they hadn't addressed every one of them, after all?

A silence fell between them. A hot flush spread up through her face, and she struggled to breathe. She needed to centre. *One. Two. Three.* She inhaled slowly through her nose. *Four, five, six.* Exhaled out through her mouth.

"You getting treatment?" she said, not unkindly.

There. She'd done it. All her nerve endings ached, but she had managed to push her menacing thoughts aside. Her savage desires were fading.

Again, the silence. Maybe he didn't want to talk about it.

"Of course I am," he muttered. He rolled his eyes at her.

Greta cursed herself for letting him make her feel so stupid.

He pointed to the styrofoam cup full of ice chips. "Already had chemo. Couldn't swallow for a week."

Greta considered the matter while he broke out coughing; a long, ragged cough that bounced off the walls of the room. She stood, glaring back at him, but even the grizzled wig perched haphazardly in seat of the wheelchair beside him was not going to deter her. She wasn't moving; wasn't going anywhere. Minute dragged into minute. When the coughing finally subsided, she straightened and told her truth. She waited for acknowledgment.

Mouth twisted, he fixed his dark eyes on her. Her father claimed he had no memory. Countered her assertion the neighbours stayed clear with his belief they lived so far away it was unfair to have asked them to visit. Rejected her story of being forced to lower her voice so as not to provoke him as dried out on the couch from bender after bender. Dismissed the scars on her back and burns on her arms as clumsy childhood accidents. Rebutted the notion the fridge was often bare, requiring her to scavenge the brush and beg for food to feed her hunger. Laughed out loud at her insistence she put on a face by the door to disguise the lies, the violence and the horrors. Held firm her mother's death was merely a tragic accident that had ended her pathetic little life.

Greta looked at him. Her father never was and never would be at fault. "You're a fucking monster," she screamed.

He turned away from her.

"How did they ever let you adopt a baby?" She lunged and kicked the side of the leather chair. "Tell me. Tell me now. And give me the papers."

"Don't know where they are. Never saw 'em. Didn't need to."

She thrust her arm forward and squeezed his shoulder hard, her nails digging into the skin. He didn't flinch. She wanted to scream. "Deny what you want, but you're full of shit." She leaned down slowly, inches from his ear, and relayed every detail she had learned the past three years.

He sat, the blood draining from his cheeks, his skin growing paler by the second. When she stood again, he raised his face to hers and smiled. "*Now* who's full of shit?"

Then, after poking holes in her story, he went into overdrive. He insisted he didn't understand why she had bothered to travel all the way back to the cabin to see him. He told her he didn't care for her counseling; claimed it softened her character. Therapy was for sissies, was what he said. And her implausible memories? They were unconvincing. Disgusting. And she disgusted him, too. Fragile as a child. Pathetic as a teenager. Now weak as a woman, as he'd always predicted. He'd expected nothing less, he said, and she had lived up to every one of his expectations for as long as he'd known her.

Detective Perez took off her glasses and rubbed her eyes. "Do you think your father believed all that?"

Greta collected herself. "His mind and memory were tack-sharp. It was all lies." When the detective didn't respond—only wrote in her notebook—she continued, "When I look back on it now, I'm sure it was willful amnesia."

Detective Perez looked up. "Did you stay?"

She shook her head. "I took off. With my unanswered questions. Without the truth. With the secrets that are going to stay buried for the rest of my life."

"The same day?"

"That afternoon. I was done."

"Were you?"

"Yes," she confirmed, her face emotionless.

The detective got her point.

Greta knew it was a place she never wanted to return to. She didn't belong there. It was a place she'd left behind a lifetime ago.

Detective Perez glanced down and opened the top-right drawer of the table. In her hand she held the thick blue file, and inside it was a manila envelope. She pulled it out. "I guess this is as good a time as any to discuss this."

Phil paled again. "Now what?"

The detective looked back and forth between them. She pointed to a box sitting against the wall behind her. "I promised I'd talk to Officer Pappas and review the ETs' evidence."

Greta looked at the ceiling. ETs? Her mind raced. Evidence Techs. She leaned forward in her chair. "Did they find something?"

Detective Perez shook her head. "*I* did."

She glanced at Phil, hopeful. Nothing was said. She turned back to the detective and waited.

"There's no easy way to—" the detective said.

"Say it," she interjected.

The detective half-smiled, uncomfortable, and paused. "There's no public record of your adoption, Greta."

"What?"

"I'm sorry."

"In Parry Sound?"

"No."

"Bracebridge?"

The detective shook her head.

Greta frowned. "Ontario?"

"I talked to Officer Pappas. He did a search, too. The techs went through every database we have. Nothing came up."

Her heart pounded through her sweatshirt. How could that be?

Detective Perez pointed to the manila envelope tagged *Ministry and Children and Youth Services* that sat on the table. "These folks can't find one either."

Greta's hands shook as she reached for her purse, slung across the back of the plastic chair. She pulled out her wallet, pried her birth certificate from its smooth plastic case, and passed it over. "Are you sure you have the dates right?"

Detective Perez didn't take it; instead, she took a deep breath, letting it go with a sigh. "There's already a copy of that in the envelope." Greta put it down. The detective stared at it. "It's a fake."

Greta slumped in her chair, and she felt a hand gently touch her shoulder. She winced. Her throat tightened, and a trickle of sweat beaded on her chest. She knew her mother had lied, but she'd lied about this, too? How could she? How *dare* she? She took a shallow breath that fluttered as she exhaled.

A pained expression crossed the detective's face. "I'm sorry, Greta."

She lowered her eyes. Who the hell was she? Who was her family? Her legs trembled and she counted inside her head.

One. Inhale. *Two. Come on. Three.* She looked at the floor and managed to let out one slow, steady breath.

"However," the detective went on, "When Officer Pappas poked around a bit, he found something else." Greta looked up at her, expectant. Detective Perez held her hand in the air. "Let's be clear from the start," she warned. "There's no evidence it's even related." Greta's heart began to race. The detective reached into the blue file and took out two pieces of white paper.

Greta gave Phil an angry nod. "Go ahead."

He shifted forward as the detective slid the documents toward them.

"What?" Greta asked after they exchanged a look, Phil hunched over the desk.

He tilted the documents towards her. Through the blur, all she could see were the words *Parry Sound North Star* followed by black lines of ink. She swiped at the wet with the heel of her hand, and reached out and grabbed them. The story spilled across the page.

August 24, 2001.

Baby girl abducted from the Parry Sound Mall.

One month old, strapped snugly into a baby seat.

In a shopping cart from A & P.

The Mother said all she had done was "turn to put groceries into the back of her car."

Honestly, how long would that take?

"It happened so fast. I only looked away for a second."

What the hell was that mother thinking?

The mother had been hysterical, it said; she'd seen nothing.

Nothing? Nothing at all?

Greta read the rest of the story and turned to the police report underneath. She scanned the information and there, two-thirds of the way down the page, her finger stopped.

Description of the baby.

One-month-old. Female. Black hair. Blue eyes.

Her heart lurched. Didn't her mother say all babies were born with blue eyes? She was sure she'd said that one night they'd been out on the back patio. Every one of them. Right? She read on.

Wrapped in a green blanket.

She froze. She reread the sentence again. A green blanket? Bile rose up in her throat. She swallowed and continued reading. The police interviewed eight people in the Parry Sound Mall parking lot that morning, and their descriptions of the subject were consistent.

Woman. Long, brown hair. Sunglasses. Thin build. Average height.

A familiar face flashed before her eyes. It couldn't be. She pushed her thoughts away.

Well-dressed. Stylish blouse. Pressed pants.

No.

"From everything you've said, it sounds like Colleen," Detective Perez said. "And she's here down the hall now, so we're going to find out."

Greta jammed her hands under her thighs. She couldn't speak; she couldn't refute anything. "But... She always seemed so innocent."

"Was she?"

"My mother's friend. Her mentor. My friend, too. I don't know anymore."

Detective Perez remained silent.

Greta's jaw dropped. "Oh my god. My mother?"

Her hands trembled. Ian wasn't the only criminal in her fucked up little family. She thought back to the day in Kindergarten when she was covered in paint to her elbows and had tried to explain the picture of her family tree. At the time, she'd hoped Mrs. Harvey would make sense of what she was trying to say. Had she actually, truly understood that she'd been abducted? Surely not at four years old. Had she? If she'd been able to articulate it, what would Mrs. Harvey have said? Would she have taken her seriously? And if she had, would she have been taken from Emily and Ian and reunited with her biological parents?

Her throat tightened. Who were they? Where were they? And who *was* she? She felt herself sink down into her chair and, thrusting her head in her hands, found herself unable to stop the tears that fell from her face. She let them fall unfettered.

THIRTY-NINE

"Was that the second last time you were with your father?" Detective Perez asked gently after they'd all taken another long and needed break.

Greta pressed her fingers to the front pocket of her jeans. The question was rhetorical; they all knew the answer. What she didn't know anymore was whom she'd really been with. Her father? Ian? Her mother's abuser? Her abductor? She couldn't speak. She didn't trust words anymore.

The detective looked at her. "Let's go on, then. That was late fall. It's April now. Tell me, what have you been doing?"

"Trying to put everything behind me, like my grandparents said."

"How's that going?"

"I started college in January. My courses are heavy. I've been working on them and I visit my grandparents on weekends." She snorted. "Everything was good. Moving along pretty well—"

"Until?" the detective said, cutting her off sharply.

"The phone call."

"From Dr. Hamid?"

She sat still. "It changed everything."

***

It was spring. It had been raining for weeks, relentlessly coming down, darkening the sky and giving the earth back what it had taken. The waves on Lake Ontario crashed violently onto the shoreline and Toronto sunk into a gray soggy mess. Sewer grates overflowed and the Don River burst its banks. The Don Valley Parkway, the most travelled artery in and out of the city, was submerged and subsequently ended up being closed. The Toronto Islands, deluged, sat under three feet of water and the families living there had been evacuated to the main land.

"Greta Giffen?" a man's voice asked after the phone rang early one evening.

She cradled it to her ear. "Who wants to know?"

The low voice softened. "Let me try again. This is Dr. Farzad Hamid from Princess Margaret Hospital. Is this Greta?"

"Yes."

"You're a hard person to track down." She listened. "Sorry to call out of the blue. I wanted to let you know we have your father with us in palliative. I assume you know he has cancer?"

"Yes, I'm aware."

"You know it's inoperable, right? There's nothing more we can do." She sighed. She knew what palliative was. "And he's here all alone?" She didn't appreciate his salty undertone and thought about hanging up. But he had no idea of the relationship they had, so she held on.

"We've been looking everywhere for his next of kin. One of the nurses dug around and found your name on the bottom of an old insurance form in his file. A document from a job he had in the municipality of Bracebridge. We searched you up on social."

They'd creeped her? Seriously? She shut her eyes, nauseated, as the doctor went on to explain they'd transported him privately two hundred kilometers from Bracebridge to Princess Margaret, Ontario's Cancer Care Centre. She imagined him being driven down the highway like some sort of king in a carriage. What a joke. The last time she'd travelled that same route had been eight months before. She shuddered at the memory.

"He's been lying in a bed on the seventh floor since he got here last week. We thought you might want to know," Dr. Hamid said.

The detective raised her eyebrows, pausing the conversation. "How did that phone call feel?"

Greta didn't know how it made her feel. Back then, what she'd felt had been stillness—and that had been all. She looked down at her sneakers and said nothing.

"Let me try again," Detective Perez said. "What is a daughter's obligation to her parents?"

Greta balked. To her father? Nothing. To her mother? The one who'd said she chose her? Ripped from a mother's arms as a baby, choice wasn't the word she'd use to describe what her mother might have done? Was she? How dare Detective Perez ask what *her* obligation was. After everything she'd learned, how the hell would she know?

***

She'd disconnected the call and put her phone down on the table. Her mind was racing.

Google Assistant told her the hospital was about twenty minutes away. She quickly considered who, of everyone she knew, could take her there. Latoya didn't have a car. She dismissed the idea of her grandparents; it was already early evening and they lived too far away. While she'd opened up a little that spring, she was still protecting them from the worst of her father's sordid history. There was no chance of asking Colleen. Plain and simple, she knew everything and hated her father, too. Last, she ruled out Kanza: had it been even slightly practical, she'd have chosen her, but she mentioned in her last text that she was on a five-day night shift at Penn. She'd be busy.

Greta grabbed her jacket off the back of the couch, locked the apartment, and walked up the street. Rain pounded around her, and she gripped the edges of the fabric and quickened the pace up to the bus stop on Queen. The doors of the streetcar swallowed her up and closed again, and she looked past the weary faces of passengers, pale in the fluorescent light, to the middle of the car in the hope of finding a solo seat. Rain thumping the windows, the streetcar travelled the rails to the downtown corridor, the windshield wipers keeping time with her heart. Beating slow. Steady. Methodical.

Had she dozed off? At University, she stood, nearly missing her stop. She walked north and squeezed her way through the large glass revolving doors pushed back into the shadows at the front of the hospital. Skin bumpy with the chill of the air-conditioning, she took the elevator upstairs. The doors swooshed open, filling her nostrils with the smell of stale air and antiseptic. Her eyes flitted around the corridor before quickly locating what she was looking for. She turned right, walked down the hall a few steps, and stopped in front of the nurse's station.

"He's in a single down the hall," said the nurse, hair salted with silver, wearing scrubs, a badge pinned to his chest.

"Room?"

"Seven fifty-six," he said.

She cocked her head. Had she heard that right? Was he kidding? She glanced at his nametag. "Larry, did you say a single?"

He nodded, confirming yes.

After the life they'd had? Always hungry? The hand-me-downs? Their cracked, mismatched plates from BFT? She wanted to laugh out loud right there on the spot. But as it was neither the time nor the place to draw attention to herself, she held in her disgust.

She made her way down the hallway. Like a runway at night time, the eerie white and green glow cascading from the beeping machines around her provided enough light to find the way.

The door to her father's room lay wide open. She peeked inside. It was as sparse as most hospital rooms were—comfortable but sterile; too much white; no curtains; no carpet; no hanging TV. A cracked fake leather chair covered with dark stains stuck down one side, remnants of whoever had been sitting there last, took one full corner. A box of latex gloves sat on the table. She slipped in and shut the door.

The detective stopped writing and held up a hand. "Stop there. Why close it?"

Greta winced. The rollercoaster feeling in her stomach returned, and she worked hard to organize her thoughts. Once she did, she looked up, smooth and unruffled. "To talk to my father, privately. One last time," she said.

The detective's shoulders tensed. "That's all you've got? Privacy?"

Greta nodded.

Detective Perez's upper lip curled. She threw her hands up in the air. "Come on, Greta. You've already told me you hated your father and wanted him dead. You've provided motive ten times over, and now you tell me, when given the opportunity to get your revenge, you close the door for privacy? How about you closed the door so there wouldn't be any witnesses?"

Greta shrugged. The only account remaining was her own, and she didn't trust herself to answer. She bit her tongue and pushed her thoughts aside. She wasn't going to be baited.

FORTY

Greta stared at the man tucked into the bed. The shadows of glory days washed over his pale face. His jet-black beard, in desperate need of a trim, lay in strict contrast to the crisp white sheet tucked tightly around him. His eyes were half-closed. His breathing was ragged, and he suddenly started to cough; a wet, phlegmy cough. It was like nothing like she'd ever heard before. He was drowning somewhere deep down in his own lungs.

If Greta didn't believe her father was dying when she'd seen him last fall, she certainly did now. His semi-conscious state allowed no window into his thoughts. Greta wondered what those memories could be. Were they reels of happier times in his life? Stories wrapped in creative half-truths? No truths at all? 'Cause it was time to be frank; time to lay it all down. There was no longer any point in pretending.

Greta stepped closer to the monster in the bed. Like the crisscrossing cracks in the walls of her childhood bedroom, a patchwork of scattered blood vessels spread across his cheeks. She dragged the stained fake leather chair from out of the corner across the room and placed it next to the bed. She then tugged off her gloves, tossed them on the seat, and sat down, inches away from him.

"Dad?" she whispered. The only sounds filling the room were the whooshing of the machines that were keeping him alive. She leaned in a little closer. "Dad. Can you hear me?"

No acknowledgement. He was lost in his thoughts. Greta closed her eyes. Well, she thought, *he can keep them. Words can't heal; there never was truth and there never will be truth.* After all, the man in the bed was a master in manipulation.

He stirred, sensing her presence. Ever so gently, he lifted his willowy hand up and pointed to the machine behind him. He mumbled something, yet his voice was reed-thin. It was too coarse to carry. Greta had to lean in just to hear him. "Pain," he rasped. "Too much pain."

Greta's eyes followed her father's knotty fingers to the machine above his shoulder. Thin lines and fat green numbers surrounded a screen lit up with child-like scribbles. She had no idea what they meant, but the numbers rose and fell as she watched. An unruly jungle of tubes tumbled out from somewhere behind, and her eyes widened as she followed each one. The smallest was stuck flat to the backside of her father's hand, while another snaked through his right nostril. The third, attached to a pump at the side of the bed, curled close to his neck and disappeared into a hole in his windpipe.

Greta watched the pump and his chest move up and down in unison, unable to stop from leaning forward. She slid her fingers along the tube that fed into her father's throat, and closed her palm around the cold plastic.

"Please," he murmured again, almost begging, "turn it off."

"What?" she said, taken aback. What was he asking?

A small green button glowed in the dim room. She could see it was turned on.

Greta froze. Memories flooded her mind with an intensity that scared her, embodying an ugly power that truly delighted her. She used to pray every day that her father would die. Now she had the opportunity to make those prayers a reality.

For her mother, who was taken away from her too soon.

For her grandparents, who had lost a daughter.

For everything he'd done to her; said to her.

For all the pain he had caused.

She squeezed her eyes shut, willing it to go away, yet reliving it all; vividly and in slow motion.

"Push the damn button," he croaked.

Greta stood, her heart beating double-time. She prayed for control. *One, two, three.* But she couldn't stop her feral side from rearing up in her mind. *Four. Five. Six.* Her rage was winning the battle—and she felt it. She wanted to take the pillow and place it over the old man's face. She wanted to push it down hard. Then harder, and harder, with all her strength. And then, as the old man's body creaked and groaned, she wanted to hold that pillow fast in place and crush the life out of him.

She tried to convince herself this wasn't what she wanted; after all, she'd come this far. She'd worked hard to move on and was desperate to have it look like she had it all together. But she didn't. There was no denying it. And she understood why. Life had no clean edges. It was her own father, the man lying in the bed, who had taught her that. He had proved it time and time again.

Although her rage frightened her, it was comfortingly familiar too. And finally she allowed herself to think the thought, as she watched him writhe in the bed: she wanted him dead.

Every ounce of control vanished. Greta drew a deep breath. She reached out for the button and touched it; lightly, at first, just to see what she might feel. It was smooth and cold underneath her finger. She smiled, and as she did, she leaned down and looked her father in the eye one last time. But his peaceful, half-smile stopped her cold.

It was more a smirk. It demeaned her.

Her face flushed with heat. She was *not* his daughter; she never had been his. And she wouldn't be his daughter now, either. Not even at the end. He'd face his own judgment day. She wasn't sorry about that. *Her* survival was all that mattered. Not *his* needs. *Hers. Her* needs.

Greta heard his breath wheeze and rattle, but she wouldn't cross that line. She sat back down on the chair, leaned back, her face emotionless, and watched the fight drain out of him.

She watched him die.

Then she ran. Out of the room. Down the hall. Out of the hospital. Out into the cool, dark night.

At last, she was free. With the kiss of rain in the wind on her face, she stepped up into the streetcar, heading east.

Detective Perez's pencil bounced off the floor. Greta gripped the arms of the chair and leaned forward. Could Detective Perez now see this whole sordid situation was on her father, and she was telling the truth? She examined her face. Cold. Still. Emotionless. How could she not give her something, after everything she'd just said? After everything she'd told her?

The detective ran her fingers gently through her hair and tucked a piece behind an ear. "So you talked to your father before he died."

"Yes."

"In my office yesterday, you said you didn't."

"Sometimes I just block stuff out when I'm stressed. Especially when it comes to Ian."

"Dissociation, Astra," Phil explained, "in the face of a threat."

Detective Perez exchanged a weary look with Phil. "I'm aware of what it is. The mind's way of saving itself from a reality it can't handle." She cleared her throat, picked up the scattered files, and placed them in a pile on the table. "I'm going to need time to a circle back on a couple of things and collect my thoughts."

"Of course," he replied. "Whatever you need. If anything comes up, we'll be right here to answer your questions."

Greta glared at him. More questions? As his advice from earlier reverberated through her head, she sat back in her chair and lowered her eyes to the floor. After the door slammed, a hush fell over the room. Phil shuffled through his papers.

"Now what?" Greta could see his hand shaking.

"We wait."

"For how long?"

"As long as it takes."

"And then?"

"You're either going to be charged with murder or you're going home."

Home?

Where was that? It had never been the curtainless cabin in the woods and it was no longer her memory of safety in her mother's arms.

The minutes crawled by. Greta's stomach rolled and her mouth went dry, the questions in her head louder than the answers. She reached for the pitcher at the end of the table. It was empty.

FORTY-ONE

Forty minutes later, the investigation room door swung open. Detective Perez strode in, put her notebook and files on the table, sat down and faced them. "Thank you for your patience. I'll get straight to the point. As there are inconsistencies in what you told me yesterday, Greta, I've gone—."

"But I told you the relevant stuff."

"I reviewed what we discussed. The evidence. What Phil's brought forward. The notes from my conversation with Officer Pappas last night. I also made calls to Mr. Parthi from your elementary school and to Mrs. Xiangzi."

"They believe me?"

"Yes. Not only that..." A lump rose in Greta's throat, and she held her breath. Detective Perez paused. "So do I."

Greta exhaled. Relief washed over her.

"But—"

She stiffened. Why was there always a *but*?

"While the evidence isn't compelling enough to bring a charge forward, we're still left with the incident that occurred yesterday in my office."

She sagged in her chair. Officer Hatten. She'd forgotten about that.

"A short fuse is no excuse," Detective Perez said.

She buried her face in Phil's shoulder. The detective was right. How could she sand away those rough edges? "I'm sorry."

"We all are. Considering the situation, he's willing to drop the charges; however, going forward, Greta, it's something you're going to have to deal with."

"Thank you, Astra," Phil said. "Pass along our gratitude to him, too."

Detective Perez gave a short nod, and then lifted a hand to her ear and fiddled with her earring. "Now, Greta, there are two other things that have come to light during this investigation that we need to address." Greta glanced up at Phil and sat up. "First, your mother's death," she said in a soft voice. "Officer Pappas did his best—a thorough job, we feel—but, without solid evidence or a confession, it's highly unlikely they'll reopen the investigation."

Greta nodded. The truth wasn't enough, but she'd learned that lesson a long time ago.

"And then there's Colleen." Her voice grew softer still. "My officers squeezed her this afternoon and she broke. She came clean and told them everything."

"Was my mom there when she took me?"

"No," Detective Perez said, opening her notebook, "but she was involved."

Greta gripped the edge of the table. "How?"

"Your father—"

She groaned. "Back to him again?" She should've known.

"When he hunted your mother down at the Bracebridge Shelter, he did everything to convince her to come back to him. At first, your mom wouldn't budge, but Colleen said that, when he got a job in town and a post at the church, she gave up."

"Why? He was only trying to hide who he really was."

Detective Perez nodded. "He was sick and manipulative. When rumours swirled about his past, things crumbled, and he was desperate to prove them all wrong."

Greta smirked. "Right. To show my parents had a stable life?"

"That he was a family man."

Her chest tightened. "By having a baby?"

"He told her he'd kill her unless she got pregnant, but she miscarried twice."

"Because of his abuse?" An image flashed in her head. Was that why her mother took such good care of the circle of smooth, white pebbles and flowers at the end of the back patio each year? What was under there?

Detective Perez nodded. "Your mom and Colleen had become close. She told Colleen what was going on. She begged her to find her a baby or she'd die. She begged for one from anywhere, apparently, however she could. Colleen was frightened. Panicked. She didn't think it through. She abducted you from that parking lot—"

"For my mother. To keep her alive."

Greta thought back to the fight she'd heard her parents have after they'd all seen Colleen in the old-fashioned candy store. Her father's words echoed through her mind. *If you ever tell anyone, I'll fucking slit your throat. All three of you.* She'd heard him right—and now she knew why. *Hers, too. Don't think I won't.* She'd never doubted it meant her. She leaned forward and shuddered. "They all knew." They'd all kept the secret.

Detective Perez took a moment to respond. "I'm sorry, Greta."

"I want to see Colleen."

"You can't. She's still in with my officers."

"What's going to happen to her?"

"At the moment, I don't know." Detective Perez tapped the file in front of her. "Based on everything I've heard the last two days, I'll use my discretion and experience to determine that. I don't think Colleen is a bad person. And I agree with you: I think she did what she did to keep your mother alive. But that doesn't take away what she's done; to you; to the family she took you from. She's likely to face criminal charges. She's breached her professional responsibilities so she'll lose her job. It's complicated, and it's going to take time to sort it out." The detective looked up at her kindly. "In the meantime, we're done here. You're done. You can go home."

Greta exhaled the breath she'd been holding since the day her mother died.

She pushed her chair back, stood, and slung the strap of her purse over her head and shoulder. She crossed the room, leaving Phil behind. As she opened the door, she turned around. Detective Perez looked up and smiled at her and closed her notebook.

Back at the apartment, Greta swiped the keypad, stepped inside, and slunk down the back of the door. Hands pressed to her chest, she crouched on her heels, taking in the light, the sound, and the smell.

Home.

It was there, where she was. It was where she belonged. In her kitchen. On her couch. Her dime box square on the living room table. After everything that had happened the past forty-eight hours, she felt it, etched deep in her bones.

She pulled herself up, dropped her purse on the table, kicked her shoes off in the hallway, branching off the living room, and dumped her clothes in a pile on the floor in the bathroom. She sniffed; they reeked of the cells, of the plastic chairs, the wiry blanket. She twisted the silver knobs, aimed the nozzle to the center of the tub, and stepped into the shower. Warm water pounded her head, the water mixing in with tears of her own. She stood, motionless, heart beating, barely breathing, unable to stop her mind from replaying every memory over and over in a loop. Fear. Confusion. Love. Anger. The nightmares. The lies she'd been repeatedly told. From all she knew now, her whole life could've been different from the one she'd actually known.

On the way back to the living room, she towel-dried her hair and tightened her robe. She sat, leaving her damp towel on the floor, and sunk into the couch, clutter everywhere, the only light coming from her phone.

There was a soft knock at the door.

"I came as fast as I could." Latoya wiped the sweat from her face and drew Greta into an embrace. "What the hell happened?"

"I'm okay," she said, red-eyed.

She took two sodas from the fridge and, out on the balcony, they sat for a minute in silence and watched the bustle on the dark street below. Cars. Bicycles. Couples arm in arm. A dog loped along the sidewalk alone.

With the wind blowing softly in her hair, Greta reached out and grabbed Latoya's hand and told her everything.

Latoya's eyebrows shot up after she'd brought her up to date. The barrage of questions came thick and fast. "Are you sure that's what the police report said?"

She nodded.

"You read every word?"

"Beginning to end," she smiled, not quite whole. It was the exact moment everything she'd worked so hard to understand turned to liquid.

"Do you think your real parents—"

"Blood parents?"

Latoya looked at her strangely. "Okay, those. Do you think they're out there?"

"I dunno. But maybe there's a chance to put an end to this."

Latoya groaned. "What happened to moving on with your life? Why can't you leave it alone?"

With a sigh, she shook her head. "I wanted to unravel my mom's history, and I did. Now I need to find my own."

Latoya's eyes widened. "G., it could be a needle in a haystack."

"I get it." Though Latoya wasn't saying anything she didn't already know, she still felt annoyed. Things were different; there were new pieces missing now. She drew a deep breath. "The least I can do is try."

"So you're leaving?"

"Hell no," she said, with a shake of her head.

"Then what's that?" Latoya pointed to the suitcase through the living room window.

She put her hand on her forearm. "I need to start in the parking lot in Parry Sound."

Latoya's jaw dropped. "You're going back?"

"Officer Pappas is meeting me there tomorrow afternoon."

"You're sure about this, G.?"

She gave her a nod. "Readier than I've ever been."

ACKNOWLEDGEMENTS

I want to thank the many people who helped with the writing and publication of this book.

Though purely a work of the imagination, this novel is inspired by the many students I had the privilege of coming to know during over two decades of work as an educator at the Scarborough Board of Education, the Toronto District School Board and at TVO. Thank you for generously sharing your voices, your lives and your stories. You are beacons of light for the rest of us—our future is in great hands!

Thanks to Maria and Gerard Doyle, Bev Freedman, Wendy McCrae, Barb Omland, Nadine Segal, Jim Strachan and Cathy Vodden for providing feedback on early drafts. You've all been amazing cheerleaders. To Donna MacKenzie and Janet Piper, for the untold hours you spent sharing your perspectives, steering me in the right direction and providing your unfailing encouragement. I'm deeply grateful. Profound thanks to Phil Tsui, Assistant Crown Attorney with the Ministry of the Attorney General's Guns and Gangs Initiative for giving me your time, expertise and answering all my questions about police protocol and the legal system in Ontario. Any and all mistakes are solely mine.

My biggest debt of gratitude is to my fabulous editor Adrienne Kerr and my mentor author Lawrence Hill.

These two literary geniuses sat perched on my shoulders month after month, year after year, through the developmental process of the novel. Both possess rare gifts for storytelling and have been great readers and even better friends. Without their insight, patience, humour and willingness to challenge me, The Dime Box would still be a document in a folder on my desktop. Adrienne and Larry set it free and let it soar. I'm forever indebted to you both for your kindness, inspiration and coaching.

Thank you to my publishing team across the pond in the UK. To Hayley Paige who believed in this story from the beginning and to Notebook Publishing for taking a chance on me. To the dream team: Mark for designing a wonderful cover, to Hayley and Riley for copyediting, formatting and marketing. You've all been a delight to work with.

Finally, thanks to family. To my husband, John, who lived this adventure with me. When I took on a little more than I could handle, he took care of the big and little things every day along the way. I could not have done this without your love and support. To Gina, for sharing her perspectives regarding counseling and serving marginalized clients; Trisha who has always been creative and encouraging; and Jaime, for stepping in effortlessly time and time again with brilliant inspiration, the right words or a new idea when I got lost. Being your Mom is my life's greatest gift. I love you all, and am so fortunate to have you in my corner.